Reginald Hill is a native of Cumbria and a former resident of Yorkshire where his outstanding Dalziel and Pascoe crime novels are set. He says he always regarded himself as a writer of some sort, but until he wrote *A Clubbable Woman* (1970), which introduced Chief Superintendent Andy Dalziel and young PC Peter Pascoe, he had managed to avoid putting his theory to the test. Since then it has received ample confirmation. *An Advancement of Learning* (1972) introduced Sergeant Pascoe to Eleanor (Ellie) Soper, and Pascoe's subsequent police career and his private life have been unfolded with wit, drama, suspense and impeccable style in *Ruling Passion* (1973), *An April Shroud* (1975), *A Pinch of Snuff* (1978), *A Killing Kindness* (1980), *Deadheads* (1983), *Exit Lines* (1984), *Child's Play* (1987), *Under World* (1988), *Bones and Silence* (1990) and *One Small Step* (1990).

By the same author

REGINALD HILL

An Advancement of Learning

Grafton

An Imprint of HarperCollinsPublishers

Grafton
An Imprint of HarperCollins*Publishers*
77–85 Fulham Palace Road,
Hammersmith, London W6 8JB

Published by Grafton 1987
9 8 7 6

First published in Great Britain by
William Collins Sons & Co. Ltd 1971

ISBN 0 586 07259 4

Set in Times

Printed in Great Britain by
HarperCollinsManufacturing Glasgow

For Malcom & Anne
Mike & Jo
Jim & Kathy

. . . to have the true testimonies of learning to be better heard, without the interruption of tacit objections, I think good to deliver it from the discredits and disgraces it hath received, all from ignorance; but ignorance severally disguised; appearing sometimes in the zeal and jealousy of divines; sometimes in the severity and arrogance of politiques; and sometimes in the errors and imperfections of learned men themselves.

Sir Francis Bacon
The Advancement of Learning.

Chapter 1

If a man will begin with certainties, he shall end in doubts; but if he will be content to begin with doubts, he shall end in certainties.

SIR FRANCIS BACON
The Advancement of Learning

There had been a great deal of snow that December, followed by hard frost. A few days before Christmas a thaw set in, temperatures rose steeply, the snow became slush. The sun greedily sucked up the moisture till it saturated the air and impinged on all the senses.

Fog.

You could smell it in the great industrial towns, its edge of carbon and sulphur biting into the windpipe.

You could see it clearly wherever you looked. But it was all you could see.

You could taste it if you walked out in it without a scarf or kerchief wrapped round your mouth.

You could feel it, damp and greasy, on your skin. Almost under your skin.

And you could hear it. No sound passed through it that it did not muffle and crush and make its own.

It made driving difficult but not impossible. If you drove with care, if your motivation was strong and impelling, it was possible to get to your destination.

Flying *was* impossible.

Airport lounges filled. And overfilled. And overspilled. Till the atmosphere of damp and smoke and noise and frustration was almost as bad as the fog outside.

Occasionally it raised itself off the ground. Sometimes long enough for a plane to taxi out on the runway.

Sometimes long enough for a plane to get away, which made the waiting even more unbearable for those still crammed in the restaurants, bars and lounges.

Confusion breeds confusion. People found themselves separated from their baggage, their tickets, their passports and sometimes even other people. Some went home and bought a frozen turkey the next day. Some cancelled their flights at the airport, some claimed refunds later. Passenger lists became as scrappy as leaves from the Delphic oracle.

Finally a light wind breathed out of the south-west a couple of times and brought back the reassuring stars.

It was a warm wind. It blew gently over half of Europe, melting what remained of the great snows at sea-level.

Higher up, however, it proved more difficult. Which was good, for it was the snow that most of the thousands marching in still dubious queues across black, wet runways were seeking.

But sometimes the wind's breath blew long enough and hot enough to loosen the grip which the long, frozen fingers of snow had fastened on the side of steep and deep.

Which was bad.

Merry Christmas.

The hot June sun glinted merrily on the placid blue sea, the long white sands, the unconscious sun-bathers and a little farther inland, the balding head of Douglas Pearl, solicitor, through the open windows of the long committee room. A neurotic motion to close the windows in the interests of security had been ignored by the chairman, who now waved Pearl and the girl who accompanied him to their appointed seats.

'Forgive me, sir,' said the solicitor, standing up immediately he and the girl had been seated, 'but before we begin, may I formally establish that all those present are

8

members of the governing body of Holm Coultram College of Liberal Arts and Education?'

'Of course we are,' said Captain Jessup, his grey eyebrows twitching in surprise.

'And you, sir, are Captain Ernest Jessup, the Chairman of this body?'

'I am indeed, sir,' said Captain Jessup with greater acerbity, understandable as he and his questioner had played golf together only two days earlier.

'And I take it, sir, that there is present here today a quorum of that body?'

'You would not be here else,' snapped the Captain. 'Is that all?'

'I think so, sir,' said the solicitor, unperturbed. 'In cases like this it is always as well to establish the standing in law of the body involved right at the beginning. There have been cases . . .'

'I'm sure, I'm sure,' said the Captain. 'Let's get a start. I may add I'm quite willing to accept that you are Douglas Pearl, solicitor, and that this is your client, Miss Anita Sewell.'

He smiled frostily at the girl who sat with her head bowed forward so that her long blonde hair hung like a curtain over her face.

'Now,' said the Captain. 'As you all know, this meeting has been convened to hear the appeal of Miss Sewell against a decision of the Academic Board of the college.

'The Academic Board at a meeting held on May 20th of this year decided that Miss Sewell should be instructed to withdraw from the college. In other words, my dear,' he said, addressing the girl directly and in a kind voice, 'you were dismissed.'

Pearl rolled his eyes upwards till the whites showed, a movement Captain Jessup did not miss.

'The grounds for this decision were that Miss Sewell's work in all subjects was of a standard sufficiently low to cause concern, and that in one subject, biology, she had sunk below a point from which it was possible for her to attain the lowest pass level by the end of her course. Miss Sewell was informed of this decision and the grounds of it. Later she decided to make use of her right of appeal to the Board of Governors, pending which appeal she has been, I believe, suspended.'

The girl nodded.

'Now,' said Captain Jessup, pressing his hands flat on the table before him. 'Now. We have already seen the academic evidence on the basis of which Miss Sewell was dismissed.'

'Suspended,' said Pearl.

Jessup ignored him.

'So I think the best interests of all would be suited if we passed straight on to the grounds of your appeal, my dear.'

Pearl coughed.

'Miss Sewell has asked that I should lay out the general grounds of her appeal to start with, Mr Chairman. Then, under my advice, of course, she will be willing to answer questions.'

'I see. Well, I suppose that's in order?' said Jessup. No one seemed disposed to question this.

'Good. Then carry on.'

The solicitor shuffled a couple of papers in front of him. Under his polite, rather mild exterior there had long lurked a desire to try his hand at the kind of histrionic advocacy popular a century earlier. Magistrates' courts offered little opportunity. Or encouragement. And looking at the row of attentive faces before him with Jessup's challenging glare in the middle, he decided reluctantly that in the interests of both his own reputation and his client's appeal this was not the time to start.

But he wasn't too worried. What he had to say contained enough built-in drama to take the complacency out of their faces.

'Mr Chairman, ladies and gentlemen,' he began quietly, 'my client has been following a bipartite course at the College and the main ground of the Academic Board's decision to instruct her to withdraw was failure in one part of the course, that concerned with biology. The main evidence to this effect was given by Dr Fallowfield, Senior Lecturer in that subject and Miss Sewell's principal tutor.'

The girl stirred slightly at the name and with an almost unconscious movement of her left hand brushed the hair back from her face. She was very attractive.

Pearl paused for effect. Captain Jessup made a moue of distaste at even this slight bit of dramatic business and Pearl was glad he had tried no more.

'Today her appeal comes before you,' he went on flatly, avoiding any undue stress, 'and it is based on two things. A piece of information and an allegation. The information requires no comment from this body, I feel. We live in a modern era. It is this: for the past two years, until last term in fact, Miss Sewell was the mistress of Dr Fallowfield, the lecturer I have just mentioned. It is with reluctance that my client reveals this. It is with greater reluctance that she asserts that Dr Fallowfield has deliberately falsified her assessment grades to bring about her apparent failure.'

The man on the ladder rested his elbow unselfconsciously on the shining brown breast.

'We could saw her off at the ankles,' he said reasonably. 'That'd be easiest. Otherwise she's likely to come apart almost anywhere.'

One of his mates guffawed. The man on the ladder shot him a disapproving glance.

Marion Cargo ignored him and concentrated all her attention on the eight-foot-high bronze nude which towered before her. She (Marion, not the bronze) was in her late twenties, as slim as the nude was Rubensesque,

11

dressed in black slacks and a loose grey sweater, her only concession to the fact that she lectured in Art at the college being her ear-rings, two crystals dangling at the end of long silver chains.

'There's a solid block of concrete down there as a foundation, you see, miss,' explained the man. 'This thing's set in it. Pretty solid too, I'd say, otherwise it'd have keeled over long since.'

'Yes, I know,' said Marion. 'But I'd rather the legs weren't cut.'

'No one'd know,' assured the man. 'We'll dig the base out separate and they can be stuck back together later somehow if the thing's not going for scrap. She might lose half an inch or so, but she can spare it, eh?'

He slapped the nude affectionately.

'Like I say, who'd notice? No one, except the joker who made it, perhaps, wherever he is.'

He laughed.

'That was me,' said Marion calmly. 'But it's not just that. We'll have to think of a way. I don't want her cut. There are other reasons.'

She bent down and looked at the inscribed plaque set into the shallow platform on which the statue rested.

TO THE MEMORY OF
ALISON GIRLING
1916–1966
Her memorial is around you.

She was conscious of the overalled men regarding her with semi-amused eyes, but she made no attempt to brush the tears from her eyes before standing upright again.

'No,' she repeated. 'I don't want her cut. There must be a way.'

Chapter 2

There is yet another fault often noted in learned men, that they do many times fail to observe decency and discretion in their behaviour and carriage.

SIR FRANCIS BACON
Op. Cit.

Conversation stopped for a moment when Fallowfield came into the Common Room. He moved swiftly to the coffee-table and waited till Miss Disney had poured herself a cup. A smile played around his lips as she replaced the coffee-pot firmly on the table and moved away without a glance at him.

He poured a cup and made a bit of business out of taking a couple of sips while he surveyed the constitution of the various groups scattered around the room.

Grouping tended to be by departments for morning coffee. The geographers sat huddled together as though plotting some government's overthrow. The English Department lay back easily in their chairs, not speaking, but with faint smiles on their faces as though someone had said, or was just about to say, something elegantly witty. Three mathematicians looked gloomily at each other like unwilling companions on a long train journey. At the far end of the room, the historians were quarrelling again, just before the stage where objective social discussion became personal infighting. Henry Saltecombe, their departmental head, almost recumbent in the deep armchair which was his own, surveyed them benignly over his swelling paunch. Glancing round, he caught Fallowfield's eye and made a pouring motion with his hand.

13

Fallowfield picked up the coffee-pot and went across to join him.

'Hello, Sam,' said Henry cordially. 'Pour us a·cup, there's a love. You're a silly fellow to be here when you could still be pigging it in bed.'

'There are things to do,' said Fallowfield non-committally. He sat down and refilled his own coffee-cup.

'Anyway,' he added, melting a little to Henry's cordiality, 'it's a rare experience to be able to feel like Lord Byron after the scandal. Though nobody actually got up and left!'

'Not quite,' muttered Arthur Halfdane, one of the young historians at the table, jerking his head so that his long hair tossed like a girl's.

Fallowfield followed his gesture and saw the slight angular figure of Jane Scotby, the Senior Tutor, wriggle out from under the menacing overhangs and promontories of Edith Disney and move across the room towards him.

'Mr Fallowfield,' she said in her high precise voice. 'I wonder if I could have a word with you?'

Fallowfield stared thoughtfully into her small brown wrinkled face whose bright blue eyes stared back as unflinchingly at his round, rather solemn features.

'Of course, Miss Scotby,' he said. 'Won't you sit down?'

'I would prefer that we were private,' she said.

'I find that hard at the moment,' said Fallowfield equably.

'Very well,' said Miss Scotby. 'It has been suggested to me . . .'

'By Miss Disney?'

'. . . that your suspension from duty makes it improper for you to be present in the Senior Common Room or indeed in the College.'

'This is outrageous,' spluttered Henry. The younger historians, constitutionalists to a man, sat forward in their

14

chairs, eager to offer an opinion at the drop of an amendment.

'I am unable to pronounce authoritatively on the legality of this,' Miss Scotby went on inexorably, 'but on other grounds I can see good reason why it might be better if you weren't here.'

She halted, just a little breathless. Fallowfield suspected that beneath the brown parchment skin a flush might be struggling to break out.

'Miss Scotby,' he said kindly, 'I have merely been temporarily suspended from my teaching duties here. I certainly do not intend trying to teach anything except perhaps a few lessons in corporate feeling and loyalty.'

He raised his voice slightly and glanced round the room.

'I am suspended. I haven't caught leprosy. So I won't wear a bell. And I shall continue to use this room as of right until I am shown why in law I should not.'

'And if that happens, you shall be my guest,' added Henry Saltecombe, his jowls shaking in emphasis.

The historians glanced at each other and raised their eyebrows in wry humour. Miss Scotby nodded as though she had expected nothing else. Which was probably true, thought Arthur Halfdane. Or at least she had the art of always giving the impression that whatever happened was expected.

A pretty young woman with a determined chin, Eleanor Soper of the Social Science department, came across in pursuit of the coffee-pot, apparently unconscious of the tension. Halfdane smiled at her and pulled up another chair beside his own. She sat down.

Miss Scotby nodded again as if this too, were expected, turned on her heel and, avoiding Miss Disney's imperious beckonings, walked smoothly out of the room.

'Nicely timed,' said Halfdane to Eleanor.

'Why?' she said. 'What's up with Scotby?'

'Gone to earth,' said Henry with a chuckle. 'Walt's furious.'

He was the only person in the college who actually addressed Miss Disney as 'Walt' to her face.

'Now, Sam,' he said, 'what's the latest? If it's not *sub judice* or something.'

He rubbed his podgy hands in mock-enthusiastic expectation.

How mock is it? wondered Halfdane.

'There's nothing new. I've agreed to go before the governors to make a statement, but not while the student governors are present. They're still trying to sort out the legalities.'

'Well,' said Henry dubiously. 'The students are after all legally elected members of the governing body. In any case, I'm surprised that you are bothering, Sam. Points of order and matters constitutional have always bored you to tears in the past.'

A general movement towards the doors prevented any reply from Fallowfield.

'What's on?' asked Halfdane.

'By Christ!' said Henry, pushing his fifteen stones breathily out of the chair. 'They're going to shift Hippolyta, her of the golden tits, begging your pardon, Miss Soper. This we mustn't miss!'

'What?'

'The statue. Al's statue. Acres of thigh swinging on high! Coming, Sam?'

'No, thanks,' said Fallowfield, shaking his head moodily, his recent liveliness in the face of the enemy now completely evaporated. 'I don't think I will.'

'See you later then.' He puffed cheerily away, followed by the slight figure of Halfdane. Soon there was only one other person left in the Common Room. She came to a halt by Fallowfield's chair.

'Yes, Miss Disney?' he said without looking up.

16

'Mr Fallowfield,' she said loudly, as though speaking to someone much more distant. 'Whatever the outcome of this business, I should like you to know I consider your admitted conduct to be absolutely deplorable. You have debauched a charming and delightful young girl. Should you be acquitted . . .'

'I'm not on trial,' observed Fallowfield, but it wasn't worth the effort.

'. . . and stay on at the college, I warn you there are other matters I may have to speak of. Other matters. You follow me, I have no doubt.'

She left in a shudder of flesh and a crash of door.

Fallowfield whistled a couple of bars of 'The Dead March'.

'Glass houses to you, Miss Disney,' he murmured. 'Bloody great glass houses.'

He finished his coffee and poured himself another cup even though it was cold.

The giant mechanical shovel-cum-crane lumbered through the herbaceous border on to the lawn of the staff garden. Miss Scotby winced visibly and Miss Disney took a step forward as though to lay herself beneath its tracks.

It was as well she didn't. The ground was baked hard by the summer sun, but still the vehicle's metal teeth left a deep imprint in the level green turf.

The college gardener, who had tended it and watered it to the last, spoke a word which normally would have caused the Disney bosom to push indignantly against the Disney chin. Now she nodded sadly as though in full accord.

'What happens now?' asked Halfdane.

'I think they've drilled most of the base out of the concrete,' said Henry, pointing with his much-chewed pipe. 'Now they'll take the strain with that thing, finish the drilling and haul away. Look. Here comes Simeon.'

The long, wirily energetic figure of Simeon Landor, the college principal, came striding from the mellow, castellated sandstone building known as the Old House which backed on to the garden.

'Hello, Principal. Come to see the fun?'

Landor shook his head in reproof.

'No fun, Saltecombe. A sad moment, this. For us all. Very sad.'

He raised his voice slightly. Miss Disney, who was standing some yards away, shot him an indignant glance and turned her back.

Halfdane had come in at the tail-end of this particular saga, but as usual with the help of the inveterate chronicler by his side he was in full possession of the facts.

The college had expanded rapidly since Landor had taken over as principal five years earlier on the death of Miss Girling, whose services to the college were commemorated by this very statue.

When he came, the place had been a teachers' training college for some two or three hundred girls, though for the first time men were being admitted the following September. Now it covered a much wider range of courses, vocational and academic, some leading to degrees from the new university of East Yorkshire, situated some fifteen miles to the south. Numbers of students, staff and buildings had risen rapidly, and now the Old House, the early nineteenth-century mansion which once housed the entire college, was the centre of a star of concrete and glass. But it was an incomplete star. In one direction lay half an acre of cultivated beauty which had once been a source of pride and joy to Miss Girling and still was to Miss Scotby and Miss Disney and many others. It was like an artifact created for a nurseryman's catalogue. It had everything, including a fringed pool and a ferned grot, and from the first crocuses in spring till the last dahlia in the autumn it was ablaze with colour. Above all, it had the long, level lawn, the finest Solway turf, five thousand square feet without a blemish. Till now.

For the Landor plan needed the garden. Where the blushing flowers had once risen in such profusion a new growth was going to gladden the eye, or some eyes at least. A biology laboratory.

The principal had tried to soften the blow by pointing out that an integral part of this was to be a hot-house for experimental husbandry. And that the fish-pool would likewise be preserved as a source of water insects and algae.

But the bruised feelings of many of his staff were not so easily salved.

And when he announced that Miss Girling's memorial would have to be shifted this seemed the central symbol of an act of needless and unwarranted desecration.

Now the moment had come. A canvas sling had been wrapped around Hippolyta, one strap passing between her legs, another two crossing beneath the magnificent breasts.

'Note how they shine,' said Henry. 'Some student wit paints a bra on them at least once a year and they always get a good polish when the paint comes off.'

But neither Halfdane nor Landor was listening. They were watching Marion Cargo, who suddenly ran forward anxiously and spoke to the man in charge of the tying operation. He nodded his head reassuringly and moved her away with a gentle push at her shoulder.

Then he waved to the man in the cab, who began to take the strain. Slowly the great arm of the machine pulled back towards the sky. The statue resisted for a second, gave a little jerk, then was swinging free in a stately semi-circle towards the truck which was waiting to take it into storage till a new site was prepared. A little trail of powdered concrete fell off its feet like talcum powder whitening the green lawn.

'A fine sight!' breathed Henry.

'Yes, indeed,' said Landor.

Halfdane turned his attention from the statue to the watchers. A contingent of students had gathered and with an instinct for the end of prohibitions were using one of the larger rockeries as a grandstand. Franny Roote, the student president, a large, quiet-mannered youth, was there, marked out by his height and his very blond hair. As usual he had three or four attractive girls crowding around him. Most of the staff were standing in a semi-circle on the edge of the lawn nearest the building. Jane Scotby looked as if she were praying. 'Walt' Disney was looking with contempt at the man next to her. He was three or four inches shorter than she was, a little man with a big, loose, Glasgow mouth. This was George Dunbar, Head of Chemistry, who shared with Henry Saltecombe the distinction of being the first man appointed to the staff. The older women hated him.

Marion Cargo had moved back to the edge of the lawn. Her face was set and tense, but no less attractive because of it. Halfdane felt a slight stirring of interest and resolved once again to get to know her better. He noted with surprise that Fallowfield had appeared beside her, though he didn't seem to be looking at the moving operation. Curious, he followed his gaze over to the students' rockery and found the answer. Behind Roote had appeared the tall long-haired girl who had been pointed out to him as Anita Sewell.

'There she goes,' said Henry as Hippolyta was deposited gently into the back of the truck.

'A perfect operation,' said Landor gratifiedly. 'Now there's just the base.'

Halfdane had turned to go but he stopped when he saw no one else was moving. The tackle had been taken off the shovel-arm and it was now swinging back along the white path left by the statue. A workman was busy at the concrete base which remained sticking forlornly out of the ground. He was removing the commemorative plaque. When he had it in his hand, he turned uncertainly towards the staff.

'Over here!' called Miss Disney peremptorily, but Landor made a small motion with his hand and the man came directly to him.

Now the mouth of the grab was opened wide, like some monster in a horror film. The driver was manoeuvring it carefully into position over the base, following the fore-man's hand signals. Finally both were satisfied and the foreman stepped back.

'He'll never drag that thing out!' said Henry, amazed. 'It must weigh . . .'

The rest of his sentence was drowned as the arm went slack and the gaping grab crashed down with all the violence of its huge weight on to the concrete slab. The shining metal teeth dug gratingly into its sides as the driver manipulated the controls.

'They can lift almost anything,' said Landor, making it sound like a personal boast.

The arm began to pull up, the machine bucked forward slightly on its tracks and Halfdane began to have doubts.

Again it tried and again the same happened.

But the third time, just when it seemed the machine must capsize itself with its own strength, the concrete block stirred, the exquisitely mown turf, which ran up to the base as though the mower had gone right through it, began to buckle and tear, the great machine sat back triumphantly on its haunches and the solid cube began to slide slowly out like a cork. The rich dark earth clung tightly to its sides, and even more solidly to the bottom, it seemed, as the great block swung free in the air. It followed the same semi-circle as before, only this time earth fell to darken the white trail below.

Earth, and something more solid than earth.

'Hold it, Joe!' cried the foreman who was nearest. The machine halted, the concrete maintained its momentum and swung forward like a pendulum dislodging yet more of the substance that adhered to its base.

'Oh, my God!' said someone as the foreman stooped, then stood up gingerly with something long and thin in his hand.

It was a shin-bone.

He poked at the underside of the concrete with it. Something like a narrow grille fell down. It might have been part of a rib-cage, but no one watching was ready to believe it. He poked again, dislodging an even more solid something. The earth fell away as it hit the ground.

Now they were ready to believe it.

It was a skull, grinning empty-eyed at them. And most hideously there was a mop of dark red hair hanging rakishly down over where had been the left ear.

Jane Scotby's hand went to her mouth, but only the dilating of her pupils showed she was not just stifling a little yawn; Marion Cargo was white as death, Henry Saltecombe gripped Halfdane's shoulder with unconscious violence, while Ellie Soper seized his other hand so he could not move.

'It's Miss Girling!' shrieked Miss Disney.

'Yes, it is,' she added in a matter of fact way as though someone had denied it. Then, unbelievably, she fainted into the reluctant arms of George Dunbar.

'Clear a space,' he shouted. 'Hey, Fallowfield, give us a hand here.'

Fallowfield was the staff medical expert, having done two years of a medical degree course before abandoning it in favour of straight biology.

But when they looked for him now, he was nowhere to be found.

Chapter 3

. . . they are ill discoverers that think there is no land when they can see nothing but sea.

SIR FRANCIS BACON
Op. Cit.

'This is what they spend my bloody taxes on, is it?' said Detective-Superintendent Dalziel, peering out of the window of the principal's study.

Sergeant Pascoe said nothing and kept his gaze fixed firmly on an area of neutral space midway between the balding, taurine figure at the window and the long, spare frame of Simeon Landor seated at his desk.

'I sympathize,' said Landor, smiling. 'I feel much the same when I see the way you go about your work, Superintendent.'

'Sorry?' said Dalziel turning. 'What's that you said?'

He cupped a large hand to a proportionally large ear.

If the buggers get clever, he had once told Pascoe, pretend you can't hear. Then pretend you can't understand. Nothing's funny if it's repeated *and* explained.

Landor shook his head, still smiling.

'Now, Superintendent,' he said. 'We want to help your enquiries in every possible way, of course. So just fire away with any questions you like.'

Oh God, groaned Pascoe. Honours even, so he extends the hand of friendship. Give the bull a scratch!

'What was going on out there?' asked Dalziel, pointing to the staff garden which the room overlooked. The mechanical digger had gone now but the deep furrows of its progress were still clearly visible. Over the cavity left

23

by the removal of the concrete base a canvas shelter had been erected. Men were moving slowly, efficiently around, watched by a silent crowd of students on the edge.

'We're extending on all sides as you can see,' said Landor. 'A new biology lab is planned there, so naturally we had to move the statue.'

'Who was out there watching?'

'The principal was good enough to make out a list, sir,' said Pascoe smartly in his best young executive manner, making a feint towards his brass-bound genuine-leather document case, an object of some derision from Dalziel when it first appeared.

'Of course, it's almost certainly incomplete,' began Landor, but Dalziel waved aside his apologies along with Pascoe's contribution and, by implication, any further interest in the list.

'Why were they watching?' he asked, scratching his inner left thigh voluptuously.

'I'm sure I don't know, Superintendent,' laughed Landor, still pursuing his sweetness-and-light policy. 'In most cases it would merely be the old hole-in-the-road syndrome . . .'

'What?'

Landor was wise enough not to explain. Pascoe gave him a mental tick.

'Was that all?' asked Dalziel as if an explanation had been given.

'Well, no. There were emotions other than mere curiosity on display, though I don't see what they can have to do . . .' He tailed off thoughtfully, then started again with renewed vigour.

'Miss Cargo of our Art Department was there for a special reason. Concern, I suppose you'd call it. You see, she had designed the statue and was naturally concerned to see it suffered no damage.'

24

Pascoe was taking shorthand notes, a skill Dalziel mocked as feminine.

'Then there were some older members of staff who were there to express their disapproval, I felt.'

'Disapproval? Because their garden was being dug up?'

'Partly that. But partly also because the statue was a memorial. They felt it smacked of sacrilege to pull it up.'

'A memorial? Who to?'

In answer Landor picked up the bronze plaque from his desk and handed it over. Dalziel read it carefully with an expression of grotesque devoutness. Like a close-up in *Songs of Praise* on the telly, thought Pascoe.

'Alison Girling,' he said, enunciating each syllable with great care like a child reading.

'My predecessor,' explained Landor.

'She wasn't old,' observed Dalziel. 'What happened to her?'

'A tragic accident,' said Landor, doing with his voice what Dalziel had done with his face. 'On holiday abroad at Christmas. She was a close friend of some of the senior staff here. They felt it deeply when the statue had to be moved.'

'Who are *they*, Mr Landor?' asked Dalziel. 'And how deeply did they feel it?'

'Well, Miss Scotby, she's my Senior Tutor, and Miss Disney, who's in charge of our divinity department, and very much the moral conscience of the college.' He gave a snort which might have been amusement or amazement. 'It was rather bizarre when those bones started to fall from the base of the statue. Miss Disney let out a kind of shriek and screamed, "It's Miss Girling!" A Gothic notion, don't you think?'

'Bizarre,' echoed Dalziel, as though savouring the word. 'Gothic. Get that, Sergeant? You mean she reacted as if it was Miss Girling's tombstone rather than just a

25

memorial? Where is Miss Girling buried, as a matter of interest?'

'I'm not certain. Austria, I believe. That's where she died. It was all several months before I first came to the place, of course.'

'Of course. Were you here when the memorial was erected, Mr Landor?'

The question was dropped very casually. Landor answered it just as casually.

'No. No, I wasn't. I didn't take up the post till the beginning of the following academic year, September that is. And now I come to think of it, I'm sure the statue was up when I came for an interview here the previous March.'

'Good, good,' said Dalziel, suddenly expansive. 'Very good.'

He came to a halt before an oil painting of a large amiable woman with warm blue eyes and bright red hair.

'Why, it's Miss Girling,' he said, peering closely at the frame. 'She's well remembered, isn't she?'

'Yes,' said Landor drily. 'She is.'

There was a perfunctory knock at the door and a large well-rounded woman burst in. She had a formidable chest development, but it looked quite solid with no hint of a central cleavage, and seemed the natural descendant of a series of fleshy outcrops which began with her lower lip and progressed downward and outward through three chins.

She looked indignant, but this meant nothing, Pascoe decided. Her features didn't seem equipped to deal satisfactorily with any other expression.

It turned out, however, that she was indignant.

'Good morning, Miss Disney,' began Landor. 'I'm rather busy . . .'

'Principal!' she interrupted, 'I really cannot tolerate this. I am scheduled this afternoon to conduct an extremely important seminar on Isaiah. But there's no one there. No one!'

She paused triumphantly.

Landor eyed her warily.

'Where are they, you ask? I'll tell you. I'll *show* you. They are there.'

A dramatic arm was stretched out towards the window and the garden beyond.

'Look at them! That boy Roote, he should have been reading a paper at my class. He has degenerated visibly since becoming President of the Union. I knew it was the beginning of the end when we admitted men in the first place. We never had this kind of trouble in Miss Girling's day!'

Once again Landor showed his quality.

'I'm glad you called, Miss Disney,' he said blandly. 'We were just talking about you, the superintendent and I. I know he wants to ask you a few questions. Please use my study for any interviews you care to make, Superintendent. I'll be with the Registrar if needed.'

He was out of the room before anyone could reply. Miss Disney seemed ready to pursue him through the door, with or without opening it, but Dalziel stepped forward smartly.

'Please sit down, Miss Disney. You have had a trying day. These things hit some of us more than others, I know. It's a question of sensitivity.'

Oh Christ, scribbled Pascoe in his neat shorthand. Extreme Unction. Oily Dalziel oozing over stormy Disney.

Neatly he scratched it out and waited.

Miss Disney glared at Dalziel, decided here was a soul-mate, and made her way round to Landor's chair behind the large desk, which seemed to swell visibly as though to take on the proportions of its new incumbent.

'Well?'

'Mr Landor told us how distressed you were this morning.'

Miss Disney was obviously reluctant to agree with any diagnosis from the principal, but Dalziel pressed on.

'I believe you were against the despoiling of the garden?'

It was a good word. Disney nodded emphatically, her chins and jowls tossing in sprightly dance.

'Indeed I was. I am! For many reasons. It has always been a place of comfort and repose for those of us not utterly unresponsive to natural beauty. It is almost the only remaining link with the college as it was before all *this*. And if this were not enough, it is in its own way, which is a very real way, a shrine to the memory of dear Miss Girling.'

She sniffed and took an absurdly small lace handkerchief from her capacious sleeve. Pascoe would have been less surprised to see her pull out the flags of the nations of Europe all strung together.

Dalziel clucked sympathetically.

'Forgive me for asking,' he said in a low, vibrantly sincere voice television interviewers use when questioning the tragically bereaved, 'but why did you say that it was Miss Girling when the – er – decedent's remains came into view?'

'It was silly, I know,' said Miss Disney almost girlishly. 'But dear Alison was so much in my mind, as you might imagine. And when I saw the bones and the hair . . .'

She broke off and looked up at the portrait on the wall.

'She had such lovely red hair, you know. You can't imagine how it used to be here in the old days. Just a handful of staff and a hundred or so girls. We knew them all by name. Al's gals, we used to call them. Such nice, decent girls too. Whereas now . . . !'

'So it was the hair . . . ?' prompted Dalziel.

'Yes, Superintendent. It was as if Alison had risen from her distant grave to reproach me for permitting all *this* to happen.'

'So you passed out?' Dalziel's tone was suddenly casually conversational again.

'I *fainted*,' said Miss Disney, moving just as rapidly from the submissive female to her previous role. 'I must say, *Inspector*, that I cannot really see how this line of enquiry is relevant. It's not the uncovering but the burying of these bones which is surely of interest. And that must have happened at least six years ago. Now I must go and teach the remnants of my class.'

She stalked to the door, but paused there a moment as if reluctant to exit on an altogether damnatory note.

'I'll tell you one thing, Superintendent,' she said, reinstating him in his proper rank. 'Those bones are not all that is buried here. This is no longer a happy place. There is godlessness at work in this college, on all levels. Good day to you.'

Pascoe managed to get the door open before she walked through it. He closed it gently behind her.

Dalziel had seated himself at the principal's desk and was dialling a number on the internal phone.

'Hello, love,' he said. 'Any chance of some tea for a thirsty policeman? In the principal's study. Oh, he has, has he? That's nice. For two? That's right, tea for two.'

He put the phone down.

'They're making us welcome,' he said. 'Well now, Sergeant, this is more your kind of scene, as they say. I'm out of my depth here in all this academic intellectual stuff. So what do you make of it?'

Pascoe did not believe a word of this modest disclaimer, but he knew better than to say so. He had a degree in Social Sciences, a qualification Dalziel frequently treated with mock-deference. But when he asked you a question,

29

he listened to what was said, despite all appearances to the contrary.

'It's not an unusual kind of situation here,' he said. 'The educational expansion programme of the sixties took places like this used to be by the neck and shook them up a bit. Government started thinking industrially about education, that is in terms of plant efficiency, productivity, quotas, etc. Small colleges such as this was could become four or five times larger in as many years.'

'Could? You mean there was a choice?' Dalziel sounded faintly incredulous.

'To some extent. You can't be too autocratic with an educational system based on liberal principles. Really what it boiled down to was the willingness of those in charge to co-operate. If you dug your heels in, progress was slow. If you went out after money and expansion, it could be relatively rapid. Landor's obviously an expansionist.'

'And her?' Dalziel nodded at the portrait.

'It sounds as if she was the other kind. A digger-in of heels.'

Dalziel suddenly seemed to lose interest.

'What do you think Disney meant by "godlessness"? Are they groping each other during her lectures, or something?'

'I don't know,' said Pascoe thoughtfully. 'Probably just that. Your modern students have come a long way from "Al's gals" I should imagine. But I can probably find out. I've been looking at the staff-list. There's someone here I was at university with. She's a lecturer in the Social Sciences department.'

He kept his tone casual but Dalziel, as always, was on to him in a flash.

'She?'

'Yes. *She*. It was a *mixed* university.'

'She,' said Dalziel again, nodding as if some dreadful

30

fear about his sergeant had been confirmed. 'A close friend?'

'Close enough. What's next on the agenda, sir?'

'Still close?'

'Hardly. It's several years now, and . . .'

'What?'

'Didn't you know, sir? I became a policeman.'

Dalziel let the sarcasm pass unreproved, though not unrecorded. But at least he left the subject.

'Right,' he said. 'Now check them all. I want to find out who was here five years ago.'

'I've made some enquiries already,' said Pascoe. 'Very few.'

'Fine. Similarly with clerical and domestic staff. Next, a list of everyone who was here five years ago and has since moved on.'

'Excuse me, sir,' said Pascoe deferentially. 'Can we really make the assumption that five years is the significant period?'

'What do you mean?'

'Can we be certain that this body was put into the hole which had been dug for the statue in the short period between its being dug and the base being dropped into it? Couldn't the body have been in the ground already when the hole was dug? Or isn't it even possible that it was buried there later, a hole dug down the side of the base, a groove scraped in the earth underneath the base, and the body pushed into this?'

Dalziel groaned dramatically.

'It's all possible, lad,' he said. 'It's possible this was a lost pot-holer trying to dig his way to the surface. But it's unlikely. I just *think* it's unlikely, but then I'm a simple soul, not over-gifted intellectually. But you're different. And when you've done all the other things you're going to do, just get yourself out there and find me half a dozen

31

good reasons why we can discount your possibilities. Right?'

'Yes, sir,' said Pascoe.

'Good. Next, I want a list of all persons reported missing in the area between, let's see, when was that blasted statue put up, January let's say, all right, between the previous October and the following April. Better make it the whole year, from July to July. And make sure I get the lab-report on the bones as soon as it's ready. I don't want any ambitious young officer working at his career prospects through it for a couple of hours first.'

There was a tap at the door. A pretty, young girl in a blue nylon overall came in carrying a tray which she placed on the desk.

'Thank you, my dear,' said Dalziel with a beam. 'We'll just be needing one cup. The sergeant has to go out.'

Pascoe ushered the girl out in front of him, then stopped and turned as Miss Disney had done.

'By the way, sir,' he said. 'Did you get a look at the statue when we arrived?'

'No,' said Dalziel, without interest. 'It's the base that concerns us here.'

'Of course,' said Pascoe. 'It just seemed a little strange, that's all.'

He made as if to go. Dalziel's expected bellow stopped him.

'In what way strange?'

'Just strange that the memorial to a woman like Miss Girling should be an eight-foot-tall bronze nude.'

He closed the door quietly behind him. Inside, Dalziel sipped his tea with noisy relish and eyed the portrait of Miss Girling with interested speculation.

Chapter 4

Men's weaknesses and faults are best known from their enemies, their virtues and abilities from their familiar friends.

SIR FRANCIS BACON
Op. Cit.

Franny Roote lay back along the window-sill, his still form blocking out the sunlight. He was wearing his usual summer dress of white beach-shoes, light cream-coloured slacks and a white shirt which was almost a blouse. This colour scheme combined with his own fair colouring somehow blurred the edges of his frame. Without moving, he dominated the room. Only twenty-three, he had developed a repose and still self-sufficiency beyond the reach of many twice his age; and these things put together gave him the indistinct almost inhuman menace of a figure magnified and blurred by sea-mist. It was an image he worked at.

'You heard nothing more, Elizabeth?' he asked quietly.

'No, Franny,' said the pretty girl in the blue nylon overall. 'Just about the lists.'

She sounded apologetic, almost distressed, at having so little to tell.

'You did well, love,' he said, nodding once, still not looking at her.

'Franny,' said the girl. 'Tonight. It is tonight, isn't it? May I come again?'

Now he turned his head and looked full in her face with his light blue eyes.

'Of course you may. We were expecting you.'

Flushing with pleasure, the girl slipped out of the

door with the expertise of one used to leaving rooms unobtrusively.

'Is that wise?' asked a long-haired sallow-faced girl with low-slung breasts.

'Is what wise, Sandra?' he asked patiently.

'Her, Elizabeth, coming along. I mean, outsiders can mean trouble.'

'What you mean is, she's a kitchen-maid,' said a small, dark-haired, moustachioed youth fiercely. This was Stuart Cockshut, the Union secretary and Franny's right-hand man. 'God, what's the point of trying to do anything if you can't shake off your reactionary concepts of an elitist society?'

'Belt up,' said Anita Sewell who was sitting on the floor staring moodily into the empty fireplace. 'Stop talking like a colour-supplement student. It's not politics that's bothering Sandra. It's sex. And she's right. Franny knows when he's on to a good thing. He gets an extra slice of juicy meat at dinner. And all the gravy he can manage, don't you, ducky?'

'Nervous, love?' Franny said to her gently. 'Don't be.'

'She'll be all right on the night,' said Sandra viciously.

Stuart sniggered. Franny spoke again, reprovingly.

'It has nothing to do with appetite of any kind, my loves. Nor with politics, Stuart. We do live in an elitist society, despite all you say. But the elites have nothing to do with class, or intellectualism.'

He swung his legs down off the sill and stood up.

'This business interests me. I've always had a feeling about that statue. Something compelled me to it.'

Suddenly he laughed and ran his fingers through his hair, looking for a moment about eighteen.

'I thought it was just the tits.'

The others laughed too, except for Sandra who was seated on the floor next to Anita. He looked down at her thoughtfully and moved his leg till his calf touched her shoulder. She leaned into his leg and closed her eyes.

'I wonder whose bones they are,' said a petite round-faced girl from a corner.

'The police will find out soon enough,' said Stuart, making it sound like a fault.

'Perhaps we can beat them,' said Franny.

They looked at him puzzled for a moment.

'Of course!' said the round-faced girl, jumping up and opening a cupboard behind her. From it she took a large box which she put on a low coffee-table. Out of the box she produced a Ouija board which she quickly set up on the table.

Franny knelt down and put his index finger on the planchette. He contemplated Sandra's pleading gaze for a moment, shook his head minutely and said, 'Anita.'

The girl touched the other side of the planchette.

Slowly it began to move.

Eleanor Soper was immersed in her favourite recurring day-dream in which her first novel had met with tremendous critical and popular success. Her elbows rested lightly on the untidy sheets of closely scribbled-on foolscap which were scattered over her desk. She was modestly accepting the plaudits of her colleagues and in particular, like a television instant replay machine, her mind kept on bringing Arthur Halfdane forward to offer his obviously deeply felt congratulations.

She was brought back to reality by a knock at the door.

'Shit!' she said. Her own subconscious was capable enough of diverting her energies away from her novel without the additional annoyance of external interruption.

The knock again.

Angrily, she opened the door.

'Hallo, Ellie,' said Pascoe.

'For Godsake,' she said, motionless with surprise.

Pascoe reached out his hand. She took it and they stood there holding hands, looking at each other.

Pascoe felt relieved and disappointed at the same time as he took in her short black hair cut to the contours of her finely structured head; her grey eyes, questioning now; her strong chin, raised slightly aggressively. He had not known what to expect, had half-feared an immediate return of all the old welter of emotions and passions. Looking into his own mind, he could find no trace of them. That was good. But still he felt sorry that something so strong could have gone so completely.

He looked again at the once so dear and familiar features. Nothing. But he knew he was keeping his mind well away from the equally dear and familiar curves and hollows lying beneath the old sweater and the threadbare slacks.

'Come in,' she said. 'Sit down. This is – well, Christ, it's a surprise. I don't know . . . what *are* you doing here?'

'Combining pleasure with business.'

'Business? Oh. You mean the statue?'

'I'm afraid so. But you're the pleasure.'

They both laughed and when they stopped, the atmosphere had become easier. They spent the next few minutes exchanging news of old university acquaintances. Or rather Ellie provided most of the news and Pascoe most of the questions. He was surprised to find how eager he was for information.

'You haven't kept in touch with anyone then?' she asked finally.

'Christmas cards. Wedding invitations. That sort of thing.'

'Summonses. Warrants. That sort of thing,' she answered, half-joking, half-serious.

'I've been spared that,' said Pascoe, wholly serious.

36

She looked embarrassed for a second, a faint flush touching her cheek-bone.

Pascoe began to reach out a hand to touch her face but stopped himself in time.

'Well, you'll be spared it here too,' Ellie said emphatically. 'The statue had been up for five years or so when I arrived. What's it all about, anyway?'

'We're still trying to find out. Who *has* been here since the thing was put up, then?' asked Pascoe casually. He didn't need the information. He had a list in his document case which told him exactly.

'I'm not sure. The oldest inhabitants, obviously. Jane Scotby. And Miss Disney. Not Landor, though. That's obvious. He came when Miss Girling died. The history man, Henry Saltecombe. And George Dunbar, head of stinks. There might be others, we're a large staff and I haven't got to know them all yet. But what's your interest? You don't think someone on the staff then was responsible?'

'Responsible for what?'

'Why, for killing whoever got killed and burying them in the garden,' said Ellie in surprise.

'Someone's responsible,' replied Pascoe. 'Any likely runners?'

The atmosphere was changing again.

'I should have thought that your best approach was to discover who it was that got killed,' said Ellie a little stiffly.

'We're working on it,' said Pascoe cheerfully.

He glanced at his watch. Dalziel would be expecting some kind of report soon.

'I must be off. Look, any chance of seeing you later tonight? There's lots to talk about.'

Ellie hesitated a moment before saying, 'Yes, surely. I'm dining in tonight and I usually pop into the bar afterwards, about eight. You'll still be around then? Good. Anyone will direct you.'

'Right,' said Pascoe at the door. 'It was nice to see your name on the staff-list. See you!'

He went out with a casual wave.

'No doubt,' said Ellie to the closed door.

She picked up her pen again but did not start to write for some time. She was trembling slightly. He looked at me like a bloody suspect! she thought. Not a sign of emotion. A useful contact! Sod him.

Convinced soon that all her trembling sprang from indignation, she began to write again but had to stop soon to light one of her infrequent cigarettes. Sod him!

Rather sticky, thought Pascoe with some regret as he walked down the corridor from Ellie's room.

But I won't work at not being a policeman. Not just to be liked. Not by anyone. It's not worth it. He congratulated himself once again on his self-possession during the encounter. Then he bumped into a large beautifully rounded girl in a frivolously short skirt.

'Sorry,' he said. She smiled and massaged herself voluptuously. He felt his self-possession crack.

Well, sometimes it may be worth it, he emended cautiously.

When he reached Landor's room, it was empty. He took the lists Dalziel had requested of him from his case and laid them neatly on the desk.

Then he stood back to view the effect. Dissatisfied, he readjusted them minutely to attain perfect symmetry.

'You'll make someone a lovely housekeeper,' said Dalziel from the door.

Five witty answers and several bluntly obscene ones ran through Pascoe's mind, but he used none of them, merely bowing Dalziel with as much irony as he dared to the desk.

'What's this lot then? Lot of bloody names. No good till we know who got the chop, are they?'

'This might help,' said Pascoe, delicately touching the central list.

'Let's see then. Persons reported missing between . . . well, you tell me, eh? There might be long words I'd have trouble with.'

It would be nice to think the sneers derived from an affectionate respect. Or perhaps not. Dalziel, according to oral tradition, had destroyed whatever lay between him and his wife despite, or because of, his almost canine affection for her. That had been before Pascoe met him. He had learned the hard way just how much of Dalziel's invitations to familiarity to accept.

Now he picked up the list and gave it an unnecessary glance. It didn't do to appear too efficient.

'Only two real possibilities so far, sir,' he said. 'Mrs Alice Widgett, aged thirty-three, housewife. Last seen leaving her home on August 27, destination unknown. She left a tatie-pot in the oven and two children watching television.

'Secondly, Mary Farish. Widow. Aged forty-five. She's the nearest. Lived all alone on the outskirts of Coultram. She had a dental appointment at 3 P.M. on November 9th. She left home at 2.15, but never reached the dentist.'

'That's what I feel like, too,' said Dalziel, sticking a nicotine-stained forefinger into his mouth and sucking noisily. 'Best reason for disappearing I know. Well, the dentist's a help. He's still around?'

'Yes, sir. I'll take details of the jaw along as soon as we get them from the lab.'

'Who are taking their bloody time. Why no one else? It looks a fair list.'

'Yes. Some of them are men, of course.'

'Why? We know the sex, don't we? Even I can tell the difference between a male and a female skeleton.'

39

'Of course,' said Pascoe soothingly. 'I just thought it would be useful to know which men felt it necessary to disappear quietly about that time. And the other six women were either seen boarding trains or long-distance buses, or some subsequent contact has taken place, a postcard, a telephone call. This doesn't cut them out altogether, of course.'

'Worse bloody luck,' said Dalziel gloomily. 'Have you got someone contacting parents, family, friends, again?'

'No,' said Pascoe. 'It didn't seem necessary. I'll get their files of course.'

'On which you'll find nothing's been done for five years. Naturally. We can't spend our precious bloody time chasing around after runaway adults. But you'll probably find half the sods have turned up again and no one's thought to tell us. They usually don't.'

'I'll get on to it right away,' said Pascoe.

'By the way. Did they have red hair?'

'Mary Farish did. And the other's described as auburn.'

'It might help. But then she might have come from a thousand miles away.'

'A central European, you mean?' asked Pascoe against his better judgement. 'That would narrow things down.'

Dalziel squinted at him calculatingly for a moment.

'Shove off,' he said. 'We've all got work to do.'

'Hey!' he called after him. 'What about that bint of yours? Get anything there?'

He backed up the double entendre with a toothy leer. Pascoe answered straight.

'Not much. I'm seeing her tonight for a drink. All in the line of duty, of course. She hasn't been here long enough to know much. I did gather they're having a bit of excitement at the moment. Some lecturer's been knocking off a student and there's a bit of a rumpus.'

'Who?'

'A fellow called Fallowfield. Biologist.'

'That figures. Was he here five years ago?'

He answered the question himself by running his gaze quickly down the list before him.

'No. Then he's of no interest. Dirty sod. Though it must be a temptation. There's a lot of it around. I think I'll take a walk and see what's going on. You can stop here. You'll need the phone.'

Jauntily he left the room. Pascoe had to close the door behind him. He jerked two fingers at the solid oak panels.

When he turned round he found two students solemnly staring at him through the large open window. They nodded approvingly, each tapped the side of his nose with the forefinger, and they went on their way. Despite the heat, Pascoe closed the window before he started his telephoning.

Chapter 5

Who taught the raven in a drought to throw pebbles into a
hollow tree, where she espied water, that the water might rise
so as she could come to it?

SIR FRANCIS BACON
Op. Cit.

Sam Fallowfield sat in a deckchair in front of his cottage
which looked down over the shingle to the level sands
and the very distant sea. When the tide went out here, it
kept on going till an onlooker could have doubts whether
it ever meant to return. The cottage was solidly built of
massive blocks of dark grey stone. It had been white-
washed at some stage but the salt and sand-laden winter
gales had long ago stripped away this poor embellishment.
It was an end cottage of a block of four, each of which
had a small garden at the front and a shared cobbled yard
behind. The other three were used only as holiday bases,
one by the owner of the block only, while the other
two were rented out by the week during the summer.
Fallowfield alone lived there all the year round and had
done so for the past five years ever since arriving at Holm
Coultram.

It was early evening. Soon the holiday-makers, temporarily his neighbours, would be returning from whatever
exciting expedition they had so noisily launched that
morning. But for the moment he had the place to himself.
One or two featureless figures were distantly visible in
pursuit of the sea. And away to his right a thin flag
fluttered on an elevated plateau to mark the outermost
boundary of the golf course. The college was completely
out of sight more than half a mile inland.

It was a situation to make a man as indifferent to society as Fallowfield sigh with contentment.

He sighed.

'That sounds as if it comes from the heart, Sam,' said a voice behind him.

'Come and sit down, Henry,' he said without looking round. 'You'll find a beer and another chair behind the door.'

Gratefully Henry Saltecombe lowered himself in the deckchair which he erected with a deftness unpromised by his podgy hands.

'Hope I'm not obtruding, my dear fellow, but I felt like a constitutional before driving back to the bosom of my family.'

Henry had a pleasant detached house on a modern estate about eight miles down the coast. It overflowed with four children, a dog, a cat, and his wife. He loved them all dearly but was rarely in a hurry to return home to them. He had married late when the habit of peace and solitude had long since moulded itself comfortably around his shoulders, and it was not easily to be torn away.

'What happened to you then?' Henry asked after he had opened a can of light ale and jetted it expertly into the O of his mouth. 'I noticed you disappeared when all the excitement started. The Law has arrived in all its majesty, controlled by a corpulence in excess even of mine. There have been comings and I have no doubt there will be goings. I have even seen one or two students with facial expressions distantly related to alert, intelligent interest. Simeon suspects it's an act of Walt, and Walt firmly believes it's an act of God.'

'And the police?'

'The police are less public about their suspicions. But it is exciting. At first I thought it was merely some animal remains. But it appears to be certainly human. I myself think the solution is simple.'

'How?'

'I have no doubt it will turn out to be a student jape. They knew all about the garden controversy. It was no secret and even if it had been, they have a supremely efficient intelligence system, if only in the military sense. So they get some bones, an anatomical specimen perhaps, and they bury them beneath the statue. What fun! Something to enliven a long, dull, very hot term.'

Fallowfield grinned wryly.

'I should have thought the term had been sufficiently enlivened already.'

Henry was immediately apologetic.

'My dear fellow, I never thought . . . that business is far too serious for anyone to be entertained by it.'

Fallowfield twisted in his chair so that he could see the other's face. Its rotundities were set in pattern of sympathetic seriousness.

'Come off it, Henry. It's the most entertaining thing that's happened here in years. One of the few consolations I have in it all is the pleasure I know I am giving my colleagues.'

Henry shook his head in protest, then began laughing. Fallowfield joined in.

'You see,' he said.

'No, Sam,' said Henry. 'It's you. You just don't strike one as a career man, so how can I worry about your career being ruined? It's the effect on you personally that matters and you give a damn good impression of not giving a damn. Which makes it easier to spectate.'

'Enjoy yourself as much as you can,' said Fallowfield. 'Who knows whose turn it'll be next?'

He said it lightly, but it stopped the conversation for a minute.

'You did bed the girl, didn't you, Sam?' asked Henry finally.

'I've never denied it,' replied the other.

'Here?' He indicated the cottage.

Fallowfield shrugged.

'Up against a tree. Out among the dunes. In the principal's study. What difference does it make where?'

'She always struck me as a nice sort of girl.'

'What difference does that make?'

'Every detail makes some difference, Sam,' said Henry earnestly. 'There's a difference between casual promiscuity and a real love affair. And between malevolence and malleability. She says you conspired to get rid of her. I know this couldn't be true. Now, does she really believe it, or is she merely being used?'

'Used? How?' Fallowfield's tone was sharp.

'Politically, I mean. Things have been quiet here for a while. They seem to have got all they wanted. But people like that youth Cockshut are never satisfied. And there's something about Roote I don't like either. They could be looking for another excuse to start trouble again.'

'Is that all?' Fallowfield laughed. 'I suppose it might be something like that.'

'You don't seem much concerned.'

'Why should I be? It's all a game, isn't it? It's about as real as that.'

He pointed towards the distant flag which was being held now by one unidentifiable figure while another tried to strike an invisible ball into the hole. From his demeanour it seemed likely he had missed.

'You're talking of the game I love,' said Henry glad to be able to shift from the seriousness of the past couple of minutes.

'I'm sorry,' said Fallowfield with a smile. 'I try never to be frivolous about other people's games, then they won't be amused or offended by mine. Games are all metaphors

45

after all, and often euphemistic at that. Ah, here comes happiness.'

A large shooting brake was jolting down the track which curved for a couple of furlongs from the metalled road down to the cottages. Even at a distance the car windows seemed incredibly crowded with faces.

'Four adults, seven children,' observed Fallowfield, 'I still don't know who belongs to whom. Adults or children. They go soon, thank God.'

'I must be off this minute,' said Henry, rising. 'Thanks for the beer. Oh, by the way, I brought you some mail from your pigeon-hole. I didn't know whether you would be in tomorrow. Not much. And one looks like your luncheon bill. You must come and have a bit of supper with us one night next week. Let me know when'll suit you. 'Bye.'

'I will. 'Bye.'

They both knew he wouldn't. He never did.

Henry made his way back through the cottage and out into the courtyard, waving his walking-stick with mock ferocity at the tidal race of small bodies which poured out of the now arrived car.

Behind him on the other side of the house, Fallowfield's face had once more lost all trace of the animation it had held during Henry's visit.

He was staring down at the single sheet of paper he had taken from the first envelope he had opened.

It was headed by that day's date. The message was simple.

'I must see you tonight.'

It was signed 'Anita'.

Dalziel did not receive the report on the bones until after 7 P.M. Pascoe, anticipating fall-out from his superior's wrath, had rung the lab at 5.30 to discover the report had been sent to the superintendent's office. He re-routed it before reporting to Dalziel, who was much less condemnatory than might have been expected.

'Limited minds,' he said. 'Specialization means you can only think about one thing in one way. I'm not specialized.'

'No, sir,' said Pascoe.

'Traffic problems to pornographic films at Buckingham Palace. I'll deal with them all. Now you, Pascoe. You're in a dangerous position.'

'Yes, sir.' Dalziel had had another half hour alone with Landor. Pascoe reckoned the principal had been foolish enough to bring out the bottles. We all learn from our mistakes.

'You've got specialized knowledge. Or think you have. Without being in a specialized job. You've got this . . . whatever it is . . .'

'Degree, sir,' said Pascoe helpfully.

'I know it's a bloody degree. But in something, isn't it?'

'Social sciences.'

'That's it. Exactly. Which equips you to work well in . . .'

'Society, sir?'

'Instead of which you have to work in . . .'

'Society, sir?'

There was a long pause during which Dalziel looked at the sergeant more in sorrow than in anger.

'That's what I mean,' he said finally. 'You're too bloody clever by half.'

Neither 'yes', nor 'no' seemed suitable here, so Pascoe preserved a diplomatic silence.

'I'm stopping here,' said Dalziel suddenly. 'Landor's fixed me up with a room. It's a long drive home.'

To nothing, thought Pascoe. Dalziel seemed to read the thought.

47

'You might as well stay too. There's no reason for you to go back, is there?'

'No, sir.'

Pascoe had had a date that night, but he had put it off hours earlier as he saw the way things were going. It had been a pity. He had felt certain he wouldn't have had to spend that particular night alone in his flat.

'Right. Then you'll be at hand. They're going to give us dinner in here. I think we're a bit low for High Table. Conversation-killers, that's what we are. Even you, Pascoe, who might have been One Of Them.'

Pascoe again skirted round the comment.

'What about the principal, sir? Isn't he going to want this room back pretty soon?'

Dalziel frowned.

'I hope we'll be able to give it to him pretty soon. But evidently part of these flash new buildings you see going up around the place is a new administrative centre. He's quite happy to have an excuse to start in there ahead of schedule.'

'Odd,' said Pascoe. 'This is . . . nice.'

He looked around the comfortably proportioned, panelled room.

'Doesn't fit the new image, I expect,' said Dalziel. 'We're still in Miss Disney-Land.'

He laughed loudly at his own joke, his flesh shaking till he started an itch in the small of his back. This he erased against the corner of the desk, grunting with satisfaction.

Dinner arrived early, about 6.45, and they were sawing through some rather stringy beef when the lab-report was delivered.

'You read it,' said Dalziel carrying on with his meal.

'Well?' he said through a mouthful of apple crumble a few minutes later.

'Female, middle-aged, been in the ground a few years, five or six would fit nicely. Skull is fractured in two or three places, probably the result of blows with a heavy instrument and almost certainly contributory factors in the death, there's a lot of technical stuff about the bones which isn't going to be of much help, she wasn't a hunchback, or lame or anything like that. Height about 5′ 6″. A big-boned woman, normal weight expectation 9 to 9½ stone, but they can't make a guess at whether she was relatively fat or thin, size 5½–6 in shoes, size 7½ in gloves. That's interesting, left leg has been broken twice, but old breaks.'

'Accident prone,' volunteered Dalziel, scraping the remnants of custard from his plate noisily. 'What else?'

'The mouth should be a help. No less than three gold fillings, one a fairly complex job.'

'We'll need that dentist. Your Mrs Farish is the only one of your probables that the age fits. Anything more?'

'Yes. That red hair. It was a wig. Or what was left of a wig. Real hair, mind you, but treated, and remnants of the binding fabric still remained. That could help.'

Dalziel was unimpressed.

'Too many bloody wigs about these days. You never know whether what you've got hold of is going to come away in your hand or not. What about clothes etcetera?'

'Well, there were traces of fabric in the earth samples we sent along and they'll let us know if they can make any definite pronouncements on the buttons, bits of metal and so on we picked up. They reckon the body was fully clothed and wrapped up in something, a blanket or a piece of curtaining. But they're still working on it.'

Dalziel poured himself a cup of coffee and stirred in two large spoonfuls of sugar.

'The first thing then is for you to go and see that dentist. It's a long chance, but at the least it will eliminate Mrs Farish. And then . . .'

'Then?'

'Then we'll have to visit every dentist and doctor in the

area. And eventually between here and Central Europe if necessary. Unless we get something else. Well, you might as well be off. You won't want to finish that, will you? It's cold.'

'I thought it was a bit off as well. Didn't you?' was the best Pascoe could do as he pushed back his chair.

Dalziel merely grinned, then grimaced as he took a mouthful of hot coffee.

'Shall I make you an appointment while I'm there?' asked Pascoe, and closed the door without waiting for a reply.

The dentist's name was Roberts. He was a round-shouldered gangling man with a small head and a hooked nose. Spider-like, was the thought which came into Pascoe's mind. He shouldn't have cared to be loomed over professionally by this sinister figure.

Roberts was not happy at being removed from in front of his television set. It was a song-and-dance show. Perhaps it was close-ups of the singers' mouths he found so interesting, thought Pascoe, his stomach moving uneasily as the smell of the surgery caught at his imagination.

Roberts had been warned on the telephone that there might be an interest in Mrs Farish's dental record.

'You're lucky,' he said in a high-pitched voice. 'I can't keep things for ever. It would have gone soon. It took me forty-odd minutes to find it as it was. And I don't need to look at it again to tell you it's nothing like this.'

He waved the piece of paper on which Pascoe had copied down the relevant details from the lab-report.

'Really, sir? Why?'

'Well; those gold fillings. Now this one, at the front here, that was probably essential, nothing else would do the trick. So you'd get it on the National Health, you see? But these two. Not necessary at all. Someone paid for that work.'

50

'And it wasn't you that did it?'

'No. Well, as far as I can remember. But I think I would, wouldn't I?'

'I've no idea, sir. I'd be grateful if you could have your records checked. We'll be asking everyone.'

'More work. All right then. I'll have a look.'

He turned to the door. Pascoe didn't budge.

'Now, sir, would be as good a time as any. While we're here. It'll save me coming back.'

Roberts was displeased.

'Look, here! I'll get my receptionist . . . this is out of working hours.'

Pascoe felt his own resistance stiffening, which he knew was foolish. He just was not in the mood for the Robertses of the world that night.

'Hello, Julian, here you are,' said a voice from the door. 'I saw a light so I came through. What's this? An emergency?'

The newcomer was in his forties, a strongly-built distinguished-looking man with an engaging smile.

'Oh no. It's nothing. The police. This is my partner, James Jackson. This is . . .'

'Sergeant Pascoe, sir. We're hoping that someone in your way of business will be able to help us by recognizing this set of teeth. Unfortunately it will probably be more than five years ago since they received treatment.'

Roberts seemed to have diminished since the arrival of his partner.

'James is more the man for you,' he said irritably. 'He gets most of our private patients.'

Jackson laughed.

'You're too modest, Julian,' he said. Pascoe doubted it. 'Let's have a look.'

He took the description of the dead woman's jaws from the sergeant's hands and glanced at it, casually at first, then with growing interest.

51

'Now wait a minute,' he said.

'You recognize it?' said Pascoe, hardly daring to hope.

'It rings a faint bell. The gold work, you see. But it's absurd . . . let's see.'

He glanced rapidly through the drawers of the filing cabinet before him.

'No, no,' he said, nonplussed.

'Perhaps where Mr Roberts got Mrs Farish's record . . .' prompted Pascoe.

Roberts pointed wordlessly to the bottom drawer of an old wooden cabinet shoved almost inaccessibly into a corner. Jackson got down on one knee and began to toss out an assortment of papers with gay abandon.

Suddenly the fountain of stationery ceased.

'Now wait a minute,' he said again, this time triumphantly. 'How about that? The artist always recognizes his own work!'

He held a record card in his hand. As he stood up, his expression turned from triumph to polite bewilderment.

'Tell me, Sergeant,' he said. 'Just what is the nature of the enquiry you're making?'

Pascoe didn't reply, but almost rudely took the card from the dentist's hands.

The diagram and its symbols meant little to him. He'd have to take the dentist's word that it checked with his own written description. And of course it would be double-checked by a police-surgeon.

But the name at the top of the card took him completely by surprise. Expert though he was at keeping a poker-face, the two men facing him would have no difficulty in reading the shock in his eyes.

The middle-aged woman, the vicissitude of whose teeth were recorded on the card in his hands, was Miss Alison Cartwright Girling.

Chapter 6

. . . sometimes a looker-on may see more than a gamester.

SIR FRANCIS BACON
Op. Cit.

'You'll never believe this,' Pascoe had said.

'I'll believe anything,' Dalziel had answered. 'But let's make sure. I don't trust dentists.'

'Who then?'

'Doctors. I trust doctors. And policemen.'

It hadn't been difficult to find out who Miss Girling's doctor had been.

Yes, the general description of height and proportions seemed to fit. Yes, Miss Girling had twice broken her left leg while ski-ing. She was an enthusiastic ski-er, went to Austria every Christmas.

And yes, he knew about the wig. It wasn't merely vanity. In one of her ski-ing accidents, she had hit her head against a tree and torn part of the scalp away. The result had been a scar and a small bald patch. Hence the wig.

'Now we can ask the question,' said Dalziel. It was nearly 10 P.M. He was sitting at Landor's desk. In his hands was the commemorative plaque removed from the base of the statue.

'And the question is, what is Miss Girling doing here, under her own memorial, when best report places her firmly in some Austrian cemetery?'

'That's a good question,' said Pascoe. 'Mind you, it did strike me as odd that she should have been left over there in the first place. Why not bring her body back to

53

be buried in the land of her fathers with all due military and civic honours?'

'Expensive.'

'She can't have been short of a bob or two, a single woman with a job like this. Someone must have got it.'

'What do you know about the way she died?' asked Dalziel. 'Or was supposed to have died?'

'Nothing. I just assumed she'd run into a tree or over a cliff or something. If I'd known she'd had two broken legs and a stripped scalp, it wouldn't even have surprised me. It's not possible, I suppose, that she could have cracked her head in the accident and some nut had her corpse brought home and secretly buried here?'

'It's bloody unlikely,' said Dalziel. 'Listen, we can't sleep on this. Someone must know. There must be a doctor's report. A death certificate. Something. I know. That woman, the senior thing.'

'Miss Scotby?'

'That's right. She was a great mate, wasn't she? Get her over here.'

'I thought it was Miss Disney who claimed to be the bosom friend, sir?'

Dalziel groaned.

'I couldn't bear them both at once. Scotby preferably, but Disney if you must.'

There was a list of staff numbers beside the internal phone. Neither Miss Scotby nor Miss Disney answered.

'They keep later hours than I'd have thought,' said Pascoe.

'Or else they're in bed. Look, scout around see if you can dig up either of them. I've got some phoning to do.'

Pascoe left, not certain where he was going. The building they were in seemed completely deserted. Outside, his gaze was immediately attracted to a row of brightly-lit windows in one of the new buildings. The curtains were only partly drawn and inside he could see what looked like a colourfully decorated lounge bar.

Ellie! The memory of their appointment for a drink after dinner rushed back into his mind. Their first encounter had not gone particularly well. This could kill it dead, he thought as he pushed open the door.

He was certain she would have left long before. Five minutes had always been her limit even in the days of their closest relationship.

But she was still there. His mind had become used even in their short previous meeting to the changes half a dozen years can make; and now, comparisons over, he was suddenly reminded of how attractive she was. She looked up and smiled. For a moment Pascoe thought she had seen him, then he saw a tall, slim young man moving from the bar clutching a couple of glasses before him.

He would have retreated at this point, not wanting to compound unpunctuality with unwanted interruption, but Eleanor glanced his way and he was forced to go on, though the smile had faded and the line of her jaw became set in an aggression as memory-stimulating as her beauty.

'Sorry,' he said. 'There was work to be done.'

'A bore,' sympathized the young man putting a gin in front of Ellie. He looked with interest at Pascoe.

'I'm Halfdane,' he said. 'Arthur Halfdane.'

'This is Sergeant Pascoe. I was telling you about him,' said Ellie, making it sound unpleasant.

'Can I get you a drink?' asked Halfdane.

'No, thanks,' said Pascoe.

'Duty,' murmured Ellie. 'Like on the telly.'

'It's quiet in here,' said Pascoe, attempting the light touch. 'I expected wild revelry.'

'It usually is pretty quiet mid-week. But even the regulars haven't turned up tonight. Roote and his mob haven't been in, have they?'

55

'No,' said Ellie. 'Not since I arrived and that was a long time ago. Perhaps there's a party.'

'Roote?' said Pascoe.

'Franny Roote, the student president. A man of power.'

'Oh. One of those.'

Ellie and Halfdane exchanged glances.

'Better clap him in irons before he demonstrates against you,' said Ellie.

Pascoe shrugged. He reckoned he'd just about compensated for being late.

'I must be off,' he said. 'I'm looking for Miss Scotby and/or Miss Disney. Do you know where I'll find them?'

'Next block,' said Halfdane cordially. 'First left through the main door. There's a Christian Union meeting. They're having a drive. It's Find-a-Faith week. I believe Walt does a nice line in turning water into Nescafé. It should be over just now. You're not going to arrest one of them, are you?'

Halfdane spoke lightly, friendlily, his attitude conciliatory. Even Ellie looked interested. Pascoe toyed with the idea of telling them what had happened. Why not? Everyone would know soon enough.

But why should he have to use tid-bits of professional information to attract friendship? No one else did.

The door burst open and a small knot of students entered.

'You'd better hurry,' said Halfdane. 'That's half the congregation.'

'Thanks,' said Pascoe. 'I'll see you again. Sorry about being late.'

The Misses Scotby and Disney proved difficult to prise apart. He made the mistake of approaching Disney first, who claimed to be irretrievably committed to an important discussion with two students who looked desperate for escape. Scotby then came into view, so Pascoe quickly switched the attack. The senior tutor said yes, she would be pleased to spare the superintendent a few minutes of her time, upon which Disney cut herself off in the middle of a reminiscence of her last tour of the Holy Land and joined the party before they had gone three paces.

So Pascoe, poker-faced, ushered them in together; Dalziel to his credit took it in his stride. He came from behind the desk to greet them like a headmaster welcoming important mothers.

All rubbery smiles like the Michelin-tyre man, thought Pascoe.

But once they were all seated, he put on his bad-news face.

'Now Miss Scotby, and you too, Miss Disney, I would like to ask you one or two questions whose relevance may not at first be apparent to you.'

'He's been rehearsing,' thought Pascoe.

'I would be grateful if you would just answer the questions, painful though this may be, without requiring from me any further information to start with.'

That's a bit tortuous, thought Pascoe. Get on with it!

'Please go ahead, Superintendent,' said Miss Scotby in her precise tones. Miss Disney said nothing.

'The questions concern Miss Girling, your late principal. Now, I believe she died in Austria, some five years ago.'

'Five years last Christmas,' said Miss Scotby.

'In a ski-ing accident?' asked Dalziel.

'Not exactly,' said Miss Scotby.

'Asshaschlange.' The strange outburst came from Miss Disney. The wisp of lace had appeared again and she was having difficulty with her articulation.

'Sorry?' said Dalziel.

'An avalanche,' she snapped quite clearly. She essayed another sob, Miss Scotby opened her mouth as though to speak, the sob was contained and she went on. 'Don't you recall that dreadful avalanche near Osterwald which

57

swept the hotel coach off the road and over the mountain-side? She, Alison . . . Miss Girling . . . was in it.'

'How dreadful,' breathed Dalziel with a light in his eyes which belied the statement. 'And her body, if you'll forgive the expression, where . . . ?'

'They never found it,' said Miss Scotby. 'There were half a dozen who were not recovered. It was a terrible business.'

'There was a service, Superintendent. On the mountainside. It was most moving,' interrupted Miss Disney. 'And quite in order. That was later, of course, much later.'

'You were present?'

'Of course.' The Disney bosom swelled. 'Where else should I be? I was dear Al's oldest friend, after all.'

Miss Scotby said nothing but shifted her feet in a minutely, eloquent gesture.

'If they never found Miss Girling's body,' said Pascoe, 'and all the passengers were killed, how were they certain she was on the coach?'

Miss Disney glanced at him coldly but did not deign to answer a subordinate. Miss Scotby had no such qualms.

'Remember it wasn't just a coach, *any* coach. It belonged to the Gasthof where Miss Girling stayed every year. They were expecting her that night. She was probably a little delayed by the fog . . .'

'Fog? Which fog?' asked Dalziel.

'Well, it was very foggy that December, I remember. There were lots of delays. I remember watching on my television and hoping the principal had got off all right. I've often thought that if it hadn't been for the fog, the coach would probably have picked her up earlier. And she would not have travelled along the road at just that fateful time.'

'I see. And the coach . . . ?'

'It was split in half, I believe, before being swept over

58

the edge into a ravine. It was one of those terrible curving roads with a precipice on one side and a cliff-face on the other. The part of the coach with the luggage boot in it was recovered almost intact. Miss Girling's luggage was there.'

She became silent. Pascoe felt that the memory gave her real pain.

Dalziel having got what he wanted was now keen to get rid of the women.

'Thank you, ladies,' he said, now a jovial inn-keeper at closing-time. 'You've been most helpful. I'll keep you no longer.'

The suddenness of the onslaught had them both nearly through the door before Disney dug her heels in.

'Superintendent! My outcry this morning (was it only this morning!) when those awful . . . *remains* were found. You cannot be taking it seriously! I was distraught. You are wasting your time. You . . .'

Words failed her, but Miss Scotby took up the burden.

'Do you really believe it might have been Miss Girling, beneath her statue, I mean?'

Dalziel nearly had them over the threshold now. He thrust his great face at them.

'Yes,' he said. 'Yes. I really do.'

They took a step back and he closed the door.

'Well,' he said rubbing his hands. 'That's better. So far, so good. It's all possible. Now we can sleep. Tomorrow we'll set about finding out *when*. Did she get to Austria and come back to be killed? Or perhaps she never got to Austria at all! But she's kept five years. She'll keep another day. Not a bad night's work, this. A bit of luck's always handy, isn't it, Sergeant? Wouldn't you say this has been our lucky night?'

But Pascoe was not at all certain that he fully agreed.

* * *

It had certainly been Harold Lapping's lucky night.

Harold was over seventy, but still in possession of all his faculties. He had served his country with common sense if not distinction in two world wars. He had loved and outlived two wives, and on certain great family festivals he could look with pride on more than twenty legitimate descendants.

Now in retirement he was a man respected near and far, a church-warden, a pillar of strength in the bowling club, the oldest playing member of the golf club though his handicap had slipped to 12, and an enthusiastic ornithologist.

He was also a voyeur.

It started by accident one spring night as he lay silently in the tough sea-grass above the beach vainly watching through his night-glasses (a memento of one of the wars, he forgot which) a weaving of grass which he had optimistically decided was a dunlin's nest. If it was, the dunlin was obviously spending the night elsewhere. Bored, Harold moved his glasses slowly along an arc, some thirty or forty yards ahead. And found himself peering into a fascinating tangle of arms and legs. It seemed incredible that only two people could be involved. Harold had no desire to disturb the happy pair, so he waited until their demeanour seemed to indicate they were completely oblivious to anything outside themselves before departing. But while waiting he saw no harm at all in continuing to view with expert approval the techniques on display.

Thereafter whenever his evening's ornithological research was finished. Harold always cast around with his glasses for a few moments before heading for home.

Tonight was different. It was far too late for any self-respecting birds to be on show. Harold was on his way home after a couple of pints of mild ale followed by two or three bottles of Guinness and the remnants of a cold pie at a friend's house. It was close on midnight, but the sun's light was not long out of the perfectly clear sky. He had turned off the road and cut across the golf course to the sea, more to prolong than shorten his journey home. The tide was half-way in, still a long way to go, and the surface of the sea was like cellophane, perfectly still. He could not recall a night so calm.

Then his sharp old eyes caught a flicker of movement among the dunes a furlong ahead.

Without thinking he halted and raised his glasses, without whose weight around his neck he would have felt only half-dressed.

What he saw sent him scrambling up a heathery bank to his right to gain a better vantage point. Then his glasses were up again, swinging wildly round in his incredulity.

In a hollow in the dunes ahead there were about twenty naked men and women dancing. At least that was the only name he could give to it. They were roughly in a circle, moving clockwise; generally in pairs, some facing each other, gripping each others arms, sinking to the ground together and leaping up again, their heads flung backwards, shaking in apparent frenzy. Others, arms linked behind; danced back to back, spinning round and round with increasing violence.

He could only see two-thirds of the circle because of the fold of the ground, and even with the clearness of the night and the help of his glasses, detail was not all that clear. But it was obvious that all the men were in a state of great sexual excitement.

A girl appeared alone in the centre of the circle. She seemed to be facing something he could not see because it was on the nearer side of the hollow. She knelt down, her arms flung wide, just in his view. Something advanced towards her from the side of the hollow, blocking her from Harold's view. Something difficult to make out,

61

dark and shadowy, a strange animal-like silhouette, like the head of a bull.

The dancing reached a new pitch of frenzy, the couples leaping high and shaking their bodies at each other with a wild abandon. Finally one pair collapsed in a tight embrace to the ground, another followed, then another, till in a few moments all lay there together, and a new dance began.

But this had no chance to reach any conclusions. Something happened, Harold couldn't tell what. But a man leapt up suddenly and looked around. He obviously said something to the others, seemed to shout it in fact, but the distance was too great for Harold to hear.

Then they were all up on their feet and moving again. Not now in the convulsive provocative gyrations of sexual frenzy, but the uncertain changes of direction of fear and panic.

The man who was first to his feet disappeared at a run out of the hollow towards the sea. Instantly the rest scattered and in seconds, as far as Harold could see, the hollow was empty. He followed one or two of the naked figures with his glasses for a few moments, but soon they had all passed completely from view.

Still he swung his glasses to right and left hoping for a brief encore. A movement to the landward side caught his attention. He stopped and focused, but immediately snorted in disappointment. It was a figure all right, but obviously fully clothed. For a moment it stood silhouetted against the night sky, just a bulky shape topped absurdly by a pork-pie hat. Then it moved forward down into a hollow among the dunes.

After that all was still.

Harold remained sitting on his vantage point for another fifteen minutes or so. Finally, 'Now I've bloody well seen it all,' he said to himself in gratulatory tones.

And, rising, he made his way back to the road and thence home.

Truly, so it seemed at the time, it had been Harold Lapping's lucky night.

Chapter 7

It is in life as it is in ways, the shortest way is commonly the foulest; and surely the fairer way is not much about?

SIR FRANCIS BACON
Op. Cit.

The next day dawned as bright as those preceding it, but by breakfast a stiff breeze had sprung up from somewhere and students and staff alike began searching for the cardigans and pullovers they had so recently discarded.

Dalziel set off early in the morning to confer with his superiors. Pascoe couldn't imagine what such a conference would be like. Who could possibly be Dalziel's superior without having dismissed him on sight? If you needed qualities of wisdom and tolerance like these to get to the very top, Pascoe despaired of his own prospects. On the other hand there was the example of Kent.

Detective-Inspector Kent, who had supervised the digging of the garden and the collection of the remains the previous day, now appeared in Landor's office and gave himself a few airs for a while. But he was too nice a man to keep it up. Pascoe liked him, but, like everyone else, marvelled that he had reached his present eminence. He was married with three young children and his family were devoted to him. But the one real love of his life was golf. It was an obsession with him. A week in which he played less than four rounds was to him a wasted week, though other men found it difficult to fit in nine holes between the demands of the job and their domestic responsibilities.

But Pascoe could feel almost sorry for the man now as

he stared out of the window in the direction of the golf course. Dalziel distrusted him and though he'd left a whole list of instructions for Pascoe, Kent had nothing but a few reports to work on and Pascoe could almost feel him working himself up to take a stroll towards the links.

Which would be foolish, but it wasn't Pascoe's business to say so. He had work enough to do.

The first thing was to get as clear a picture as possible of Miss Girling's movements on the day of her departure for Austria.

It is remarkable how difficult it is to reconstruct one particular day after five years. Pascoe tried it for himself and found it impossible.

The actual disaster had taken place in the early hours of December 20th. A Tuesday. Pascoe had arranged for copies of relevant press reports to be discreetly obtained for him. There was no point in provoking interest before they had to. The discovery of the bones had created a small stir, but generally speaking the public preferred fresh, warm blood.

Examination of the relevant year book which had provided much help with his lists the day before revealed that term had ended on Friday December 16th.

This seemed late to him. He consulted Landor who came in from time to time in search of files to take to his new office.

'We are not a university, Sergeant,' he answered drily. 'I am realistic enough to fear that many of our students will not deign to open a book once away from us for the vacation. So we keep them here as long as we can. And in Miss Girling's day, the place was very much a ladies' seminary.'

Pascoe was growing to like Landor. Before leaving, Dalziel had told him of the previous night's discoveries. Landor was unamazed.

'How clever of you, Superintendent,' he had said. 'May we expect an early solution? It has taken a mere five years to discover that poor Miss Girling was murdered.'

Landor now suggested that Miss Scotby might have preserved some record of the sequence of end-of-term events. He himself was quite unable to help. Nothing in the registrar's office was of any assistance either.

But before he could even start another Scotby-hunt, there was an interruption.

A small aggressive man with a Scottish accent burst in.

'Where's the other, the fat one?' he demanded.

'You mean Superintendent Dalziel?'

'Dalziel? He's a Scot?'

'Only by birth. He's not here at the moment. Can I help?' The man looked doubtful, then nodded.

'Why not? I'm Dunbar. Chemistry.'

He said it as though he were the science's personification.

'Yes, Mr Dunbar?'

'What's all this about Girling? That fool Disney's been twittering about her all morning evidently. She's a dreadful creature, dreadful. But they all are. It's an occupational hazard. But what about Girling? The daft creature was hinting at a connection between our late lamented principal and those bones out there?'

He pointed dramatically into the garden. His short arm didn't seem to stretch as far as he would like.

'We have reason to believe that the remains discovered yesterday are Miss Girling's,' said Pascoe officially.

'There's a thing,' said Dunbar. 'Well, now. I didn't believe the others, but this is horse's mouth stuff, eh?'

'Others?' said Pascoe.

'Aye. Disney yesterday. I had to hold her up. "It's Girling!" she cried. Man, I near ruptured myself. Then some students this morning. They were convinced. Said

66

they had it from a weejy board or some such nonsense. You're certain, it's true?'

'Yes,' said Pascoe in some exasperation. Dunbar nodded as if reluctantly convinced. He pulled a disproportionately large pipe from his pocket and began to shred what looked like brown paper into the bowl.

'She had it coming to her, y'know,' he said. 'I thought it was the hand of God, but this . . .'

He struck three unsuccessful matches.

'You knew Miss Girling then?' asked Pascoe. He knew full well that Dunbar's name was on the list of staff surviving from six years before.

'Aye. Well. Too bloody well. Me and Saltecombe – you've met him? Fat chap in charge of history – we were the first men ever appointed here, you know. 1965. Must have been mad. She didn't want us, I'm pretty sure. But there were pressures. Others could see the way things were going, so we were a kind of concession. Reckoned we were pretty harmless. Mind, I think Disney would have had us operated on if she could. There was a girl got pregnant that year. She didn't speak to us for days.'

He laughed loudly and his breath scattered charred shavings from his pipe.

'I don't know how I've stuck it all this time.'

'But now . . . ?'

'Now? We exchanged one old woman for another.'

'You speak very frankly, Mr Dunbar.'

'It's my nature, laddie. Look, how the hell did it happen? I mean, what's she doing here when she should be feeding the edelweiss in Austria?'

'That's what we wish to find out. Tell me,' said Pascoe, 'when did you last see Miss Girling. Alive?'

'Man, that's a hard one! Let's see. That morning. The last day of term.'

'December 16th?'

'If you say so.'

'Friday.'

Dunbar looked at him puzzled.

'Ah, no!' he said. 'That would be when the students went off. But not us. Oh no. We used to hang around over the weekend so we could have a cosy little post-mortem at a staff meeting on the Monday morning. The 16th, you said? Then it would be Monday 19th.'

'I see. So all the academic staff were there on Monday 19th. Have you any idea when Miss Girling would have set off on her holiday? She was flying to Austria, you'll recall.'

'No recollection at all. The day is dead to me. I'd be off myself as soon as I humanly could.'

'A pity. Perhaps Miss Disney, or someone on more friendly terms . . .'

Dunbar stood up, letting loose his unpleasant laugh once more.

'Disney! Friendly! Man, you've been propagandized!'

'But I understood . . .'

'It's a myth. She's got no friends among the living, that one, so she appropriates the dead. One of the few things in Al's favour was that she couldn't stomach Disney. Good day to you!'

'Goodbye. I'm sure the superintendent would like to talk . . .'

But the door was already slamming shut.

'Not a very nice kind of man,' said Kent from the window-seat. Pascoe had forgotten he was there.

'You handled him well, Sergeant. I think I'll take a little stroll around the estate and soak up a bit of atmosphere. Back in half an hour if I'm wanted.'

Pascoe watched him stride purposefully out of the room. Perhaps I'll be like him with a year to go to retirement, he thought wryly.

He turned back to his work. Dunbar had been interesting. But first things first. At what stage did Miss Girling

68

cease to be Miss Girling on her way to a winter holiday and become a corpse ready for its grotesque interment beneath her own memorial? Any point you cared to choose on the road from the college to Osterwald seemed as impossible as any other. Only the reasons changed.

At least this wasn't one where time was of the essence. There was no freshly killed corpse to be examined, no relatives to be informed (perhaps there were? but it wasn't the same), no frantic rush to track down a killer, while the traces were still fresh. There was no need to browbeat witnesses, to cut corners.

This one could be taken leisurely, almost academically (not that Dalziel would approve of either of those words!).

But it was true. Pascoe felt almost happy as he went about his work. There was a feeling of cosiness in the old panelled room with the wind outside pushing vainly against the window-pane.

Perhaps he should have gone in for the life scholastic after all. These boys knew what they were at, arriving at their (qualified) conclusions after taking the long way round.

Welcome aboard! he told himself.

Down near the shore the wind was stronger than ever, gusting with violence off the land.

Captain Jessup was having difficulty in coping with it. It blew his drives into the rough, his approach shots into bunkers and even his putts he was willing to swear were being steered inches off course by the malevolent blasts.

The captain's lips pressed together in a tighter and thinner line beneath his sadly ruffled white moustaches.

Douglas Pearl on the other hand had discovered the secret of the perfect golf swing.

Again.

It was a cyclical business this, like the old religions. An

endless circle of discovery and loss, death and resurrection. And to be conscious of the gift was often the prelude to losing it. So he viewed the fourteenth fairway uneasily. It ran along the sea shore, separated from the beach by a range of steep-sided dunes, vicious with tangled heather and gorse. The fairway ran round inland in a wide arc; the wise man followed it. The brave and the stupid attempted to carry the broad peninsula of dunes which lay between the tee and the hole.

Pearl stood uncertain. The wind galed forth in new fury. The captain sniffed impatiently. He made his mind a blank, and swung.

It looked good for the first hundred yards. Then like a Spitfire in a dog-fight, it seemed to accelerate upwards and banked violently to the right, finally crashing out of sight beyond the dunes.

'Oh, bother!' said Douglas, much distressed. But his careful solicitor's mind took close note of the last-known position of the ball.

The captain sent his shot on a flat trajectory one-hundred-and-seventy-five yards down the fairway. It ran on another thirty.

He spoke for the first time since losing two balls at the fifth.

'This letter you've sent me. You know it can't be done?'

'It's not asking much, I feel,' replied Douglas. 'An early decision, certainly before the end of the month, is necessary if my client is going to have a chance of finishing her course this year.'

'Naturally we'll come to a decision before the exams,' said the captain. 'She can still carry on with her private work now, can't she?'

'Oh, don't be absurd!' said Douglas excitedly. 'Think of the strain she's under. In any case, while under suspension, she can't attend lectures, as you well know.'

'Well, these students spend most of their time saying they're a lot of bloody nonsense anyway, as far as I can see,' said Jessup unrepentantly. 'And you know what's holding things up as well as I do. Fallowfield's protests have brought up a pretty complicated constitutional position. It's not at all clear whether "college representatives" means the student members of the governing body as well as the staff. They've taken advice, I believe. I thought they might have come to you.'

'They did,' said Douglas. 'I couldn't help them. It might have conflicted with my client's interests.'

Jessup pondered the implications of this as they trudged up the fairway together.

'I can understand Fallowfield though. It's like a court-martial with midshipmen sitting in judgment,' he said finally.

'It's a college, not one of Her Majesty's ships,' observed Douglas ironically. 'I think he's deliberately delaying things. The longer he spins things out, the more likely it is the girl will jack everything in.'

'But he's admitted he slept with her!'

'He's not a doctor, Captain. She's over age. No, the real thing here is this question of maliciously trying to get her out of the college. If that's proved, then he's had it. Perhaps he's hoping she'll have a change of heart.'

'And will she?' asked the captain. 'I'm not prejudging, mark you. Nothing's proved. She may yet turn out a liar. But could she have a change of heart?'

Douglas considered, then shook his head.

'No,' he said. 'I haven't really been able to make her out yet. She's a very reserved girl in many ways. But, true or not, something very powerful drove her to make these accusations in the first place. And it's my reckoning that it would take something even more powerful to stop her now. I can't imagine what. But certainly more

71

powerful than any blandishments of Fallowfield. I reckon it was just about here.'

He turned off at right-angles and began to climb through the heather up the dune.

'Give us a hail if you don't spot it,' said the captain. 'I'll save my old legs an unnecessary walk.'

'Right,' said Douglas.

At the top of the dune, he paused. There was a narrow parapet of scant, wiry sea-grass, then the dune fell steeply away in a bank of fine white sand. He stood staring out across the white-flecked sea for a moment. A few gulls wheeled and hung in the turbulent air.

'Any luck?' shouted the captain.

'Not yet,' said Douglas. 'It might be a bit farther. It wasn't a bad hit.'

On the seaward side of the dunes, wind and waves had scooped out a series of semicircular bays which provided ideal situations for bathing parties. Usually in the summer there were some students around, but the chill edge of the wind seemed to have kept them all away today.

Or nearly all. Douglas walked a little farther along and looked down into the next bay. He drew in his breath sharply. Lying on her side in the white sand was a girl. She had her back to him and seemed to be asleep. She was also naked.

His ball lay gleaming, challenging, a few inches from the smooth curve of her young buttocks.

Absurdly his mind began wrestling with the difficulty his next shot presented. Should he awaken her and ask her to move? Or perhaps he could claim a drop without penalty.

But the non-golfing part of his mind was beginning to notice other things. There was no pile of clothes nearby, for one thing. And there was an awkwardness about the sprawl of her limbs and a strange stillness about the whole body which he did not like.

'Shall I come up and help?' called the captain.

Douglas did not reply but, laying down his golf-bag, he jumped into the bay, half-falling, and reaching the bottom in a slither of sand. Down here out of the cut of the wind, it was quite warm.

But the coldness of the girl's skin as he gently touched her shoulder told him she felt nothing of this. He knew at once she was dead.

And as he turned her over and looked down into her stiff contorted face, he knew he had been right.

It had taken something very powerful indeed to stop Anita Sewell from carrying on along her chosen course.

Chapter 8

The parts of fifteen are not the parts of twenty; for the parts of fifteen are three and five; the parts of twenty are two, four, five and ten. So as these things are without contradiction and could not otherwise be.

SIR FRANCIS BACON
Op. Cit.

Now there was twice as much work and more than twice as much activity. Pascoe had visible evidence that he had been right to feel that old bones didn't produce the same sense of urgency as a fresh corpse. It was Kent's finest hour. For the second time in a quarter of a century he had been in the right place at the right time. (The first occasion had given him the promotion momentum which had brought him to his present eminence.) He had come across Pearl and Jessup in earnest conference by the fourteenth fairway. By the time Dalziel arrived everything needful had been done, down to a list of those who had played a round that day, and a methodical search of the dunes and the beach was taking place.

All Pascoe wanted to do was to re-immerse himself in his (so-far, unproductive) researches into the last movements of Miss Girling. But Dalziel didn't seem in the mood for demarcation disputes.

'These are distinct and separate enquiries, sir?' said Pascoe hopefully.

'If you mean, is there any connection, the answer's yes,' snapped Dalziel. 'Two bodies in the same place means a connection to me. It might be accident; but coincidence is like the bastards we pull in, assumed

74

innocent till proved guilty. And we do that by finding two distinct and separate killers. Right?'

'I suppose so,' said Pascoe.

'Anyway, how are you getting on? Any progress?'

'Precious little. I was just getting into it when news of the girl came in. I've got an outline of the day here. Look. Mostly from Miss Scotby's old diary of events. She hoards them. The students had gone down the previous Friday. There was a staff meeting on the Monday morning and a governors' meeting in the afternoon. Now Miss Girling was catching her flight at 11.30 P.M. or thereabouts. She was evidently a believer in starting the vacation as soon as humanly possible. Anyway, Miss Scotby saw her after the meeting, about 5 P.M. and she says she waved to her as she drove out, presumably on her way to the airport, about an hour later.'

Dalziel grunted. 'She didn't leave herself much time. It's well over a hundred miles.'

'That's what I said. But Scotby says she thinks the governors' meeting may have been arranged late in the term, after Girling had made her holiday plans. The ink confirms this.'

'Ink?'

'It's not the same as the stuff she used for the other major events. So she deduces she noted the meeting later.'

Dalziel rolled his eyes. The whites were quite revolting without the little brown pupils to hold the attention.

'So what are you doing now?'

Pascoe was ready for this.

'What I'd like to do is check at the airport. The big question is, did she get that far or not? They may still have records. And at the other end, Austria, too.'

'All right,' said Dalziel. 'But remember, it's tax-payers' money, lad.'

75

'It's the tax-payers' bodies as well,' said Pascoe, but only after Dalziel had gone out of the door.

His destination was the golf clubhouse where Kent had set up a temporary HQ. He found the inspector gazing dreamy-eyed at a large gilt-framed photograph of Harry Vardon in mid-drive.

'Look,' he said. 'He had his jacket on. And a tie.'

'Was he playing here today?' asked Dalziel.

'No. Of course not.' Kent returned to earth. 'Sir.'

'Anything new?'

'Nothing much. The p.m. report won't be through for a while yet, but I'm sure they'll confirm what the doctor said. Death by asphyxiation. Her mouth and nostrils were full of sand.'

He grimaced at the memory.

'Next of kin?'

'Her parents. They live in Newcastle. They'll be on their way.'

'Have you seen Mr Landor? I couldn't find him at the college and they said he might have come up here.'

'That's right. He's through there.'

Kent nodded at a door to his left.

'He doesn't look well.'

'Right. How's the search?'

'Nothing yet. Or rather, a great deal. Those sand dunes are pretty popular evidently, by day and by night. But nothing obviously relevant.'

'I'll have a look later,' said Dalziel.

He went through to the next room where he found Landor leaning against a billiards table, sightlessly flicking a red between the opposite cushion and his hand.

'Hello, Principal. I asked for you in the college.'

'Superintendent. I had to come up here. They had taken her away. I was glad really, I would not have liked to see her. As it was, I had to come through here and be by myself for a moment. That poor girl! Why her? On top of all her other troubles . . .'

Dalziel interrupted in his turn.

'What other troubles?'

Landor looked surprised.

'Didn't you know. Anita, Miss Sewell, she's at present in the middle of an appeal against dismissal from her college course. She has – had – made certain allegations against a member of my staff . . .'

'Oh, that. It's that girl? That's interesting.'

'Why? You can't think there's a connection? Oh, it's vile!'

Landor turned away and with a single convulsive movement hurled the ball away from him down the table. Dalziel noted with interest that it went into the farthermost pocket without touching the side.

'What kind of girl was she?'

'I'm not sure. Who can tell these days? She seemed an amiable young thing, quiet, well-mannered, not one of our high-fliers academically, but intelligent. Then last Autumn term, there started a falling off in the quality of her work which soon reached serious proportions. I talked to her, of course. She appeared quite unchanged from the description I have just given you, agreed that there was cause for concern, could offer no explanation but gave assurances of renewed diligence, then went off and continued as before. We don't work on exams alone here. Course assessment plays a very important part in all our courses and it was clear by the end of the Easter term that she was in desperate straits.'

'What did you do then?' said Dalziel.

'I wrote to her in the vacation suggesting she came up early to have a talk with me. She didn't reply. She didn't come early. Indeed she didn't turn up till almost a fortnight after the start of term. Her case was discussed at a meeting of the Academic Board. There was nothing else to do but ask her to go.'

'High time from the sound of it,' said Dalziel.

'We try to be humane,' said Landor coldly.

'And then she appealed to the governors? And brought out this story about . . . whatsisname?'

'Fallowfield. That's right. She alleged that her relationship with him was the major factor affecting her work.'

'Did he deny it?'

'No,' said Landor sadly. 'He admitted freely that they had been lovers.'

'Is that unprofessional conduct?'

'In the eyes of some, yes. But not in any legalistic sense. Our humanity doesn't stop at the students, Superintendent.'

'I'm glad to hear it. So?'

'She claimed also that they quarrelled, he wanted rid of her. And alleged that his assessment of her work in biology was unfairly weighted against her.'

'I'm a bit thick,' said Dalziel, scratching his pate as though to prove the point. 'But couldn't someone else just have a look at what she'd done?'

'Of course,' said Landor. 'This has been done. It's of a very low standard. But just as important in that course is practical work, laboratory work done under supervision, experiments, dissections, that kind of thing. It was here that Mr Fallowfield was most critical. It was here the suggestion was made that he had allowed his personal involvement to outweigh his academic judgment.'

'Which could be serious for him? Real unprofessional conduct?'

'That's true,' said Landor. Suddenly he looked at Dalziel sharply. 'But you can't think . . . you're not *motive-hunting*, Superintendent?'

'We're always doing that,' said Dalziel.

The door opened.

'Can you spare a moment, Super?' said Kent.

Dalziel joined him in the other room.

'What is it?'

Triumphantly Kent held up a flimsy white brassiere.

'They've just found this. In some gorse bushes about two hundred yards from where they found the body.'

'So?' said Dalziel.

Kent was a little nonplussed to find his own enthusiasm so little shared.

'Well, it might help to pin-point where the actual killing took place.'

'If it's hers.'

'Oh,' said Kent. 'Yes, of course. But it seems likely. It obviously hasn't been lying long.'

'No,' said Dalziel, taking it from him. It was slightly damp from the dew. But the metal adjusting rings and fastening hooks were bright and shiny still.

'May I see?' It was Landor, at the door. Dalziel looked at him in surprise, but held out the garment without demur. Landor took it between his thumb and index finger.

'No,' he said. 'I don't think it's hers.'

Kent opened his mouth and began to say something, but Dalziel silenced him with a glance.

'Now, why do you say that, sir?'

'She, Miss Sewell, was larger,' he said, enunciating the last word with meticulous precision.

'I see. Well, thank you, Mr Landor.'

He took the brassiere back and laid it on the table.

'Still, it will be interesting to find out who it does belong to,' he said.

Franny Roote woke instantly as he always did, with no interim stage of gradual revival. It was late. He was already missing his only lecture of the morning. Not that it mattered. It was only people like Disney who moaned about absentees. In any case as President of the Student Union, his official duties often kept him otherwise engaged. He smiled.

This morning, he thought as he dressed, Miss Cargo. About the art exhibition in the Union building. That would do. An attractive woman, Miss Cargo. He must keep an eye on her.

Someone tried the handle of his door. It was, as always, locked.

'Who?' he called.

'It's me, Stuart. Open up, Franny.'

'Wait.'

He fastened a single button of his white silk shirt, leaving it open from the throat almost to the navel. There was a speck of dirt on his white tennis shoes which he flicked off before fastening them, making sure the laces were nowhere twisted.

A careful glance in the full-length mirror fixed behind his wardrobe door; he held his own gaze steadily for half a minute; the door handle was rattled impatiently, but he did not move.

'Franny! For Godsake!'

He closed the wardrobe door and turned the key in the main door to admit Cockshut.

'Nothing is worth hurrying for, Stuart, love,' he said amiably.

'You moved as fast as anyone last night,' snapped Stuart. 'Listen, haven't you heard? About Anita? They've found her. Dead! Out in the dunes. Oh Christ, this is terrible.'

He sat on Franny's bed and put his head between his hands. The other did not move but stood stock-still, a pale outline in the light of the single heavily-shaded lamp which was the room's only source of illumination.

'Can't you open these bloody curtains?' said Cockshut finally. 'It's the middle of the bloody afternoon.'

80

'No,' said Franny. 'There is an ambience I wish to preserve here. Besides, now it is fitting. Tell all you know.'

It came pouring out of Stuart. It was all over college. The plain fact of Anita's death was certain, and the place – there were policemen all over the golf course. The rest was rumour. Her body was naked, half-clothed; she had been drowned, strangled, stabbed.

'Take your pick,' said Stuart. 'What are we going to do, Franny?'

'I must go and have a word with Landor,' said Franny. 'There'll be things to do. The poor love won't know whether he's on his arse or his head.'

'But what about the police? Shouldn't we . . . ?'

'Anything we do must be a democratic decision, Stuart. Surely I don't need to tell you that? We meet for recall this evening. Then we'll talk. Now I must act as befits a President of the Union. You, I suggest, should be thinking as befits a pragmatic Marxist. There could be a new basis for action here.'

Cockshut looked at him with distaste.

'You're a cold bastard, Franny.'

'No,' he replied with something like passion. 'I live in balance. I am all I should be, but not in each part of me. There is no place for weeping in that part of me which wishes to survive.'

Stuart shrugged his shoulders.

'You can't survive without humanity.'

Franny laughed.

'Go and start a revolution, Stuart.'

The door opened again and Sandra Firth rushed in, her hair more dishevelled than usual and a flush burning through her sallow skin at the cheekbones.

'Franny, have you heard? What are we going to do?'

Roote looked at her long and steadily.

'No-thing,' he said, giving each syllable a full value.

81

'Later we will talk. There are things we must talk about, you and I, Sandra.'

The flush ebbed away from the girl's face.

'Stuart, we'll need a full Union meeting. Tomorrow night; no, Saturday. Get the word around, posters up, you know the drill.'

'Surely it's up to the committee . . . ?'

'Oh, see them first then,' said Franny impatiently. 'But arrange it.'

'It's a bad night, especially at short notice. You might be pushed for a quorum.'

'Quorum forum,' said Franny. 'Just get the notices out. Right? I've got to go.'

He took Sandra by the hand and smiled at her, the smile lighting up his whole face.

'Don't look so down, love,' he said pressing her hand reassuringly.

She responded instantly, coming close to him, pleasure and relief in her face.

'Oh, Franny,' she began, but he interrupted her, still smiling.

'After all, you didn't even like Anita, did you? So why so glum?'

She pulled away from him, her face set again, and ran out of the door without replying.

Franny waved Stuart out before him, then followed, locking the door behind them.

'What the hell do you keep in there, Fran?'

'Memories,' said his companion. 'The distillation of experience. See you later, love.'

Stuart Cockshut watched him stride confidently away through the windy sunlight, strangely indistinct in the shifty dapplings cast by the old beeches which had survived the building programme. Turning back into the hostel building they had just left, he ducked into a plastic-shielded telephone booth, an unnecessary movement for one so small. With the end of a pencil, he dialled the London coding, followed by a number he knew by heart.

'Hello,' said a non-committal voice at the other end.

'Cockshut,' he said. 'Let me speak to Christian . . . Listen, Chris, we've got a situation here which might be useful . . .'

The trouble with a college, Dalziel was finding, was that you had a hell of a job putting your hands on people. If they were teaching, they were reluctant to be interrupted and Dalziel was reluctant to provoke open antagonism. Yet.

If they weren't teaching, they might be anywhere. In their rooms if they lived on the campus; at home if they didn't. In libraries, laboratories, bathrooms, bars or beds.

There was a copy of the staff time-table on the wall of Landor's room but he gave it up after ten seconds. He found he was missing Pascoe. There were plenty of other 'leg-men', uniformed and CID, at his disposal, but Pascoe knew his ways and was at home in this kind of territory.

Kent he had left up at the golf club.

Landor had been in and out a couple of times. At first Dalziel had suspected he was going to turn out to be a 'twitterer', but he was obviously doing a fairly efficient job of keeping the college in balance. The news would be in the evening papers, on the television. Already reporters were beginning to pester. Soon it would be anxious parents. Dalziel had already arranged with the local exchange that one of the college lines was to be kept completely free for his own incoming and outgoing calls.

'I've called a staff meeting for first thing tomorrow morning,' said Landor. 'If the staff are informed, it helps to cut down student rumour.'

'Good idea,' said Dalziel, uninterested. 'At least I'll know where the bugg . . . they are.'

'I wondered if you could perhaps spare five minutes. Just a statement, you understand. It could help.'

Dalziel laughed shortly and rudely, but stopped before translating the noise into words. It might not be a bad idea to see this lot as a group.

'Right,' he said. 'I'll try. Now listen, Principal, I'd like to get hold of . . .'

There was a knock at the door, Landor opened it. Outside stood Halfdane with Marion Cargo coming up behind him.

'Oh, you'll do,' said Dalziel. Halfdane, aware now of Miss Cargo's presence, stood back and indicated that she could go in first. She shook her head.

'Both of you!' snarled Dalziel impatiently. 'Together. And if one of you is superfluous to requirements, I'll decide.'

Landor smiled wanly at his colleagues and left.

'I'm Arthur Halfdane,' began Arthur. 'I wondered if Sergeant Pascoe . . . ?'

'He's away. Working. He has a full-time job. You'll have to make do with me.'

Dalziel's supporters claimed his rudeness was calculated; others, impressed by his record, were willing to concede it might be intuitive; Pascoe asserted it was merely digestive.

Whatever it was, Halfdane didn't like it.

'No thanks,' he said icily. 'I'll wait till later.'

'Please yourself,' said Dalziel indifferently, looking at the young man's long hair with distaste. 'I presume you're not withholding information relevant to our enquiries?'

'No. I merely wanted to ask something.'

'Oh. And you, Miss. Are you giving or just asking?'

Marion Cargo was obviously not reacting very strongly to external stimuli. The expression on her classical features was brooding, inward-looking. She would never have won a run-of-the-mill beauty competition, but she

had a fascinating face and a figure which invited speculation. Halfdane, who had no further reason to stay,
made no move to go but looked at the girl with open
admiration. Dalziel was suddenly conscious of his paunch,
his bald patch and his short-sightedness.

He scratched his right thigh viciously.

'I'm asking, I'm afraid, Superintendent. It's about Miss
Girling.'

Another! groaned Dalziel inwardly.

'Miss Disney screamed it was Miss Girling when those
bones were dug up. It just seemed absurd, and I thought
it was just the result of this when I heard the students
talking about it later. They, the ones I heard, were certain
it was Miss Girling.'

Again, thought Dalziel. Interesting.

'But now Mr Dunbar says he's seen you and you
confirmed it was. But I don't see how . . .'

There was real pain on her face, Dalziel was surprised
to see.

'You knew Miss Girling then?' Dalziel asked gently.

'Yes. Of course. She was very very kind to me. And
it's worse because of the statue somehow. If it was her,
that is. But I don't see how it could be?'

Dalziel turned on what Pascoe called his vibrantly
sincere voice, with matching expression.

'Nor do we yet, my dear. But I'm afraid there's no
doubt. It was Miss Girling's body. I'm sorry.'

The girl shook her head in bewilderment. Halfdane
began to usher her to the door.

'Come on, Marion,' he said. 'I'll buy you a cup of tea.'

'One moment,' said Dalziel. 'What did you mean about
the statue? Why was it worse because of the statue?'

Halfdane looked disapproving but halted, his arm sup-
plying quite unnecessary support to Marion Cargo's waist.

'It was my statue,' she explained. 'I designed it. I never
thought . . . But who would want to kill her?'

85

Now there were tears in her eyes and Halfdane's arm was not altogether unnecessary.

'We'll find out, my dear. Never fret.'

The girl seemed to pull herself together and even managed a watery smile.

'I'm sorry. It's just that it all seemed so long ago. Dead. And then it came back. That's all. At the time it seemed like the end of everything. And when Miss Scotby didn't get the job and we knew everything would be changed from the way Al wanted, I never thought I'd want to see the place again. But you've got to keep moving. I'm glad things are going forward instead of standing still.'

Dalziel nodded approval of this plucky-little-trouper philosophy but his thoughts were elsewhere.

'Miss Scotby applied for the Principalship, did she?' he asked.

'Oh yes. She was hot favourite. There was even a sweepstake and we thought whoever got The Scot was home and dry. But Mr Landor ran home an easy winner.'

She was quite recovered now and disengaged herself from Halfdane with a small smile of thanks.

'Thank you,' said Dalziel. 'And good day to you both.'

He closed the door behind them and stood still for a moment, something Pascoe had suggested about the statue and something Marion Cargo had said almost coming together. But not quite.

He had no time to manipulate the pieces. There was another knock at the door. His hand was still on the handle and the speed with which he opened it obviously surprised the two men standing outside.

Dalziel was sufficient of a realist about his own appearance to recognize one of them was built just like himself. Big, bald and beery.

The other was shorter, slimmer, much more restrained a figure in every way.

'Yes?' he said.

'Superintendent Dalziel?' said the fat man. 'Salte-combe. Head of history. And this is Mr Fallowfield of our biology department.'

'Ah. You'd better come in.'

So this was Fallowfield, debaucher of youth. Dalziel had seen too many cases where girls much younger than Anita Sewell had been much guiltier than the men accused of debauching them for him to make a quick judgment. But some old Puritanical streak, doubtless traceable to some not so remote part of his Scots ancestry, still made him disapprove.

But Fallowfield was high on his list of people to be talked to. He had already sent someone round the college in search of him without success.

'Sit down, gentlemen,' he said. 'Everyone seems to be coming in pairs this afternoon. What's it for? Protection?'

'That may not be funny in Mr Fallowfield's case,' said Henry, rather pompously. Fallowfield shot an annoyed glance at him but Henry shook his head.

'No, Sam. It's true. You got some nasty looks.'

'And why should people look nastily at Mr Fallowfield?' asked Dalziel.

'Don't be coy, Superintendent,' said Henry, with a Laughtonesque world-weary sigh. 'You've been here long enough to have heard about Mr Fallowfield's connection with Anita Sewell.'

Fallowfield, as though growing tired of having Salte-combe do all the talking for him, leaned forward and handed a pink envelope to Dalziel.

'Read that,' he said.

With conditioned carefulness, Dalziel removed the single sheet of paper from the envelope and read what was written on it.

'Anita,' he said. 'This was the dead girl?'

'Yes.'

87

'There's no date on it. You received it when?'

'Yesterday,' said Fallowfield almost inaudibly. Then more loudly. 'Yesterday. Henry came to tell me what had happened. I couldn't believe it. He asked me about the note.'

'Why?' snapped Dalziel.

Saltecombe cleared his throat.

'I'd taken it down to Sam's cottage early yesterday evening. I recognized the writing. It was none of my business, of course, but when the poor girl was found murdered, I had to say something, even though it was probably quite irrelevant. So I mentioned it.'

'Very public-spirited of you,' said Dalziel evenly. 'Tell me, Mr Fallowfield, did Miss Sewell come to see you last night?'

'No.'

Dalziel said nothing but continued looking steadily at Fallowfield till he felt impelled to qualify his answer.

'I sat up till after midnight but she didn't appear. Then I went to bed.'

'I see,' said Dalziel. 'Where is your cottage, sir?'

Again the other man's voice was low, almost inaudible.

'Just above the shore. About a quarter of a mile down from the end of the golf course.'

Well now, thought Dalziel. I should have known that. Someone should have told me that by now.

There was a brief silence which did not have the chance to stretch into significance because Saltecombe leaned forward and tapped the desk.

'You see what that means, Superintendent? She might have been on her way there when this terrible thing happened.'

'Thank you, sir. Indeed she might. Mr Fallowfield, have you any idea what the girl wanted to see you about?'

'No. No idea.' The man looked quite ill.

'When did you last have any communication with her?'

88

Fallowfield shrugged, as if forcing his memory to function.

'Weeks ago,' he said. 'The last time I spoke to her privately was when she came back at the start of this term, or rather not at the start but several days late. She had been under discussion at staff meetings. I wanted to tell her personally that I could not in conscience grade her practical work as of a satisfactory standard.'

'How did she take this?'

'Quietly. She knew I was right, you see. She is – was – a very bright girl.'

'And since then?'

'I have seen her, of course; but never alone. Since the appeal, of course, we have consciously avoided each other.'

'She gave you no warning of the appeal; made no threat about its nature?'

Fallowfield hesitated a split second.

'None,' he said.

'You're certain?'

'Quite certain,' he said.

Dalziel felt this was just a beginning, but there was other information he'd like before going further. And he didn't like interviewing two by two. It was a case he was building, not a bloody ark.

'I'll keep this if I may,' he said, waving the note. 'Thank you for coming, gentlemen. Perhaps we can talk again later.'

They stood up, both he was interested to note looking relieved.

'Tell me, Mr Saltecombe,' he said as he walked them to the door. 'When the candidates for the principal's job were being interviewed five years ago, who was your favourite for the appointment?'

Henry laughed unforcedly.

'No question,' he said. 'It was me!'

Another gap in my knowledge, thought Dalziel. I'm slipping.

'But the popular favourite was Scotby,' went on Henry. 'Not for me though. I always reckoned a man. Female emancipation results in free competition and in ninety cases out of a hundred, that means a man. So Simeon stepped in.'

'I see,' said Dalziel. 'Who else applied internally?'

'Just the three of us.'

'The three?'

'Yes. Scotby, Dunbar and myself. The women thought it was bloody arrogant of Dunbar and me. We were the only men on the staff at the time. But, apart from Simeon, another four started the following September, including you, eh, Sam?'

'That's right,' said Fallowfield. 'Look, I think we'd better move now. The superintendent must be frightfully busy.'

'All right. Cheerio, Super.'

'Good-bye to you,' said Dalziel, again whipping open the door very smartly.

Standing there, his fist upraised as though to knock, was a slim blond youth dressed all in white.

'Hello, Franny,' said Henry. 'You look like a symbol of White Power.'

He stared incuriously at Dalziel who found himself vaguely intimidated.

'Wrong place. This is police HQ now,' said Henry.

'The principal's in the new admin. block,' said Dalziel.

'Thank you, sir,' Franny said politely. 'Good day.'

He padded silently away in his tennis shoes.

'What was that?' asked Dalziel.

'That was Roote, our student president. An interesting boy,' said Henry. 'Don't you think so, Sam?'

But Fallowfield, Dalziel observed, was only half listening, staring after Roote with a troubled look in his eyes.

. . . the first great judgment of God upon the ambition of man was the confusion of tongues; whereby the open trade and intercourse of learning and knowledge was chiefly inbarred.

SIR FRANCIS BACON
Op. Cit.

'I'm sorry,' said Sergeant Pascoe helplessly. 'Would you say that again?'

Up till now his sympathy with those living near airports had been casual, unthinking. But for the past hour, ever since he had arrived at the airport, he seemed to have been interrupted either in his talking or his hearing every five minutes.

It wouldn't have mattered so much if he had been getting anywhere, but the net result of all the repetitions and amplifications was so far nil. Only the presence at one of the reception desks of a Giant, Unrepeatable Offer, Super-Size pair of breasts had prevented his visit from being utterly pointless. Noting his interest as they walked by to the sound-trap they rested in now, the airport's Deputy Executive Officer, a cheerful, middle-aged man called Grummitt, told him that the girl had wanted to be a hostess, but according to rumour no airline was willing to risk her presence on a plane.

Grummitt remembered the Christmas in question quite well. He had been lower down the airport hierarchy then, out at one of the desks himself.

'It can be hell if you get a bit of fog just as the holiday planes are starting. It's bad enough in the summer, but at Christmas it's always worse, not just because it's more common, mind you, but because it's so bloody short for most people. It's . . .'

The rest was noise.

'I'm sorry?' said Pascoe.

'I said, it's a matter of four or five days for many of them, so if they get held up here for half a day or even a few hours, they see a substantial chunk of their holiday disappearing. And they get mad. Now, I've checked as much as I can, and if my memory is correct, that particular day it was thick. Hardly anything got off till the early hours of the next morning. But it was a late-night flight you were interested in, wasn't it?'

'That's right.'

'Not that that makes any difference if I've got the right day. Everything would have piled up. There'd be bodies lying around everywhere.'

'That's what we're interested in,' said Pascoe drily.

Grummitt looked puzzled, but continued, 'Of course, as you'll realize, even in normal conditions, after all this time it's unlikely anyone would recall your Miss-whatsit-Girling? – but in circumstances like that, it's impossible.'

'Flight lists? Customs?' suggested Pascoe without hope.

'No use, I'm afraid. It's too long ago. Contrary to popular belief, no one stores up great sheaves of paper for ever. Do you know what flight she was supposed to be on?'

'No,' said Pascoe gloomily.

'Not to worry,' said Grummitt, trying to cheer him up. 'Even if you did, it probably wouldn't help. Everyone would be desperately trying to jump up in the queue, trying to get an earlier alternative flight. It'd mostly be families, of course, and they would stick together. But someone alone would stand a better chance. She was alone, you say?'

'Yes. We think so.' Pascoe realized guiltily he had not really thought about it at all. Had Dalziel? Naturally.

'What do you mean, an alternative flight?'

Another metal cylinder full of fragile human flesh lifted itself laboriously into the air.

'I'm sorry,' said Pascoe. 'Again, please.'

'I said, if you were due on a flight at midnight and shortly after midnight the mid-day flight finally got away – to your destination of course – you'd obviously be interested in getting a seat on it. Or you might even take a flight to another airport and hope to move on from there.'

'There wouldn't be any record kept of people changing flights?'

'Oh no. Not now,' said Grummitt with a laugh.

Pascoe scowled back at him. But a new idea was forming.

'What about baggage? Your baggage is checked in for one flight. You change to another. Does your baggage get shifted automatically?'

'Yes. Of course. It's a matter of weight, old boy. Someone may pick up the ticket you've vacated and he'll have baggage too.'

'Oh,' said Pascoe, disappointed.

'Mind you, I'm not saying that baggage and passengers never get separated. Especially in conditions like the ones we're talking about, anything's possible. But they'd end up at the same destination. Unless the passenger changes destination as well as flight.'

He laughed again. His cheerfulness was beginning to get on Pascoe's nerves.

'So you can't help?' he shouted through the incipient uproar of another jet.

'Afraid not, old boy. Have you tried the Austrians? They probably keep lists for ever. Very thorough fellows. Or travel agents?'

'What?' screamed Pascoe.

'Travel agents. Probably someone fixed it all up for

her. It might even have been a charter. Perhaps they had a courier running around, ticking off names.'

The noise became bearable. It's too early in the morning, thought Pascoe. What else haven't I done?

'You've been very helpful,' he said to Grummitt as they walked out together through the reception area.

'Sorry I couldn't be more useful,' said Grummitt. 'What's it all about? Or must I just watch the papers?'

'I wish I knew what it was all about,' said Pascoe. 'I'll watch the papers with you.'

They passed the Giant Super-Size Unrepeatable Offer. Grummitt nudged him.

'No wonder they built Jumbo jets, eh?' he said.

'You can say that again,' said Pascoe lasciviously.

Grummitt with a look of polite resignation began to say it again.

Superintendent Dalziel had breakfasted early and well. Unless the college domestic staff were putting on a special performance for his benefit, they did themselves rather well here, he thought. As he was still segregated from the communal breakfasters in the dining-hall, he had no chance to make comparisons. And, a cause of relief, no need to make conversations.

Perhaps this was the reason why his wife had left him. Often breakfast was the only waking period they spent together during the whole day, and try as he might (which hadn't been very hard) he could not force himself to be sociable.

Unwilling to cause offence by leaving anything (there was another school of working class gentility which believed that something always *should* be left, but not in his family, thank Heaven!) he took the last slice of toast from the rack, spread the remaining butter on it to a thickness of about a quarter-inch, scraped his knife round

95

the sides of the cut-glass marmalade dish, and took two-thirds of the resulting confection into his mouth at one bite.

The door opened and the pretty young girl in the blue nylon overall entered. She seemed to have been told by the powers that were in the kitchen to look after his needs. Dalziel approved. Paternally, of course, he assured himself, dismissing a mental image of himself slowly unbuttoning the overall which in the height of summer was probably over very little. His fingers compensated by unbuttoning his waistcoat, leaving dabs of butter on the charcoal grey cloth.

'Are you finished, sir?' she asked.

He swallowed mightily.

'I think I am, my dear. My compliments to whoever prepared it.'

She began to gather together the dishes.

'Tell me,' he said, 'what's your name?'

'Elizabeth,' she said. 'Elizabeth Andrews.'

'Well, Elizabeth, have you been here long?'

'Over a year,' she said.

'Do you like it?'

'It's all right,' she said.

'It'll fill in the time till you find a lad and get married, eh?' said Dalziel jovially. If they're going to regard you as a bloody uncle, you might as well act like a bloody uncle, he thought.

The girl didn't reply. Slightly flushed, she swiftly piled the remaining dishes on her tray and moved gracefully out of the room.

Even in his faint surprise, Dalziel was able to admire her figure in retreat, which was more than he could do for the advancing form of Detective-Inspector Kent which appeared through the door before the girl could close it.

'Lovely morning, sir,' said Kent happily, peering through the window at the sun-drenched garden, whose border and rockeries were ablaze with colour. The winds of the previous day had quite abated and only the canvas cover over the hole left by the base of Miss Girling's statue obtruded into the pastoral idyll which lay without.

Had things gone according to Landor's plans, the garden would by now have been trenched and torn by foundations for the new laboratory. Dalziel had asked for the work to be postponed. He was almost certain now that nothing new could be learned from an examination of the earth. But you never knew – and in any case it was much pleasanter to sit here undisturbed by the unbeautiful cacophony of the building trade.

'Sergeant Pascoe not here?' asked Kent.

'No,' said Dalziel. 'He's off doing some work.'

There was little subtlety in his stresses, but Kent took it in his stride.

'Just thought I'd call in before going up to the club-house,' he said. 'I've brought in the medical report on the girl.'

'Stick it on the desk,' said Dalziel. 'Does it confirm what the doctor said on the spot?'

'Yes. Not nice. Suffocated in the sand,' said Kent. 'Her throat and nostrils were absolutely blocked up with it.'

'Anything strike you?'

'Not really. Just the obvious. Between 10 P.M. and 3 A.M. And no sexual assault. That's a bit odd.'

'Why?'

'Well, in the circumstances. I mean, why take off her clothes?'

'Why, indeed? Well, you'd better get on with it. Though I doubt you'll find anything more up there. How's the questioning?'

'The difficulty is finding anyone to question,' said Kent. 'It's not exactly overcrowded out there. By the by, talking of finding, is there anything on that bra?'

'What? Oh that. Yes,' said Dalziel, annoyed at having

97

to be asked. 'You're looking for a girl with a 34 inch bust whose initials might be F or E, N or A. They had been marked, but many washes ago. It's probably nothing to do with this anyway. It must be a popular spot in those dunes and a few articles of clothing are bound to go adrift.'

'Ay,' said Kent gloomily. 'We found any number of old French letters. But a bra's a bit different, isn't it? And if it had the owner's initials on, that must have been for a reason. Like identification in communal living, I mean. Like here.'

'We'll make a detective out of you yet,' said Dalziel only half sarcastically. 'Have a look at the student list. See if any of the initials fit.'

'OK, sir,' said Kent. 'Well, I'm off. Who's for golf, eh?'

He went out of the door making minute swinging motions of the arm and clucking his tongue against the roof of his mouth.

Dalziel turned to the desk and began organizing his day's business. Already he had accumulated an amazing amount of paper in the form of reports, statements, directives, instructions etc., etc., and the two drawers vacated for him by Landor in the filing cabinet were quite full. The principal had by no means completed his removals to the new administration centre and even Dalziel felt reluctant to urge him to get a move on.

He called in a uniformed constable to help sort things out and to answer the telephone. He was beginning to feel the irritation which always grew on him if he found himself cooped up unproductively for no matter how short a length of time.

It came as a relief when Simeon Landor arrived in mid-morning and reminded him about the staff meeting.

'You said you'd come and say a few words,' he said apologetically. 'I just want to put everyone formally in

98

the picture, that's all. It's just ten minutes during coffee-break so that everyone can attend without cutting lectures. If you're too busy, please say so, and I'll . . .'

'Not at all,' said Dalziel expansively. 'I'll be glad of the chance to meet them all collectively. After all, you're the people who must know what goes on round here. You've a right to all the information we have.'

He gave a few quick instructions to the constable, then left with Landor, enjoying the feel of the sun on his balding pate as they made their way towards the building which housed the Senior Common Room.

Conversation stopped for a moment as Landor ushered him into the crowded room, but almost immediately some of the more ancient inmates, the Misses Scotby and Disney much in evidence, demonstrated their good breeding by continuing their conversations at a higher pitch than before and looking fixedly away from Dalziel.

Landor supplied him with a cup of coffee and led him to a chair behind a table at the far end of the room.

'May we begin?' he said in a voice so conversational that Dalziel imagined he was being addressed directly despite the fact that Landor had half-turned his back on him. But he quickly realized that the principal was addressing his staff. Evidently in these circles you didn't shout or ring a bell to bring a meeting to order, you merely spoke to those nearest you and by some aural osmosis the message eventually reached the other end of the room.

'Thank you,' said Landor. 'Now this is not a formal meeting so there will be no minutes either read, or taken. But as far as possible I suggest we stick to our usual modes of procedure. Most of you will know, by sight at least, Superintendent Dalziel. He has kindly agreed to come along today to put us in the picture, as it were. Everyone here will be aware of the double set of tragic circumstances which have necessitated his presence in the

99

college. However, it is often difficult to separate truth from rumour and the better informed we are, the better informed the student body will be. Superintendent Dalziel.'

Dalziel stood up heavily and viewed his audience. Up until this moment he had had no real idea of what he was going to say. Now, faced by this polite blank of faces, he reacted to their common denominator (bloody clever bastards, all of 'em, he thought mockingly) by selecting a role Pascoe would have recognized with an inward groan. The blunt, unsubtle policeman.

'I'll be brief,' he said. 'First things first. The remains found in the college garden on Wednesday have been identified as those of Miss Girling, the former principal of this college. We are treating it as a case of murder.'

He paused. One or two shifted slightly in their chairs. Miss Disney's face was a mask of stoically-borne grief.

'Yesterday, Thursday, the naked body of a student, Anita Sewell, was found in the dunes by the golf course. She had died of asphyxiation as a result of having her face forced down into the sand some time late on Wednesday night or early Thursday morning. She had *not* been sexually assaulted. This too we are treating as murder.'

He paused again. Now there was a general shifting of position. Several cigarettes were lit. Halfdane leaned over to Henry Saltecombe and said something. The older man nodded vigorously. A man recognized from Pascoe's description as George Dunbar was smiling faintly with the complacent look of one to whom this was all very old stuff. He couldn't spot Fallowfield at all, but the pretty woman sitting between Marion Cargo and Halfdane (triumphantly?) was possibly Pascoe's old mate.

Miss Disney opened her mouth to speak. He let the first syllable get out, then continued, overriding her without a glance in her direction.

100

'I've told you nothing you won't read in the newspapers. Probably have read already. But it's often useful to have it from the horse's mouth, so to speak.'

A slight ripple of laughter.

'You're the people who ought to know. You're the ones who can reassure the students here.'

'You haven't really given us much to reassure them with, Superintendent.' It was Halfdane. 'And don't you propose to talk to them direct? After all, they're just as important as we in this institution. Perhaps more so.'

A couple of mutters of agreement. More indignant snorts.

'I can't talk to them all at once. Not without turning it into a rally. In any case, you're the ones who are paid to talk to these youngsters. You're their teachers.'

Halfdane started up again indignantly, but Dunbar beat him to it.

'Tell me, when did you find out it was Miss Girling in the garden?'

'This was confirmed on Wednesday evening,' said Dalziel. 'Why?'

'I just wondered how half the college seemed to have this information on Wednesday afternoon?'

Dalziel nodded for the want of anything else to do.

'You mean, staff?'

'I mean students.'

There was a confirmatory murmur from half a dozen places in the room.

'You surprise me,' said Dalziel. 'As Miss Girling died nearly six years ago, I should have thought it unlikely that any *student* could have known anything about it.'

The implications of the stress were caught immediately, but Dalziel was not impressed by this display of sharpness of wit. Anyone with half a mind must have realized days earlier that he'd be interested in the old-established members of staff.

101

Landor obviously decided he must take back control of the meeting.

'Thank you, Superintendent. I know we will all assist you in every way we can. What is important I think is that we carry on as normal, and I know that you will be eager to assist us in this.'

'Of course,' said Dalziel, still standing. 'But our work comes first. Let's be clear about that. Disruption of your work is unfortunate. Disruption of mine amounts to obstruction of the law.'

Again the raised eyebrows bit, the exchange of glances, the pursing of lips. Henry Saltecombe stood up waving his pipe apologetically, scattering warm embers over his neighbours.

'One question,' he said. 'Do you think these two dreadful businesses are connected in any way? Or is it merely some terrible coincidence?'

Pascoe had asked this. Dalziel wondered how he was getting on at the airport. Even if he got nowhere, he'd get there thoroughly. He would probably have made a damn sight better job of this side of the business as well. He might have some understanding of these people. Dalziel tried not to despise them because that could easily lead to underestimation of ability (criminal, of course), and misinterpretation of motive. But six months' holiday a year and a working life centred on reading books . . . ! The scientists he could go along with to some extent, but surely someone, some day, was going to sort out the rest!

'As a policeman, I distrust coincidence,' he replied.

'And I, as a historian,' said Saltecombe. Those about him smiled. He must have made a funny, thought Dalziel.

The woman who might be Pascoe's friend now rose with a suddenness that suggested she had been hurled by a spring through a stage trap-door.

'What I'd like to know is how we're expected to maintain hard fought-for personal relationships with our students in an allegedly democratic institution when we permit the civil authorities to so blatantly take control of our decision-making. I would remind the principal that his loyalties ought to be to the college and its members,' she rattled out at a great rate, then sat down as abruptly as she had risen.

Miss Disney swelled visibly, as though someone was pumping air into her body through some inimaginable orifice, but she took too long about it and it was Miss Scotby who stood up, arrow-straight, and spoke first.

'I would suggest that Miss Soper thinks less about *personal* relationships and more about *pastoral* responsibilities.'

She sat down. Dalziel did not have the faintest idea whether this was a match-winning riposte or not. There was a small outbreak of probably ironic applause from the back of the room. Ellie Soper rolled her eyes upwards in mock despair.

Landor rose.

'Yes, I agree there are one or two purely internal and academic matters we ought to discuss, but I see no reason to keep Superintendent Dalziel from his very important duties.'

He wants me out, thought Dalziel. Before they get too rude. Perhaps he thinks I'm sensitive!

The thought pleased him and he smiled benevolently at the staff who were obviously sitting in tense expectation of the hand-to-hand fighting which seemed likely to follow his departure.

'It's been a pleasure, Mr Landor,' he said. 'No, I can find my own way back. Good day to you all. Ladies. Gentlemen.'

It might be interesting to hear what they say, he thought as he closed the door behind him. But it'd only have curiosity value. He rarely questioned his own powers of perception, but he now admitted he'd probably have

103

difficulty in taking in whatever the hell it was they were going on about. They seemed to treat words as things of power, not as tools. They could get stuffed. He had work to do.

A girl started walking by his side as he descended the stairs. He glanced sideways at her. Long hair, sallow skin, hive-shaped breasts inadequately supported under a darned grey sweater.

'I want a word with you,' she said casually.

Lords of the bloody earth, he thought. First that lot back there. Now this.

'Why?' he said, not slackening his pace. They passed through the main door of the building out into the sunlight. She made a concession to it by thrusting the sleeves of her sweater up over her elbows, producing as a side effect a gentle breast-bobbing, which caught his eye.

'I was a friend of Anita's.'

She didn't look as if she were about to cry on his shoulder, so he continued the hard line.

'So what?'

'So either bloody well listen or not.'

He stopped and faced her.

'Haven't you got a bra on?' he asked.

'No. Does it disturb you?'

'What's your name?'

'Sandra. Sandra Firth.'

'Oh,' he said, disappointed. 'All right. I can give you five minutes.'

They set off walking once more.

'Thanks,' she said. 'Do you wear a corset?'

'Please,' he groaned as he led the way into Landor's study. 'Just one thing. My interpreter's away at the moment. So just keep it simple, eh?'

'All right,' she said. 'Are you sitting comfortably? Then I'll begin.'

* * *

'Hello? Hello!' said Pascoe. '*Ja. Ja. Ich bin* Pascoe. Pascoe! Hello! *Was ist* . . . oh, for Christ's sake!'

He resisted the temptation to slam the 'phone down only because he knew that the small beach-head he had achieved would then have to be laboriously re-established.

'Hello?' said a female voice, loud and clear.

'Yes? *Ja. Ja.* Pascoe *hier*.'

'This is the operator, Sergeant Pascoe,' said the voice in icy tones. 'Your call to Innsbruck will be through in one moment. Please wait.'

'Thanks,' he said. 'Hello! *Hier ist* Pascoe!'

He was beginning to have doubts about the wisdom of his actions in all kinds of ways.

The previous day he had with Dalziel's authority tele-graphed a request for assistance to the Innsbruck police. It had seemed a good idea at the time to suggest the information required be transmitted through a direct telephone link twenty-four hours later.

Now he recalled uneasily how keen Dalziel was on economy in matters of public money. Other people's economies, of course; Dalziel himself was very ready to spend any money thus saved.

In addition, Pascoe was having doubts about the adequacy of his German. It had been some years since he had used it and he was beginning to fear the old fluency had gone.

The next couple of minutes seemed to prove him right. The 'cribs' he had surrounded himself with were more of a nuisance than a help. The carefully looked-up words for 'flight list', 'immigration officer', 'passport control', even 'avalanche', seemed to present considerable diffi-culty to the man at the other end.

'*Wiedersagen bitte*,' said Pascoe for the fifth or sixth time. '*Ja. Ein Moment.*'

He began ruffling through the pages of his English-German dictionary once more, unable to discover anything vaguely resembling the word he had just heard.

Finally there was a strange noise from the receiver which might have been a polite cough squeezed and contorted through several hundred miles of telephone cable.

'Say, Sergeant, how would you like it if I tried my English out on you? It's a vanity of mine and I'd appreciate the practice.'

The shame of the moment was almost lost in Pascoe's surprise that the words were spoken with a strong American accent.

'That would be fine,' he said, with relief. He hoped the operator was not listening in.

The only difficulties now were minor variations of American usage soon overcome.

'We checked out the airport and the hotel without much joy from either. No records of arrivals here are kept for so long and I can't discover that anyone made a formal check that your Girling did in fact arrive that night. Why should they? If someone gets listed as dead, and they ain't, you'd think they'd come running, wouldn't you?'

'What about the baggage?'

'It seems the hotel bus was expecting a full load that night, both from the rail-station and the airport. It's a distance of about fifty kilometres from Innsbruck to Osterwald. Some of the guests arrived both at the station and the airport well before midnight. We know this because when they realized they weren't going to get on their way till well into the morning because of the delays in the English flights, some passengers insisted on hiring cars to take them or spending the night in Innsbruck and being picked up the following day. They were the lucky

106

ones, the way things broke. Anyhow, they filled us in on the story at the time.'

'Look, Lieutenant, could the coach-driver have picked up Miss Girling's luggage without picking up Miss Girling?'

It was a silly question. It must have happened unless someone had dug Al out of an Austrian avalanche and smuggled her back to England to bury her under her own memorial.

'Yeah. Why not? It'd be labelled. Do I gather you've got a corpse you think might be this dame?'

'That's right.'

'You don't say! Now your other questions. No, her passport wasn't in the baggage removed from the wreck. It seemed likely she'd have it in her hand-luggage which would be with her in the coach. At least, that's what was thought at the time. They got the driver's body out and a list. Girling's name was on it, and ticked off. But that might just have meant the luggage in the light of what you say. And that's about it.'

'Oh,' said Pascoe. He was sure there was something else he ought to ask before cutting off finally (at least it seemed an act of finality) this connection.

'Hey, you still there?'

'Yes.'

'At the hotel there was evidently another dame, a particular buddy of Girling's. It seems a group of them, half a dozen or more, used to meet up for the winter sports every Christmas vacation, but this one was a special friend. And they usually travelled together, the manager thought.'

'Did she now?' said Pascoe with interest. 'I don't suppose . . .'

'You want her name? Miss Jean Mayflower. Like an address? It's old; she stopped coming after your girl bought it. 17, Friendly Villas, Doncaster, Yorkshire. Got it?'

'Got it. Many thanks. I don't suppose the hotel had any correspondence from Miss Girling herself?'

'Oh no. I checked. All they had was a confirmatory note from her travel agent. He did all the arranging every year.'

'I don't suppose . . .' said Pascoe again.

'Hey, I like that "I don't suppose", I can use it. Wait. I've got an address. Super-Vacs Ltd, Harr-oh-gate, that make sense?'

'Very much so, I can't say how grateful we are.'

'Think nothing of it. It breaks the routine. Let's know how you make out, huh? I mean, if she ain't at the bottom of that ravine, then that's one less cadaver we've got lying about.'

'I will. Goodbye.'

'OK. *Gruss Gott.*'

Oh, I will, I will, thought Pascoe as he heard the receiver go down 900 hundred miles away. Public money well spent!

'Are you finished?' asked the cool, efficient, female voice.

'Oh no,' said Pascoe in a husky, passionate whisper. 'We're just starting.'

The line went dead. He replaced the receiver with a smile.

Perhaps things were beginning to break for him after all.

Sandra Firth had been a grievous disappointment. Something somewhere had gone wrong. She had carried on for a while in the cool, self-possessed manner in which she had started, but after offering a brief outline of her own background and position in the college, there had been a hiatus.

Finally Dalziel had tried his earlier bluntness once again.

'Look,' he said. 'Sandra, Miss Firth, whatever you want me to call you, if you've got something to say, then say it. If you haven't, then we're wasting each other's time.'

'I just wanted to find out,' she began. 'I mean I was a friend of Anita's . . .'

'So you said. Were you with her last night?'

'No!' she said sharply. 'I mean, when?'

'Any time?'

'No.'

'Wasn't there a party on somewhere?'

Pascoe had mentioned the emptiness of the bar to him earlier.

'No.' Again very sharply.

'Nowhere? You surprise me. I thought there were always parties!'

'Not that I was at, I meant.'

Exasperated, Dalziel struck the desk with the flat of his hand.

'Is there anything you *do* know about these murders?'

'Murders?' She stressed the plural.

'That's right. There's been two.'

She looked at him frightened.

'Your friend, Miss Sewell. And Miss Girling, the late principal.'

'Oh, *that*.' She laughed, relieved.

'Doesn't *that matter*?' he asked.

'No. I didn't mean that. I mean, we didn't know her, so it didn't bother me when the name came up. It was interesting really, rather than tragic.'

'When the name came up,' echoed Dalziel. 'What does that mean?'

'Nothing really,' she said.

'Why were so many students certain it was Miss Girling's body?' persisted Dalziel.

'No reason. Oh, it was nothing. Coincidence, I expect. It's just that some of us – them – play around with the wineglass thing. And the letters. Or a ouija board.'

'You mean, you had a seance? Asked the bloody spirits?' asked Dalziel incredulously.

'That's right. Not really a seance, just a bit of fun.'

'And it – this thing – told you it was Miss Girling?'

'Yes,' she said defiantly. 'It spelt it out quite plainly.'

'Well,' laughed Dalziel. 'You'd better ask it about your friend!'

Something about her silence made him lean forward and peer closely into her face.

'You're going to, aren't you?' he said gently. Then with greater violence, 'Aren't you?'

'I don't know. We might!'

'My God,' he said sadly. 'To think of the money that's being spent on educating your tiny minds.'

She stood up, breasts swinging disturbingly.

'Thanks for seeing me,' she said. 'I'll be off now. I have a lecture.'

'You didn't do it, did you?' he said shaking his head.

'Do what?' She looked frightened.

'Tell me what you wanted to tell me. Or ask me what you wanted to ask. Why not? I'm sorry if I've put you off. Why not sit down, lass, and let's try again?'

For a second he thought she was going to agree but after only a perfunctory knock, the door burst open and Kent strode in, his face awash with good tidings.

'Excuse me, sir,' he said. 'But we've come up with something, a chap who was out along the dunes last night and saw something which could be relevant.'

Through the open door, Dalziel saw a white-haired man, with a sun-darkened face in which a pair of bright blue eyes flickered and darted glances of alert interest at the scene before him.

'It's a Mr Lapping,' continued Kent, but Dalziel raised his hand in a silencing gesture.

'If you could just hang on a moment, Inspector,' he said with suspicious gentleness. 'I'm rather busy . . .'

'No. Don't bother about me,' said Sandra. 'I'm finished, and I have to go anyway. Goodbye.'

Head bowed so that her hair covered her face, she walked quickly from the room, past the old man who turned to look at her with undisguised interest.

What was she going to tell me? wondered Dalziel. If only that fool Kent hadn't come in . . . But it was more than just the interruption, he felt. It was the content of the interruption, perhaps . . .

'Will you see Mr Lapping now?' asked Kent. There was little choice. The old man had wandered into the room and was peering around with interest. Round his neck hung a large pair of binoculars. Dalziel sighed inwardly, wondering what Kent had let him in for.

But two minutes later as the old man described what he had seen the previous night, all his little half-formed plans for tearing Kent limb from limb had disappeared.

Harold Lapping told his tale with great gusto, not disguising his whole-hearted enjoyment of the show he had so unexpectedly stumbled upon.

'Ah'd niver seen owt like it. Niver in all me days. Some on 'em had paps as'd have made World Cup footballs!'

He paused, bright-eyed in reminiscence then his expression became sombre.

'But when ah heard about that lassie . . .'

He shook his head distressfully.

'Ah niver thowt, niver . . . when they all ran . . . it seemed a joke, someone walking by the shore . . . like meself.'

He paused as though to study the implications of his last remark.

'Like meself,' he repeated sadly. 'I expect he were.'

'I doubt it,' said Dalziel in his kindly tone, cursing Kent once again for an unthinking fool. What kind of checking on this old man had he done? Was there enough strength in those thin arms to hold a well-built young woman face down in the sand till she choked? Enough desire in that seventy-year-old body to drive him to such a deed?

'You saw someone?' he asked, breaking the silence which was beginning to run on too long.

'Ay. Just a glimpse through the glasses. Just afore they all ran. Just an outline.'

'Well?' said Dalziel.

'Nay. It's no good,' said the old man sadly. 'It was just an outline, like ah telt him.'

He nodded at Kent who smiled encouragingly.

'The hat,' said Kent.

'Oh ay. The hat. This fellow that ah saw, or it might've bin a woman, wore a hat. A . . .'

He made a gesture over his head.

'Pork pie,' said Kent. 'We did some drawings, didn't we, Mr Lapping? A pork pie hat.'

That was that. A mysterious figure in a pork pie hat disturbing what sounded like a Roman orgy. It might mean something or nothing. It was very intriguing whatever it meant.

'Mr Lapping,' said Dalziel as Kent led the old man off to have his statement typewritten and signed. 'Would you recognize any of those taking part in this dance?'

Lapping thought a moment.

'One perhaps,' he said. 'The one in the middle by herself. Ah had a good glimpse of her. But none of t'ithers.'

He turned once more before he left, his original lively smile arcing across his face.

'Not their faces, anyway, mister. Not their faces.'

You know, said Dalziel to himself when alone, you could make a name for yourself. You could have the identity parade of the century.

The thought made him happier than anything else he had heard that day. And there was still the educated, efficient Sergeant Pascoe's report to come in.

Pascoe was also feeling happy as he pushed open the door of Super-Vacs. (You Take The Trip We Take The Trouble) Ltd. (Prop. Gregory Aird).

After his abortive trip to the airport he had felt uneasy at the prospect of confronting Dalziel with nothing but negatives. Particularly when they did not remove even one of the many possibilities concerning the movements of Miss Girling and/or her corpse.

'Elimination is the better part of detection,' Dalziel on occasion uttered with the smugness of a man specially selected to proclaim an eternal truth.

All Pascoe had eliminated by his journey to the airport had been some public time and public money. But his continental telephone call had opened up new possibilities. He had instigated enquiries in Doncaster as to the present whereabouts of Miss Jean Mayflower, while he himself drove into Harrogate. The bright sunshine and a comfortable intuition that somewhere in the old records of Super-Vacs Ltd would be useful and revealing information revived in him a pleasure in his work based on a conviction of its positive social usefulness. He had once told Dalziel in an unguarded moment that it was his social conscience which had brought him into the police when many more comfortable careers were open to him.

'Well, bugger me,' was the fat man's only comment at the time. But a week or two later Pascoe had found himself 'on loan' to a neighbouring force who were drafting in extra men to help control an Anti-Racial-Discrimination demonstration. It had been very unpleasant for a few hours.

'How's your social conscience?' Dalziel had asked him on his return, but did not stay for an answer. Then, as in the last couple of days, the academic life had seemed very attractive.

Now as he pushed through the plate-glass doors, the lives of those in places like the college seemed pale, thinly-spread, lukewarm by comparison with his own purposeful existence.

The young man behind the counter looked with pleasure on the sergeant and smiled welcomingly, obviously seeing in his demeanour a customer ready, willing and eager to be satisfied.

'Good afternoon, sir. How may we help you?'

Pascoe felt in his wallet for his warrant card.

'I'm interested in ski-ing holidays,' he said. 'At Christmas.'

'Certainly, sir,' said the young man. 'I am sure we'll be able to . . .'

He stopped in puzzlement as Pascoe held out his card for inspection.

'I'm a police officer,' he said. 'I'm interested in ski-ing holidays five years ago.'

'Oh,' said the young man, taking a step backwards. 'I don't know . . . please wait a minute.'

He turned and went through a door behind him which obviously led into an inner office. Pascoe heard a half-whispered exchange but could not catch what was said. The young man reappeared followed by a slightly older man, smartly dressed, his hair beautifully set in shining undulations, who stretched out his hand to Pascoe with a slice-of-melon smile.

'How do you do? I'm Gregory Aird. I didn't catch . . .?'

'Pascoe, sir. Sergeant Pascoe. I wonder if I might have a few minutes of your time?'

'By all means. Step in, Sergeant, do.'

The inner office was sparsely furnished. A desk, a couple of chairs, a filing cabinet and a small safe.

Pascoe took this in at a glance and felt uneasy. There seemed little space here for long-term storage of old records.

'How can I help you?' said Aird, putting on the serious, co-operative look Pascoe usually associated with the desire to make a good impression in court.

'You can tell me first of all how far back your records go, Mr Aird.'

'To the beginning. To when it all started, my dear fellow. To the day I took possession.'

Pascoe felt relieved.

'I'm interested in a woman who booked a ski-ing holiday through you. It wouldn't be the first time, you understand; it was something she did every Christmas, but I believe your firm handled the arrangements.'

'Aha,' said Aird. 'Well, let's see. Let's see.'

He jumped up and strode across to the filing cabinet which he unlocked.

'Now,' he said opening a drawer.

'I'm interested in her flight number,' said Pascoe, delighted by this display of efficiency. 'And I wondered if for instance it was a charter flight, you might not have had a courier who would have made his own check list at the airport. It's a Miss Alison Girling. And the date was Christmas 1966.'

Aird's reaction was surprising. He crashed the drawer shut with a flick of his fingers and returned to his seat, shaking his head.

'I'm sorry,' he said. 'I can't help you there.'

115

'Why not, sir?' asked Pascoe, half-suspecting the answer.

'I've only been here three years,' said Aird. 'Since March '68. You're before my time, Inspector.'

'Sergeant. But you said . . .'

'Ah. I see your difficulty. No. The Super-Vacs you want went out of business in '67. No scandal, nothing like that, you understand. The parent firm in Leeds folded up, so their half-dozen branches went too.'

'But the name?'

'As I said, there was no scandal. No dissatisfied customers, not here anyway. So when I became interested in the premises for my own agency, well, among other things I found stored here enough stationery for four or five years. All with the Super-Vacs heading, of course. So I just kept the name.'

He smiled again, brilliantly, apologetically.

'What about the rest of the stuff that was here? Files, records, that kind of thing?'

'We had a clearing-out. And a bonfire. I'm sorry, Sergeant.'

He stood up and escorted Pascoe to the door. Disappointed though he was, Pascoe still sensed the man's relief at getting rid of him. Vindictively, he promised to mention Aird's name to the locals. There might be something there.

But that didn't help his own present investigations. Nor would Dalziel be very impressed.

Perhaps the academic life wasn't so bad after all.

When, on his return to Headquarters, he found waiting for him a message from Doncaster saying that Miss Jean Mayflower had died four years earlier as a result of a brain tumour, the academic life appeared as a very desirable haven of peace in a storm-battered, thunder-thrashed, Dalziel-haunted sea of troubles.

Chapter 10

. . . the arts which flourish in times while virtue is in growth, are military; and while virtue is in state, are liberal; and while virtue is in declination, are voluptuary.

SIR FRANCIS BACON
Op. Cit.

That gentle voyeur, Harold Lapping, would have found much to please him in the college precincts that night. At 7.30 P.M. the sun was still bright and warm and young bodies turned towards it on every patch of greenery. Even the staff garden, once patrolled with protective fury two or three times an evening by Miss Disney, was now regarded as common ground in its state of limbo between holy land and a building site. The area immediately around the hole left by the statue was for reasons of decency or superstition unoccupied. But half a dozen small groups were scattered around the rest of the lawn, many stripped for sunbathing, those in swimming costumes practically indistinguishable from those who had merely taken off their outer garments, happy with the doubtful protection of their underclothes.

If Harold, dissatisfied with anything less than total nudity, had been able to glide unnoticed through the college buildings, he would not have been disappointed there. It had been a long, very hot day and there was a growing heaviness in the air, promising thunder. The pleasures of a cold or at least lukewarm shower were attractive even to the least Spartan. The shock to an incorporeal Harold of drifting through the walls of Miss Disney's flat would have been great, but not prolonged. The advantages of complete nakedness while actually showering were too great to be ignored, but it was not a state she chose to remain in for longer than was necessary. Two minutes after turning off the water she was sufficiently clothed to be able to face herself in the mirror.

Something that she saw there, not in her physical proportions because she had long since come to terms with her lack of beauty, but in or behind her eyes filled them momentarily with tears. But they didn't fall. Instead she picked up from her dressing-table the old Bible which was so often her only comfort and let it fall open at random. Frequent reading in certain places may have reduced the truly random element in some degree, but this did not occur to her. In any case, Miss Disney did not believe in random openings of the Good Book.

It was one of her favourite passages.

'Blessed is he whose transgression is forgiven,' she began to incant, her eyes full now of a very different light.

Harold, had he remained so long, would have surely drifted on at this stage.

Thirty or forty yards down the corridor from Miss Disney he would have struck oil.

Marion Cargo too had just taken a shower, and she had none of the older woman's inhibitions. Lighting a cigarette she sank naked into a capacious easy-chair. Light filtered through the incompletely drawn curtains laying bars of gold across her brown body, turning her into a nymph of summer.

But her mind was contemplating a cold and foggy day nearly five years earlier when her life had changed. She stirred uneasily and made a movement towards the telephone. She felt the time had come to talk to someone.

The ringing of the doorbell prevented her. Quickly she rose and took a towelling wrap from the bedroom. She was still tying it one handed as she opened the door.

'I'm sorry,' said Arthur Halfdane. 'It's inconvenient? I

118

just thought; well you said, come and have a drink some time.'

'Of course it's not,' she said. 'As long as you don't mind. Look, come in. I'm glad you're here. I'd like to talk to you.'

Obviously there would have been no point in Harold's remaining there for the moment anyway. Had he struck off at a right-angle and drifted through the evening air till he penetrated the next block, he might have found a much more promising situation.

Sandra Firth lay naked on the bed. Beside her, standing looking down at her, was Franny Roote, his shirt in his hands. She reached up and pulled it from him.

'My word,' he said. 'You're impatient, love. Is it my manly charm?'

'The others will be coming soon,' she said.

He glanced at his watch as he took it off and put it carefully on the bedside table.

'So they will. Perhaps we shouldn't bother?'

She turned her face away from him and he laughed, undoing the heavy brass-buckle of his trouser-belt.

'By the way, love,' he said, 'what were you saying to that nice fat policeman today?'

'Nothing,' she said, pushing herself up on her elbows. 'Nothing. I just wanted to ask, well, you know, what they were doing.'

'Oh,' he said, still again.

'Yes,' she said urgently. 'I just wanted to see what I could find out.'

'And what did you?'

'Nothing, of course. What do you expect?'

'I expect discretion.'

'Discretion! Don't you want to know who killed Anita!' Her voice rose and he reached out his hand and caressed her gently.

'Of course I do. Very much.'

119

Something in his voice chilled her.

'Listen, Franny, let the police do it. It's their business.'

'Everyone to his trade, eh?' He laughed again. 'Well, you stick to yours in future. I thought I could trust you. Everyone's getting all independent. Stuart thinks he's laying the base-work of the people's bloody revolution. Now you're off Sherlocking about the place.'

'I'm sorry, Franny. Really.'

'All right,' he said, pushing his trousers down.

Harold would have been puzzled to observe he did not seem in the slightest degree excited. But Sandra seemed capable of remedying that.

Unfortunately once again there was an interruption, a sharp banging at the door.

'Franny? Open up. Stuart here. I wanted to see you before the others arrived.'

'Hang on a sec! Sorry, love,' he said to Sandra as he rolled off the bed. 'I don't think I can concentrate with Cockshut listening at the door. Later, eh? OK?'

With a blank expression almost amounting to despair Sandra rose up and began to dress.

Harold with a shrug of resignation would surely at this point have launched himself seawards to the more certain delight of bird-song and the golf club.

Miss Scotby and Simeon Landor were strolling in the garden of the principal's house, apparently admiring a fine display of roses. The house itself standing on the edge of the college grounds was only two years old. The long line of spinster principals had been easily accommodated in a flat in the Old House. But the ready availability of college-employed labour had already turned the garden into a thing of beauty.

They had been discussing matters of college business. Miss Scotby still held a writing-pad in her hands in which she had been jotting down notes.

'Roote came to see me today,' said Landor. 'Very polite. He expressed student concern. He said they were worried.'

'Aren't we all? We must be careful. That boy Cockshut will be out to cause trouble. Roote's just a pawn.'

'You think so?'

'Yes. I saw him today. Cockshut. Mr Fallowfield was passing. Some very unpleasant things were said. Mr Fallowfield looks quite ill which was a blessing in a way as I don't think he heard them. But he ought to see a doctor.'

'I'll speak to him,' said Landor. 'But it's a hard one this. He's still officially suspended, but now of course . . .'

'With the girl dead,' concluded Miss Scotby, 'there's not much that can be done.'

'No. Well, I think that's all, isn't it? Shall we go in?'

They turned back to the house. Behind a closed upstairs window, the pale gleam of a face was visible, staring down at them. Landor raised a hand in acknowledgement and it turned away.

Among the roses the principal and the senior tutor stood still for a moment before moving over the lawn to the open french window.

'Nice of you to come back,' said Dalziel. 'I was beginning to think you'd bloody well gone to Austria.'

It wasn't as bad as Pascoe expected. Dalziel listened to his report with hardly a comment till he came to the end.

'So,' he said. 'We're no further on? What about her car?'

Pascoe was ready.

'At the airport in the long-term car-park. Where you'd have expected it to be.'

'You spoke to the attendant?'

'It's five years, almost,' said Pascoe protestingly. 'What can *you* remember about that Christmas?'

It was, to say the least, an unwise question. By itself it smacked of impudence when directed at a superior officer. In terms of Dalziel's broken domestic life, God knows what significance it had. Once again Dalziel's reaction was surprisingly mild.

'Not much,' he agreed. 'But you asked?'

'Yes. Nothing.'

'So all we have is that Disney saw her drive off into the fog that night, and that is that, till her bones turn up back here two days ago.'

'What about the girl, sir? Anything there?' asked Pascoe hoping to strike a more promising vein.

'Not much. What there is is bloody puzzling.'

Briefly Dalziel filled his sergeant in on the events of the day.

'That's very interesting!' said Pascoe when he heard Harold Lapping's story. 'It sounds like a coven.'

'A what?'

'Witches, sir.'

'You mean black magic? That stuff? Perhaps.'

'What did the autopsy say?'

'If you're thinking it's a nice ritual murder, you can forget it. It was a straightforward case of jumping on her back and holding her face in the sand till she stopped breathing. No frills. No white cocks, black candles or any of that how's-your-father.'

'No. Well, there wouldn't be, would there? Obviously something or someone disturbed them and it was after they all split up that this happened.'

'Likely. The time fits,' said Dalziel without much enthusiasm.

'Do we know who else was in on it?' asked Pascoe.

'Nothing definite. I've a feeling this girl, Firth, can tell us something. But everyone seems to have shut up tight as a virgin's knees. We've been asking around. Nothing. Landor expresses amazement at the thought of such goings-on. I'm beginning to think he's as wilfully blind to realities as Disney and Scotby. Perhaps more.'

Moodily the superintendent pulled a bottle of scotch and a couple of glasses out of a desk drawer. He filled them both and pushed one towards Pascoe who took it quietly and raised it to his lips.

He had seen this pessimistic, almost self-doubting mood come upon his superior before but was still at a loss how best to deal with it. Nor was he certain whether his presence at these sessions was a mark of favour or a potential source of disfavour when Dalziel recalled his own weakness.

The sun was still bright outside, though now the shadows lay long. Very distantly there came the mumble of thunder.

The sound seemed to rouse Dalziel.

'Look,' he said. 'I've a feeling I'm missing something about this bloody place. Perhaps that's what comes of leaving school at fourteen. I talked to those buggers this morning but I'm not sure we really made any contact. They're meant to be educating these kids about society, but all the time I could feel they didn't trust me themselves. Not that I give a toss about that. I'm not looking for love.'

Pascoe essayed an expression which he hoped could pass for either amused appreciation or serious agreement depending on what Dalziel's comment required.

'But it worries me, not knowing what makes the place tick. I thought I had it sorted out. An old guard, represented by Disney and Scotby and what-have-you, and a new guard represented by Landor and his supporters. Reaction and radicalism. Christ, I come from a good trade-union background, I know all about that. But suddenly people start making nasty cracks at Landor, as if he belongs in the dark ages. And he's obviously shit-scared of the students. Someone wants to tell him about appeasement in the thirties.'

'He has a degree in history, I believe,' ventured Pascoe.

'Christ, what's that mean? Flint axes, stately homes and kitchen gossip! That's the trouble, most of these sods have spent all their bloody waking lives in schools and colleges and universities. It's all inbreeding, like a Welsh village'

Dalziel refilled his glass but didn't offer a second helping to Pascoe. It was pure malt, *Glen Grant*, and not to be wasted.

'I don't think you're quite fair,' said the sergeant diffidently. 'It's the nature of the institutions which matters rather than people's backgrounds. You're bound to get a certain special kind of underlife developing. Like in a prison.'

Dalziel studied the analogy for a moment.

'You mean there'll be gangs? tobacco rings? that sort of thing?'

'Not quite the same, but something like it. Initiation ceremonies for instance. An encouragement to belonging, a threat to not belonging. Food fiddles. Gambling schools. Witches' covens even.'

'But OK so that could happen, well, but why isn't something done? I mean, there are rules. Who knows? If *you* know, then a hell of a lot of other people must have worked it out too.'

'Of course,' said Pascoe impatiently. 'But *knowing* and *acting*, or even *admitting* are different things.'

'No,' said Dalziel, finishing his drink once more. 'It sounds – well, there's something not right. It isn't a prison after all. They don't seem to have any rules at all here!'

'Perhaps not,' said Pascoe. 'But in a place like this, it can be more than just rule-breaking. There must exist whole areas of shadow where self-deception is necessary because clarity would be too awkward to deal with.'

Dalziel slapped his broad knee violently, evidently found it pleasurable, and did it again.

'Like me at school!'

'Pardon?'

'When I was a lad at school, about ten, I was supposed to be an innocent little boy, playing football and so on with other innocent little boys. But what I was really interested in was chasing girls into the lavatories and if possible having a look at their crotches. But no one ever seemed to notice this. They all must have known, parents, teachers and all, but no one ever said owt!'

'That's the kind of thing,' said Pascoe drily.

'So what you're saying is that those buggers on the staff probably know a lot more about what the students do than they let on?'

What did I expect? Pascoe asked himself. A nice philosophical discussion on the nature of institutions?

'That's about it, sir,' he said. 'And vice-versa, of course. There's a whole range of non-official relationships which offer access to areas of privacy like baby-sitting, car-washing, that kind of thing.'

'And we mustn't forget friend Fallowfield,' said Dalziel. 'He seems to have been offered plenty of access.'

He glanced at his watch.

'Right,' he said. 'It's not late. Let's get to work.'

'What at?' said Pascoe.

'Well, you go and exercise that charm of yours on the staff. Take a trip down memory lane with your Miss Soper, see if you can soften her up. Oh, and that lad, Halfdane, the one who looks like a consumptive haystack, he was after you earlier. Wouldn't say anything to me.'

'And you, sir?' prompted Pascoe. 'Where will you be?'

'With my own kind,' said Dalziel rising and patting his paunch. '"They hate us youth." That shakes you, eh? Erudition in unlikely places. I'll be with the top student brass. I think there's something on tonight. Something that girl Firth said. We'll see. Give us a hand to clear this stuff away, will you?'

He began to shuffle the papers which lay on the desk before him. Pascoe hurriedly joined him, knowing from experience who would be held responsible for the superintendent's chaos.

Rapidly, efficiently, he began transferring material to the appropriate files in the large cabinet Landor had loaned them. One piece of paper caught his eye and he paused to read it.

'What's that?' said Dalziel whose own sole contribution to the clearing-up operation had been the careful removal of his bottle of scotch from the table.

'It's just the information from CRO,' said Pascoe.

'Oh, ay. We sent them all in, staff and the student officers just for good measure. Don't want to discriminate, do we?'

'And nothing's known. Only to be expected. Except . . .'

'That lad, Cockshut? Yes. Quite a list, isn't it? Obstruction. Damage to property. Resisting arrest. A big demo man. And I bet the bloody state subsidises him heavily enough to pay his fines.'

'I've heard of these people.'

'The International Action Group? Student bloody communists. We've had our eyes on them,' said Dalziel darkly.

Pascoe smiled, wondering whether Dalziel would shed his Fascist Beast role before he started talking to the students. Possibly not. He worked mainly through antagonism.

'Still I can't see any political motives for what's happened here.'

'Someone probably said that about Lincoln,' said Dalziel.

He dropped the bottle he was still clutching into the top drawer of the filing cabinet, slammed it shut, tested it and nodded.

'Safely stowed,' he said. 'Now to work!'

The room was heavy with smoke. The heat of the day, fading now outside as the evening wore on, was trapped in here by the heavy richly patterned curtains which also cut off the mellow light echoed from the sun. The only lumination here came from two candles on a double-branched candelabra on the mantelshelf above the boarded-in fireplace.

The room was full of people. Overfull. It could take at the most half a dozen in any kind of comfort. Now there were over twenty. The smell of smoke had to compete with the smell of human sweat.

'All right, my loves, now hear this,' Franny Roote was saying. He was seated cross-legged in the middle of the floor.

'I didn't expect much from recall tonight. Interruptions like that shatter all the links. But not to worry. There'll be other times. As for what happened later, to poor Anita, we know this has nothing to do with any of us.'

He paused. Somewhere outside a girl laughed.

'Help the police, my loves. Even you, Stuart. It's your bounden duty under the state.'

There was a slight murmur of amusement at the heavy irony of his tone.

'But remember our responsibilities to each other. Beware especially of the fat man. Let me know instantly if you are approached.'

Sandra Firth shifted uneasily. Franny clapped his hands once.

'Now off you go,' he said. 'Remember what we decided. We have done nothing wrong.'

There was a general rustle of movement about the room as people stood up and made for the door. But no one spoke. Shadows flickered wildly on the walls as the open door let in a draught of slightly cooler air. Even the

127

heavy curtains stirred, though the window behind them was closed, and suddenly the candles went out. The last few to leave stumbled in the darkness as they made for the narrow rectangle of light visible through the half-open door. Finally one of those who remained pushed the door shut at the same time as Stuart Cockshut relit the candles.

Only five faces were now revealed by the flames. Franny still sat motionless on the floor. Sandra seated herself beside him. Two other girls sat facing them and Cockshut pulled from under the bed a highly polished square of wood on which rested a crystal wine-glass and a pile of plastic letters from a Scrabble set. These he arranged swiftly in a large circle round the glass, placed the board in the centre of the seated group then retired to sit on the bed.

'Thank you, Stuart,' said Franny. 'Now, let me see.'

He closed his eyes and bent his head. The others followed suit, breathing deeply through the nose. After a full two minutes, Franny slowly stretched out his hand and laid a finger on the glass. One by one the others did the same. The glass stirred uneasily as though eager to move.

'Who is there?' called Franny in a clear, steady voice.

Again the glass stirred, then suddenly set off sliding round the table, emitting a vibrant, bell-like noise as the rim rubbed against the polished wood.

'Too fast. Too fast,' said Franny.

The glass came to rest again in the middle of the board.

'If it's Anita, she won't have had the practice yet,' said Stuart from on the bed, a touch of scepticism in his voice.

'Hush, hush,' said Franny. 'Anita. Are you there?'

Slowly, jerkily the glass began to move again.

'Yes!' breathed one of the girls. There were beads of sweat on all their faces now, except for Franny's.

'Ask who killed her,' said Sandra fiercely.

128

'Hush,' repeated Franny.

'No. Ask!' said Sandra. 'Anita! Who did it? Who did it?'

The glass moved rapidly round the ring of letters, pausing nowhere, gathering speed all the time. At first its path followed the circle itself, but suddenly it began to dart across from one side to another, till finally it broke through the barrier of letters, scattering them violently, and ran off the board altogether. It fell sideways as it caught the pile of the carpet and the stem cracked. One of the girls shrieked and started to suck her cut finger.

'It's no good,' said Franny. 'There's too much fear there. The ambience is not right somehow. There's some interference somewhere.'

He peered intensely around the room. A dark shadow moved from behind the Chinese screen which stood against the wall by the corner nearest the door.

'I expect that's me,' said Dalziel, flicking the light switch on. 'Let's have outward illumination at least.'

He moved over to the window, wrinkling his nose like a bulldog, pulled back the curtains and with some difficulty threw open the window.

'There!' he said, breathing deeply. 'That's better.'

Cockshut stood up from the bed and approached him fiercely.

'What the hell right have you got in here? Have you got a warrant?'

Dalziel looked puzzled.

'Mr Cockshut, isn't it? Ah yes. You'd know all about warrants, wouldn't you, laddie? No, we never use them these days, we prefer illegal methods as I'm sure you know. Now shut up or I might demonstrate a bit of police brutality.'

He turned to where Franny was still seated on the floor. The girls had all risen.

'This is your room, isn't it, Mr Roote?'

'Yes.'

'Forgive me if I've intruded. There were a lot of people coming in and out earlier so I just joined them. I could see you were busy, so I sat and waited rather than interrupt. You don't mind, do you?'

'Not at all.'

'There!' said Dalziel triumphantly to Cockshut. He squatted down cumbersomely beside Franny and looked with interest at the board and the letters.

'This is interesting,' he said. 'Did you know some police forces go in for this kind of thing in a big way? I believe you yourself had a bit of success. Over Miss Girling's body, wasn't it?'

'That was the ouija board,' said Franny.

'Ah. I see. But tonight didn't go so well?'

'No. There was interference. You see, Superintendent, these lines of spiritual communication are very sensitive to the presence of scepticism, especially when its physical embodiment is gross and earthy. Now, what can we do for you?'

'Mr Roote,' began Dalziel. 'You're the President of the Students' Union in this college, right? You've got the students' interests at heart. So have I. I want to find out who killed Miss Sewell. And quickly. For all we know, he might be building up to killing someone else. That's my interest. I'm not concerned with questions of morality and discipline, at least not officially. Let me give you an example. If a group of people over the age of majority care to run around naked in the middle of the night in a remote area of countryside, far removed from the public view, that's their business. I've no interest in publishing lists of names, or writing to anxious parents. If I can do things quietly, I will do them quietly. On the other hand, if I've got to stir things up, they'll hear the stirring from here to the Brocken.'

'You're not a warlock by any chance,' asked Franny

130

with a faint smile. 'Of course I'm eager to co-operate in any way I can. This story about naked dancers now, where did you get hold of that, I wonder?'

He eyed Sandra speculatively. She shook her head with pleading eyes.

Cockshut could contain himself no longer.

'You're threatening us, Dalziel,' he said. 'You talk about stirring things up. You're not the only one who can stir, you'll find out before the week-end's done!'

Franny shot him a warning glance. Dalziel merely smiled.

'Perhaps we could talk more comfortably in my office, Mr Roote?'

'Why not? Stuart, tidy up for me, there's a love.'

Cockshut bent down and helped himself to a handful of letters from the board.

'Big man!' he shouted after Dalziel as he went through the door. 'Here! Make a name for yourself!'

The letters whistled past Dalziel's head and scattered along the tiled corridor. He glanced down at them as he passed.

There were four of them; a U, a C, a T, and an N.

When Roote caught up with him, he was mildly surprised to find the fat policeman shaking with laughter.

'You looking for me?' asked Ellie behind him.

'Well, I can't find anybody else,' said Pascoe before he could stop himself. His remark wasn't directed at Ellie but arose from his growing annoyance at the way in which these academics seemed to disappear at will. Perhaps they're all practising witches, he had thought. Perhaps the entire staff of the college are at this very moment chasing each others' naked backsides round the dunes.

Ellie surprisingly did not take offence. Indeed she seemed glad to see him.

'You'd better make the most of me, then,' she said. 'Fancy a coffee?'

'Thanks.'

They were outside the block in which Ellie's flat lay. He had indeed been on his way to call on her when she came up behind. He had left her to the last from a reluctance to be rebuffed once again for apparently using their old friendship for cold professional ends. But no one else seemed to be around. Knocks on doors had produced no replies and the staff common rooms were deserted.

He experienced a strange feeling as he followed Ellie into her flat, but he was too well trained not to have it isolated within a few seconds.

It was a kind of misty familiarity. There were a couple of pictures, an ornament, a Chinese bowl, a small rather threadbare Persian rug, one or two other things, which had at one time in a different room been as familiar to him as his own possessions.

His eyes returned to the rug again, remembering more. On that very scrap of woven fabric he had laid Ellie down for the first time, ignoring the institutional divan shoved into a corner.

'Take a seat,' she said with a grin. 'I'll make the coffee.'

He had an uncomfortable feeling that she had followed the direction of his eyes and his thoughts very accurately.

'Had a nice evening?' he asked, sinking into an old armchair.

'Not very,' she called. 'I've been to the local Film Society. Some dull bloody Polish film. Rotten projection, illegible sub-titles and hard wooden chairs. What I would have given for John Wayne, red plush and a tight clinch in the back row!'

'You should have said,' he answered lightly. 'Many there? From the college, I mean?'

'Not from nowhere. There's usually half-a-dozen from here but they all wisely stayed away tonight.'

'Does Halfdane go?'

'Sometimes.' She came in with the coffee. 'Why do you ask?'

'I heard he had been looking for me. I've been away most of the day.'

'Oh yes. The great detective. How's it going?' she asked sarcastically.

He welcomed the change of mood. It gave him a chance to ask questions without appearing to take advantage.

'Slowly,' he said. 'There's a lot of space to fill in.'

'For instance?'

'Well, there's the intangibles. What kind of place is this to work in? In normal conditions I mean. Everybody draws together in the face of the enemy.'

'Not everybody. It's a funny atmosphere. All happy and Butlins'-Redcoats on the surface. But lots of oddities. We're very isolated for a start and instead of improving on lines of communication with the university, socially and administratively I mean, there's been a kind of contraction into an even tighter little circle. Or groups of little circles.'

'For instance?' asked Pascoe in his turn sipping his coffee and trying to concentrate on what Ellie was saying rather than on her brown, well-fleshed legs draped lengthily over the arm of her chair.

'Well there's all kind of odd little societies for a start. In the prospectus it looks very good, opportunity to pursue a wide range of interest and activity in the college, that kind of thing. But it's not really like that. It's hard to break into these tight little circles. You've got to prove you fit, almost. And I suspect you need more than just a proven interest in stamp-collecting or whatever it is.'

'What for instance? You mean some special sex variation, that kind of thing?'

She made an impatient gesture.

'Christ, man, you've had the fine intellectual edges rubbed off you, haven't you? Sex sometimes, of course. But more often as a symptom than an end in itself. It's a matter of belonging. How you belong is unimportant except that people generally take the line of least resistance. Anyway I don't know why I'm bothering to tell you all this. You can read it in my book.'

She gestured at a fairly bulky file which jutted out of her book-shelves.

'I'll look forward to that. What is it – a thesis?'

'Christ, no! Thesis faeces! That kind of crap's all behind me now. No, it's a novel,' she replied, a defensive note in her voice.

'Really?' He was uncertain whether to go on talking about it or not. He decided not. If she wanted to talk about it, she would. The only other novelist he had ever known seemed willing to stop complete strangers in the street and force chunks of his indigestible prose down their throats.

'What about the staff? Don't answer if you'd rather not,' he said. Dalziel would have torn out what remained of his greying hair at such delicacy. Or worse, perhaps admired his hypocrisy. 'There seem to be a few feuds here. Disney and Fallowfield, for instance.'

She hooted with derision at the names.

'What d'you expect? There's nothing queerer than two old queers. No, there's bloodier battlegrounds than that.'

She paused enticingly, but Pascoe was not to be drawn by hints. If she wanted to say more she would. But she *had* made a firm assertion and that was worth pursuing.

'Disney and Fallowfield, two old queers? Why do you say that?'

She looked at him incredulously.

'Come off it, Sherlock. Walt's so butch she might as well advertise in the local paper.'

'Is this guesswork?' he said, allowing disbelief to colour his tone.

'Guesswork nothing! When I first came she tried to charm me into her magic circle. What a thought! Poor Walt. It's mostly sublimated now, I guess. Just girl-talk and confession hour and a bit of shoulder-patting and hair-stroking. She was hit bad when old Girling died, so they tell me.'

Pascoe was surprised.

'I thought they didn't get on all that well? That this friendship thing was just a posthumous fantasy.'

Ellie shrugged.

'I heard different. Who told you that?'

'Dunbar.'

'That little Scotch git! What'd he know anyway? I bet they paid money to get him out of Scotland.'

Pascoe pressed on, ignoring this other invitation to divert.

'And Fallowfield? What about him? Surely this business with the girl . . .'

'Yes,' she said slowly. 'That surprised me, I admit. I hadn't known him long, of course, or well. But I'd have guessed differently about him. What the hell, perhaps he's just got catholic tastes!'

'Perhaps. But why . . .'

She jumped up. Again the legs were much in evidence.

'Enough's enough! Drink your coffee and either stop being a policeman or go.'

She went over to a record-player pushed beneath a small sideboard, pulled it out and put a record on.

Pascoe reached into his wallet and produced his warrant card.

'There you are,' he said placing it on the mantelpiece. 'I now have no official standing.'

Feeling incredibly ham, he took Ellie in his arms and they began dancing, pressed close together.

135

'Why aren't you married?' she asked suddenly. 'Or are you?'

'No,' he said. 'No time. Besides I don't mix with a very nice class of person. You?'

'God no! Half a dozen offers though; I shouldn't like you to think no one else had ever asked. And a host of odd boyfriends. But nothing ever clicked.'

'No one now?' he asked diffidently. 'I wondered perhaps about that chap the other evening, Halfdane . . . ?'

She drew away slightly, then laughed.

'We hardly know each other. But while there's life . . . Still, he's a bit young.'

'Rubbish,' he said drawing her close again. 'You're perfect. Mature.'

'Like a good cheese. I'm over thirty now. Hell, I don't want to be like the others, like Disney and Scotby. Christ, I'm sometimes really sorry that we split up when we did. I even dream about it! Mind you, we'd probably have been divorced by now!'

'Probably.'

She stopped dancing and looked at him.

'Anyway, I wouldn't like you to get the idea that I'm desperately thrashing around for a husband. Especially you.'

'Of course not,' he agreed.

'Good. As long as that's clear,' she said, coming back into his arms. 'You are stopping the night, aren't you?'

'Perhaps not all the night,' he said cautiously.

'Enough of it,' she said in his ear. 'We'll take a trip down memory lane.'

He awoke at two in the morning. They had been too warm to be covered by anything other than a single sheet and even this had been thrust off in the night. He looked down at her sleeping form on the bed beside him. They had started off on the Persian rug, but eventually transferred here, admitting that comfort came before sentiment. She opened her eyes now.

'I'd like you to read my book,' she said.

'It'll be a pleasure,' he said taking hold of her again.

He left at five. It was light outside. She sat naked in an armchair watching him comb his hair in front of the mirror.

'The book,' he said.

'If you like.'

He watched with pleasure as she stood up and went over to the bookshelf.

'Thanks,' he said.

'Don't forget your card,' she said.

He picked it up from the mantelshelf.

'They say you always leave something in a place you want to come back to,' he said laughing.

'You've left something,' she said, opening the door. She seemed keen for him to go, but returned his farewell kiss with enthusiasm.

Outside in the corridor they heard another door open. Pascoe peered out cautiously. A few yards along stood a man, carefully closing a door behind him. It was Halfdane.

Pascoe glanced enquiringly at Ellie, but her face showed no emotion.

They waited in silence a few minutes till Halfdane had moved cautiously away.

'Cheerio, love,' said Pascoe, kissing her once more. 'See you later.'

She still didn't speak and he left, moving swiftly but quietly down the corridor, pausing only to glance at the name on the door Halfdane had come out of.

It was Marion Cargo.

The next name was Miss Disney's and normally Pascoe might have noticed that the door-handle was not quite at the right angle as though someone was standing inside, holding it tightly. But he was pleasurably tired, his mind and body full of pleasant impressions.

He paused outside to breathe in the balmy morning air and listen to the birds.

It looked like being a red-hot day. But he could be wrong. For instance yesterday, for all its early lack of promise, had turned out very fine indeed.

Chapter 11

With arts voluptuary, I couple practices jocularly; for the deceiving of the senses is one of the pleasures of the senses.

SIR FRANCIS BACON
Op. Cit.

'What the hell happened to you last night?' asked Dalziel. 'I went round to your room three times.'

'I'm sorry, sir,' said Pascoe. 'I got held up.'

Dalziel looked at him critically.

'Held up, eh? It must be age. Anyway, you should be old enough to look at this.'

Pascoe had found his chief wandering around, apparently merely enjoying the morning sunshine, in an area just beyond the large beech hedge which marked the farthermost bourne of the staff-garden. A couple of old garden-sheds stood against the hedge and, as he spoke, Dalziel dramatically flung open the door of the larger.

The sun poured in and ricocheted off the broad flanks of the woman who lay there on a bed of sacking. Upright she might have been dramatic; on her back she was almost obscene. Pascoe had last seen her on the back of a builder's truck.

'So this is where they put it,' he said, patting the statue's upraised left knee. 'So much for Miss Girling's immortal memory.'

He looked enquiringly at Dalziel.

'You told me to have a look, Sergeant,' he said. 'So I tracked her down. That was a good point you made. Not before time, I might add. Why should a woman like Girling have a memorial like this? And furthermore, how

139

did they manage to get it up so quickly – February someone said. It usually takes ages to organize anything like that – deciding on a design, getting someone to do it, the artistic work – it all adds up. There's many a Great War memorial just got finished in time for 1939.'

'Yes, sir,' said Pascoe, sensing a reminiscence coming on. 'How do you think they managed it?'

Dalziel scratched his navel then, as though in comparison, did the same to the statue.

'Tell me, lad,' he said, 'you've got an eye for the girls. That lass, Cargo, how old would you say she was?'

'Cargo?' said Pascoe. 'Which is she?'

Dalziel looked at him in disgust.

'The best thing on the staff,' he said. 'Your Miss Soper must have strong powers of attraction. Let's see. I would say, at a guess, without actually handling the merchandise, that she can't be any more than twenty-seven or twenty-eight at the outside. Probably twenty-seven. Does that suggest anything to you?'

'Wait a minute!' said Pascoe. 'She wasn't on the list of staff employed when Girling was boss!'

'So!'

'So . . . I don't know. Perhaps she was just commissioned to do the job and got a full-time post later?'

'Commissioned for a job like this at twenty-one?'

'Twenty-one? Yes, twenty-one. Of course!' said Pascoe. 'She must have been a student.'

'Well done! Yes, one of Al's famous gals. And here, if I'm not mistaken, she comes.'

Pascoe looked along the beech hedge. At the far end a uniformed constable appeared with Marion Cargo. He pointed towards the two detectives, put a finger to his helmet and went on his way.

'Very gallant,' observed Dalziel. 'Miss Cargo, how nice of you to come!'

He had to raise his voice as she was still some twenty yards away. Pascoe watched her approach with interest.

Nice, he thought. Not built on traditional art-mistress lines, all bum and bosom, but none the worse for that. She could go to the vicar's tea-party dressed like that and still put a bit of strength in the sexton's arm. Oh, yes.

His thoughts turned rather guiltily to Ellie. What the hell. There were no ties there. Last night's encounter had been the chance-in-a-million crossing of orbits which now would spin them light-years apart.

He liked the image. Perhaps Ellie could use it in her book. He had tried the first chapter over breakfast. It hadn't held him but he felt he ought to persevere.

'Why do you want to see me, Superintendent?' asked Marion. Then she saw the statue through the open door.

'Oh,' she said in neutral tones.

'It's a pity,' said Dalziel, 'that it should be lying here out of sight. Like all that stuff in the basement of the National Gallery.'

That's it, thought Pascoe. He'll mention 'The Stag at Bay' then he's shot his bolt.

'Not really,' said Marion. 'It's not very good.'

'You mustn't say that. I'm no judge, but I know what I like, and this looks fine to me.'

Dalziel nodded sagely as though he had just bestowed a Nobel Prize.

'But,' he went on, 'if you place so little value on it, why were you so upset when it came down? Everyone remarked on it.'

'Everyone,' had been Landor.

Marion flushed.

'Not because of the statue itself,' she said. 'I know it's absurd but, well, it had a sentimental value. That's all.'

'Really? You mean, because of Miss Girling?'

'Yes. It was her idea, you see . . .'

141

'*Her* idea!' broke in Pascoe. Dalziel looked at him reprovingly.

'. . . and she gave me so much encouragement. She was really super. The others didn't want it, you know, they didn't think it was the thing. I thought they'd have banned it after it all happened, but instead they decided to use it as . . .'

She stopped and turned away.

'There, there,' said Dalziel, patting her shoulder avuncularly. But his eyes were glancing smugly at Pascoe.

'I'm sorry,' she said finally, moving from under the next of Dalziel's blows.

'Not at all. Quite understand,' he said. 'So, Miss Cargo, you started work on the statue in . . .'

'. . . September. It should have gone up before Christmas, but the weather was so awful that they didn't get the hole dug for the base till the last week of term.'

'You'd be a final year student at the time?'

'That's right.'

'And after Miss Girling's reported death, it was decided to use your statue as a memorial to her?'

'Yes. Like I said, not everyone agreed. Miss Scotby was very much against it.'

'And Miss Disney?'

'No, actually. It was her and Henry Saltecombe who talked the others into it. It *was* a bit absurd. I mean, the thing was meant to symbolize youthful drive and energy.'

'And the base,' continued Dalziel, 'when did they put the concrete base into the hole?'

'I'm not sure,' said Marion. 'Is it important?'

'Yes,' said Dalziel.

She thought hard.

'I can't say, I'm afraid. There was a hole there when we left for the hols, and the base was in when we got back. That's all I can say.'

'Sergeant Pascoe, perhaps you could . . .'

Pascoe did not wait for him to finish, but nodded and began to step out rapidly towards the college.

'And when did you come back to the college?'

'Oh, just a year ago. I'd done a bit of teaching, got some extra qualifications on part-time courses, then this job came up. It seemed like fate somehow. I'd said I'd never come back after the last year. But that all seemed such a long time before. Now it's all started again.'

She slammed shut the door of the shed, frightening a blackbird which had been perched on the roof, observing them.

'Sorry,' she called contritely after it, but it didn't look round.

'Thank you very much, my dear,' said Dalziel. 'Let me walk you back to college.'

He turned to the low archway cut in the hedge which led through into the garden.

'No thanks,' said Marion looking through the gap. 'I think I'll stroll around here for a while.'

These artists have bloody sensitive souls, thought Dalziel as he watched her go. She even came the long way round.

He found Pascoe in Landor's study in the act of replacing the telephone receiver.

'Easy!' said the sergeant. 'Very nice for once. It was the builders who are doing the work here now. I gave their office a tinkle and got right in touch with the man who supervised the job. He remembered it well.'

He paused dramatically. Dalziel belched.

'The base was lowered into place on Tuesday the twentieth of December.'

'There's a thing,' said Dalziel.

'She never left.'

'Or didn't go far if she did.'

'Scotby saw her driving off at 6 P.M.'

'Saw someone driving off at 6 P.M.'

143

'Or *says* she saw someone driving off.'

'What do we know about her movements that day?'

'We've got an outline.'

'We need more than a bloody outline. Sergeant, let's get to work and fill it in!'

Filling it in proved more difficult than it sounded, but not more difficult than Pascoe had come to expect. If getting hold of staff on a working day was difficult, getting hold of them on a Saturday morning proved almost impossible.

Landor was nowhere to be found. His wife, a pale skeletal woman, denied all knowledge of his whereabouts. She was only certain he would be back for lunch.

'We have guests,' she added defensively as though Pascoe were holding her certainty against her.

It's all I'd hold, thought Pascoe.

Scotby, the main source of what little information he already had about the course of events on the nineteenth of December, had likewise disappeared.

He banged on the door of her room, then Disney's, and finally Ellie's.

'Hi,' she said. She was still in her dressing-gown. 'Coffee?'

'I'd better not,' he said. She seemed to be expecting to be kissed so he obliged. The dressing-gown fell open.

'I'm looking for Scotby. Or Disney,' he said hurriedly, averting his eyes.

'It takes all sorts to make a world,' she answered, fastening her belt.

'Any ideas?'

'Well, Scotby'll be down on the beach with a great lump of animality between her legs.'

'*What?*'

'Riding. She rides. Horses. It keeps her fit,' said Ellie lighting a cigarette and coughing violently. 'And it sweats out her refined little lust for Simeon.'

144

'Landor? You're joking!'

'Please yourself. I've watched her. She'd love to get her saddle over him,' said Ellie coarsely. 'Anyway she makes do with Black Beauty every Saturday and Sunday morning. There's a riding-school beyond the golf club.'

'And Disney?'

'Hair. Every Saturday. You didn't think it could look as unkempt as that by nature? No, it's a wash and set and a bit of capital titillation from the fingers of some epicene young man.'

'Thanks a lot,' said Pascoe gloomily.

'You're welcome. In fact,' she added, dropping her voice to a husky whisper, 'you're very welcome.'

She laughed after him as he retreated back to Dalziel.

'It's no good,' he said. 'They're all out of reach, those who might be some good to us.'

'That's all right,' said Dalziel. 'They'll all be back. I just rang the chairman of the governors.'

'Oh?'

'You did say there was a governors' meeting that day, didn't you? It might be interesting to find out what it was about, when it ended, that sort of thing.'

'And was it?'

'I said it *might* be. He was out.'

'Having his hair done or riding?'

'Is it a dirty private joke?' asked Dalziel. 'No, he's on his way here for lunch with Landor. There's a cricket match this afternoon, college versus the locals. Landor's bent on keeping up the appearance of normality. So we'll see him then. And the others likely. Meanwhile . . .'

'Yes, sir?'

'You can catch up on your reading. This is what I got out of Roote last night. While you were busy.'

According to Franny's statement, a small group of students, Anita Sewell among them, had gone down to the beach for a midnight bathing party. No, there hadn't

145

been anything odd or sinister going on. Witches' dances? That was absurd. Mr Lapping must have mistaken some very ordinary 'pop' dancing – he was an old gentleman, wasn't he? Music? Yes, they had had a transistor. There was *always* pop music on the radio, no matter what time. As for nudity, well some of them wore very skimpy costumes. At night, from a distance . . . Why did the party break up? Somebody disturbed them. It was silly really, they weren't breaking the law, just a couple of silly college regulations perhaps, if that. But it was dark, and late, and someone panicked and ran. Then they all grabbed their clothes and made off. It was a bit of fun. Exciting. That was all. They mostly stuck in groups, no one wanted to be alone. He'd been with Stuart Cockshut, Sandra Firth and a couple of others. All the time? Yes, all the time and all the way back to college. They'd had coffee in Sandra's room. Sat and talked for half an hour. No, he couldn't remember noticing what Anita did when they scattered. Perhaps one of the others . . . certainly he would make out a list of their names.

'Anything there, sir?'

'I should be very much surprised. I've got a couple of the lads sorting round them; there's always a chance. I went back to see the girl Firth, and Chairman Cockshut last night. They confirmed Roote's story.'

'Is it true then?'

Dalziel snorted contemptuously.

'You're joking! No, our Mr Lapping had it right, I reckon. Harmless dancing indeed! There was obviously some kind of pretty abandoned sexual rollicking going on. I don't know what we're coming to. But the important bit, about the party breaking up, and Roote and the others coming back here, now that's true, I'd say. The girl was too obviously relieved when she got on to that bit of the story. She might as well have stuck up a notice

saying, "Here endeth the lies and beginneth the truth!"
So we're nowhere.'

'What do you reckon happened?' asked Pascoe. 'She
runs off into the night without a stitch on, comes back for
her clothes a short while later when things are quiet,
meets Mr X, perhaps the one who interrupted them in
the first place, and is quietly done to death?'

'That's a good question,' said Dalziel. 'Perhaps you'll
try leaving a bit to answer in future. Anyway, you didn't
tell me in your question what happened to her clothes.'

'X took them.'

'Why?'

'Kinky?'

Dalziel shook his head.

'This doesn't smell like a kinky one to me. Look, get
Roote, Cockshut, any of them that were in on this bathing
party. No, not the lot, any *one* of them. I'll pick up Mr
Lapping and we'll all go and see exactly where it was
they were dancing. I want to see how far it was from
where the girl was found.'

'Right, sir,' said Pascoe.

Outside he met one of the constables Dalziel had set to
checking up on the names on Franny Roote's list.

'Anything?'

'Not a glimmer, Sarge,' said the young man
lugubriously.

'All right. Look, take a quick walk up to the golf club
and tell Mr Kent the super's on his way. Make it snappy.'

From behind the half-open door, Dalziel watched the
scene with interest. He too had noted Detective-Inspector
Kent's unnecessarily sporty looking outfit that morning.
But now he nodded in approval.

He liked loyalty in junior officers. He was sure Sergeant
Pascoe would have done as much for him.

Almost sure.

* * *

Miss Disney and Miss Scotby were very differently situated, and neither would have changed with the other for love or wealth.

Miss Disney sat under a hair-drier like a science-fiction monster with a badly fitting space-helmet. For a while the dextrous hands and tongue of Neville, her favourite hair-artist, had soothed her mind, but now with only herself and an absurdly frivolous magazine for company, her thoughts were beginning to chase each others' tails again. She tried to concentrate on the only readable part of the glossy magazine on her lap – the Reverend Ronald Rogers's weekly message to the housewife – but even this was distasteful, quoting St Paul in support of his advice to mothers on dealing with the sexual problems of the adolescent.

It would have been even more distasteful, however, to be where Miss Scotby was. Her face animated in a way which few students would have recognized, she rose and sank rhythmically with the body of her horse as it cantered through the shallows of the outgoing tide. As it approached the groyne which was the usual limit of their outward ride, it slowed down of its own accord, but Miss Scotby urged it on. Surprised, it scrambled over the groyne, sinking fetlock-deep in the drift of soft sand piled against the farther side, and Miss Scotby was almost unseated. She recovered expertly, however, and brought her mount to a halt, facing out to sea.

In a moment she would ride back and experience once again the fierce exhilaration of the gallop. But now she sat in thought, a grey-haired little woman with a face long practised at keeping the counsel of the mind that worked so busily behind it.

To be confined in a hairdressing salon on a morning like this would have been a blasphemy beyond anything ever touched upon by Reverend Ronald Rogers.

But so very differently situated though Miss Scotby

148

and Miss Disney were, they did for a brief time have a thought in common. It was a deep-down thought, almost unacknowledged, certainly never to be brought out into the light of day.

They each wished someone dead. But for only one of them was the wish to come true that particular day.

Pascoe was having lunch at the golf club with Detective-Inspector Kent, who in the space of a couple of days had established himself as *persona* very much *grata* in the clubhouse. His readiness to admire shots, exchange anecdotes, and sympathize over the malevolence of fate, had won golden opinions from the members.

Pascoe's message had in fact been unnecessary. Kent had been going about his legitimate business when it arrived, but he appreciated the thought.

Sandra Firth had been the only student concerned that Pascoe had been able to pick up quickly. She and Harold Lapping had very soon agreed on the location of the midnight dance. No reference had been made by either to the difference between their two versions, but Pascoe noted with interest that Sandra's nonchalant air was beginning to wear a bit thin under the amused glances from Harold's bright eyes.

The hollow in the dunes where Pearl had found Anita was nearly a quarter of a mile away, almost at the bottommost end of the golf course.

'Some way from where she left her clothes,' commented Dalziel.

'Perhaps the killer picked them up and then went after her, knowing she wouldn't go too far,' suggested Pascoe.

'Why not just wait near the clothes?' replied Dalziel.

'Or she might have taken them with her when she ran and have stopped here to get dressed and *then* he came upon her.'

149

'Perhaps,' said Dalziel. 'I'm off after some lunch, then I think I'll watch the cricket. Thanks for your help.'

He flung the last remark over his shoulder as he strode off back towards the college. Lapping grinned broadly after him, Sandra looked thunderstruck at his apparent callousness.

Pascoe had been about to follow when Kent had issued his invitation.

It was a pleasant lunch. Kent had chatted amiably about a variety of subjects, with golf not unbearably predominant. Pascoe who had hitherto regarded the man as a slightly risible example of what not to be in the police-force, found himself enjoying his company. When talk got round to the case (or cases) in hand, he listened appreciatively to Kent's assessment. He didn't say anything new, but he missed nothing out either.

'It's motive we're after, not murderers. Not yet. Motive. It's a truism, Sergeant, but it's true. Find out why and you'll like as not find out who.'

'Agreed,' said Pascoe, starting on his second pint. 'Cheers.'

'Your astonishingly good health,' remarked Kent, before carrying on his theorizing. 'And to find out why, it helps to eliminate why not. Take the girl, for instance. Obvious thing is sex. But he never bothered. Never touched her. Now why not?'

'Perhaps it was a woman,' suggested Pascoe.

'She'd need to be a hefty one,' said Kent. 'No. Something else, I think. Now who'd have a motive for killing her, if it wasn't just a nut?'

'Fallowfield?' said Pascoe.

'Who?'

'Fallowfield. Lectures at the college. Don't you know?'

His new-found respect for Kent began to evaporate. Somehow the man had contrived never to have heard of the relationship between Fallowfield and Anita. It would

150

be Dalziel's fault partly. He didn't believe in spoon-feeding his men. Certainly not Kent.

Pascoe filled him in quickly, efficiently. Kent supped his beer and chewed on his cheese and biscuits with a distantly worried look in his eyes. Finally he swallowed and shook his head.

'No,' he said. 'No. Are you sure?'

'Of course.'

'His mistress?'

'He admits it.'

Kent began to look really concerned.

She must have brought out the father feeling in him, thought Pascoe. They can all look so innocent when they'rc lying there, dead.

'No,' said Kent again. 'She was a virgin.'

'Don't be daft.'

'It said so in the medical report. A virgin.'

'No,' said Pascoe in a kindly voice. 'She hadn't been sexually assaulted. That's what it said. Not quite the same thing.'

'A virgin. It said she hadn't been assaulted that night. And it said she was still a virgin. I should know. I read the bloody thing to the super.'

Pascoe froze, his glass in mid-air.

'You read it to him?' he asked. 'Didn't he look at it himself?'

'I don't know. Not when I was there. You know he hates to be bothered reading things himself. Always gets someone else to do it if he can,' said Kent defensively.

'A virgin? You're sure?' said Pascoe, adding 'Sir' as he saw Kent react to his tone.

'Yes! But listen, Sergeant . . .'

Pascoe carefully put his beer on the table and stood up.

'Thanks for the lunch, sir. I'd better be getting back now.'

Swiftly he moved out of the room before Kent could reply. It might have been a kindness to let him do his own reporting to Dalziel. But one kindness a day was enough for the likes of Kent.

Someone shouted at him as he marched across a beautifully-kept green, and he broke into a trot.

Dalziel wouldn't be pleased. Kent would have some explaining to do.

But that would be nothing to the explaining that Dalziel would surely expect from Mr Sam Fallowfield.

'The reason the English love cricket,' said George Dunbar in his loud, guttural voice, 'is that it structures their bloody indolence.'

'Or masks their machinations,' added Henry Saltecombe.

'Oh aye. You all like to think you're so bloody clever,' sneered Dunbar.

Looking round, Pascoe had to agree with Dunbar's theory, much as he disliked the man. The thinly delineated oval of spectators, some in brightly striped deck-chairs, others recumbent in the grass, was positively Keatsian in its projection of indolence. But, he thought, as in all great works of art, realism alone did not do the work; realism only existed at a single level. What was needed for art was the living symbol at the centre, and the almost motionless white-clothed figures inside the oval were precisely that symbol. Yes, it was more than just a demonstration of indolence, it was an act of worship.

But Pascoe also saw with a policeman's jaundiced eye; and that part of his mind was very ready to accept the hypothesis that machinations were being masked.

Roote, for instance, and that little gaggle of students almost hidden in the tall grass at the end of the oval farthest away from the pavilion. They looked as if they were merely enjoying the innocent pleasures of sun on flesh. A bit perhaps of the less innocent pleasures of flesh on flesh. But nothing more. Yet he wished he could listen in on their talk.

Or Miss Disney. Her deck-chair as upright as it would go, her long skirt pulled challengingly low over her short, chubby legs. Her face showed nothing except the usual indignation at life's insults it always seemed to bear. She spoke to a passing girl, Sandra what's-'er-name, who paused, obviously reluctant even at a distance, shook her head twice, answered briefly, and moved on towards the Roote group. The Disney basilisk gaze shot after her, but, happily, she did not look round. What had been said? What was she now thinking? And why, even as Pascoe watched, did she stand up and stride purposefully away?

Or Halfdane, still to be talked with, but now reclining elegantly between two deck-chairs in which Ellie and Marion Cargo were competing in a whose-leg-goes-far-thest competition. Ellie, he felt, was just inching ahead, but looked to have little in reserve. Perhaps he should stroll over and talk to them, but if Ellie still had ambitions in the Halfdane area, he was unwilling to butt in. Or worse still, despite the previous night, appear as a competitor. Though why it should be worse still, as memories of the previous night flooded back, he could not really imagine. In any case, the point was, what was really going on inside those three minds?

Or Jane Scotby, listening with the obvious dislike sometimes called deep interest to Mrs Landor's sparrowy voice twittering from under the eaves of a broad-brimmed hat, which was supplemented by a fringed parasol of golf-umbrella dimensions. The principal himself sat slightly apart, though still in his wife's penumbra, and viewed the two women thoughtfully. Perhaps, thought Pascoe, he and Scotby are busily deceiving poor Mrs Landor and

153

even now are throbbing with frustrated lust after a brief passionate embrace behind the pavilion.

The thought made him smile but his policeman's eye continued on its beat and the next tableau it paused at swung him wholeheartedly towards Henry Saltecombe's view of the situation.

Two elderly gentlemen, one corpulent, bald, jolly, the other spare, white-haired, straw-boatered, their heads, wreathed in cigar smoke, nodding like mountain peaks through the mist as some piece of action in the central ritual caught their attention, their hands clapping, once, twice, even three times in moments of wild excitement; old friends relaxing together watching the youngsters carrying on in ancient, revered tradition.

One was Captain Ernest Jessup, chairman of the governors. The other was Superintendent Andrew Dalziel.

Of one thing Pascoe was convinced – however involved in a ritual of indolence the others might really be, here at least there were mental machinations a-plenty.

Not a bad sort of chap, Jessup was thinking. Self-made of course, with the stitching poorly concealed, but there was nothing wrong with that. He himself belonged to a service with a long tradition of advancement through merit. And at least the fellow could relax. He had feared total interruption of his afternoon's cricket when Landor had introduced the man. Not that he wouldn't have been willing to talk with Dalziel all day and all the next day too if it promised to help get to the bottom of this business.

But all was going well, it seemed. The assistant chief's confidence in the man seemed justified (though he had been less than warm about his personal merits) and their conversation so far had been restricted to the field-changes between overs. It looked like being a good game.

What a bloody way to spend an afternoon! groaned Dalziel to himself. Rugby he could enthuse over, soccer could move him deeply, but these flannelled fools moved to a music too refined for his coarse ears. And the deck-chair! A direct descendant of the rack out of the Iron Maiden!

He had not yet recovered from Pascoe's news about the dead girl. That had come dangerously close to being a blunder. He didn't normally make blunders. He prided himself on being able to extract from all the usual scientific twaddle in these reports the few important facts. These generally confirmed his own observations and deductions. Or often there were none at all.

Pascoe would have noticed and subtly drawn his attention to it. But stuff Pascoe! He didn't want a kind of constabulary Jeeves hanging around all the time. Yet if poor Pascoe were to be stuffed, then what of Kent? Lash him naked in a deck-chair with his back to the eighteenth green at St Andrews during the Open? It would bear further thought.

As for the information itself, that the accusation made against Fallowfield by Anita Sewell could not possibly have been true, the implications were far from clear. Fallowfield's reason for admitting the truth of the accusations, or at least that part of them which said he had been knocking the girl off for a couple of years, would bear investigation. But he had no intention of rushing in like the bear he was popularly reputed to be. With a bit of luck he'd run into Fallowfield during the course of the afternoon, though there was no sign of him yet.

But this old goon on his right had to be kept happy for a while. He had been quite unable to remember a single thing about the meeting at which Miss Girling had made her last public appearance. He probably had difficulty remembering the way home, thought Dalziel savagely and quite unjustly. But he had agreed to telephone the clerk to the governors who had promised to dig through

155

the records and send any pertinent information to the college that afternoon.

Meanwhile an hour and a half, two wickets, and thirty-eight runs had trickled away with agonizing slowness. But despite his discomfort and his boredom, Dalziel had felt curiously enervated and quite unable to rise from his chair to do something useful. In any case everyone was here, everyone that mattered. Nearly everyone. Big wheels were moving elsewhere, and all those who had left the college since Girling's death were being traced and interviewed. But Dalziel was somehow certain the solution was here somewhere.

'Well hit, sir!' boomed Jessup. 'I think that's our man, Superintendent.'

'Oh, yes, indeed. Very promising,' said Dalziel.

'By the pavilion. The man with the minutes,' said Jessup patiently. 'Let's go and see.'

The shade of the pavilion was a relief. Dalziel realized his shirt was wringing with sweat; Jessup on the other hand in his absurd hat looked quite cool as he glanced through the papers he had been given.

'No, I'm sorry,' he said. 'It doesn't bring anything back at all, except very vaguely. Certainly nothing which might help you, Superintendent. Though I see now why it was so late in the term. It was an appointments meeting and obviously we hadn't been able to convene the full interviewing panel earlier in the term. Miss Girling would be eager to get things like this done as soon as possible, before the good candidates got offers elsewhere, you understand.'

'Interviewing?' said Dalziel sharply. 'For what?'

'A post, of course. It was a short list, only three. For a lectureship in the Biology Department.'

'Let me see,' said Dalziel, unceremoniously removing the papers from Jessup's hand.

Quickly he flicked through them till he found what he

wanted. A list of three names. One stood out as though embossed on the paper.

Samuel Fallowfield.

'Excuse me,' he said, moving quickly out of the pavilion leaving Jessup tugging his moustache in exasperation.

Dalziel's cry of 'Sergeant!' as he strode round the outer oval of spectators almost certainly caused the fall of the third wicket. But by the time the angry batsman had returned to the pavilion, Dalziel had disappeared in the direction of the sea and only Pascoe's head was visible as he went in hot pursuit.

Chapter 12

For many are wise in their own ways that are weak for
government or counsel; like ants, which is a wise creature for
itself, but very hurtful for the garden.

SIR FRANCIS BACON
Op. Cit.

The dismissed batsman was not the only one who noticed
Dalziel's sudden departure. Halfdane and his two female
consorts did.

'Perhaps he's off for a swim,' he suggested.

'That's not a bad idea,' said Ellie, watching Pascoe
picking himself up from among the daisies.

She stretched herself voluptuously, back arched, breasts at maximum projection, legs at maximum exposure.

'I wouldn't mind myself,' she added, watching Halfdane
carefully. She saw she had his interest.

Something's happened to me recently, she thought.
Suddenly I'm a huntress! I've been eyeing this poor
bastard hungrily for a month or so now. Then last night;
that was me. And what *do* I want anyway, for God's
sake? Some memories for a lonely old age? Or something
permanent? It's too late for that with PC Pascoe, even if
he doesn't know it yet. And I'm not really going about it
the right way with this one. Any lasting erection must
have a firm foundation, so they say.

She giggled at herself, let her body relax and pulled
her skirt down.

'Do you think they'd miss us if we did?' said Marion
Cargo from the other chair.

Quietly confident! groaned Ellie inwardly.

'Who cares?' said Halfdane. 'Anyway we might see the

158

bold gendarmes again and I want a word with Ellie's mate. Let's get our things.'

Ellie's mate! Perhaps Pascoe was the only hope after all. The beach might tell. It was ground of her own choosing. In or out of the water she knew she was physically superb.

'Let's go,' she said.

Landor rose to adjust his wife's parasol against the threatening manoeuvres of the sun. He had met her and courted her in the long winter of 1947. Curled up deep in an armchair before a roaring fire, or muffled against the snow in layers of clothing which permitted only the slight pale oval of her face to show, she had appealed deeply to his protective instincts. They had married in the spring and the tremors of doubt he had felt even then had been confirmed in every summer thereafter.

He looked at Jane Scotby and received from her a cold impersonal smile in return. She had resented him deeply when he first took up the post, he suspected. But he had met the senior tutor on the beach one morning more than a year ago, perilously perched on the back of a huge brown horse, her face slightly flushed with excitement, her eyes brighter than ever. It had seemed odd at first, almost ludicrous, till he realized how completely in control she was. And the beast was no milk-horse, it terrified the life out of Landor. The meeting had subtly changed their relationship.

His wife on the other hand controlled nothing, not even the running of the household. Lunch today had been all right. Salad and strawberries were difficult to spoil.

'That young policeman was most brusque this morning, I felt,' she said, watching Dalziel and Pascoe depart. 'The police are not what they were.'

Landor caught Scotby's bright blue eyes again. She

159

gave no sign of any reaction to his wife's inanities, for which he was grateful. But comfort was pleasant, it was good to be comforted from time to time.

He watched Ellie Soper and Marion Cargo sinuously rise from their deck-chairs, helped by young Halfdane.

He sighed deeply, felt the gaze on him of both the women by his side, and turned his sigh into a yawn. Comfort would be nice, but not at the expense of discretion. He glanced over his shoulder back to the complex of buildings which formed the college. That was his comfort. Nothing could come between him and that.

'What did Walt want?' asked someone after Sandra had been lying in the grass for ten minutes.

'When?'

'When you came over just now.'

'Nothing. I don't know. Just to talk. You know what she is.'

'No, I don't really,' said the youth who had asked the question. 'She's never bothered me. *I* don't get invited on the Tour of the Abbeys trip.'

There was a general laugh. Miss Disney's annual long week-end among the ruins of Yorkshire's abbeys with a group of specially selected girls was the subject of a great deal of scurrilous folk-lore.

'Poor you,' said Stuart Cockshut. 'Where's that fat bastard off to?'

They watched Dalziel and Pascoe heading towards the dunes.

'I hope he keeps walking and drowns.'

'You don't like him, Stuart?'

'I don't like policemen, period. And this one's out of the original mould. Thick as pig-shit and twice as nasty.'

'Stuart love,' said Franny who was lying on his back chewing a daisy, 'you are far too positive for a politician. You are as clear and uncomplicated as a pane of glass.

160

Yon Dalziel saw through you at a glance. I have no doubt he has a file thicker than Miss Disney on your many misdemeanours. And probably knows better than you the membership and background of these odd little societies you belong to. You must dirty the window a little, keep the inside polished but let rain-drops and bird-crap stop others from looking in.'

'He doesn't know what'll happen at the meeting tonight,' snarled Stuart, angry at the reproof.

Franny sat up.

'But surely no one knows that? Isn't that one of the mysterious joys of the democratic process? Well now, everyone seems to be heading for the beach.'

The others peered through the grass at Halfdane and the two female lecturers.

'Perhaps there's an orgy going on,' said someone.

'Oh, I took my organ to an orgy, but nobody asked me to play,' sang Franny softly.

'Anyone fancy a walk down there?' said Sandra. 'To see what's on?'

They looked at Franny who lay down once more and resumed his daisy-chewing again.

'Not me,' he said. 'I'm enjoying the cricket far too much to drag myself away. If someone will substitute a smoke for this flower, I'll be perfectly content.'

There was a pause. He lay with his eyes closed till he felt the thin cylinder of paper put to his lips. He inhaled deeply.

'Of course,' he said, 'if anyone else wants to go, don't let me keep you.'

No one moved. Only a breeze touched the grass and died with the touch.

Pascoe was sweating as much as Dalziel by the time he caught up with him.

'Where're we going?' he asked.

'Fallowfield. Look,' said Dalziel, waving Jessup's papers at him. 'He was here, being interviewed. The day Girling probably got killed. How's that for coincidence? Just like the coincidence that he had a date to see the girl he wasn't really sleeping with the night she got killed. That's another coincidence, eh?'

'It might be,' said Pascoe, cautiously.

'We're just going to *ask*,' said Dalziel, as though answering a warning. 'There's no harm in *asking*, is there?'

'No, sir,' said Pascoe, a little breathlessly. The previous night must have taken more out of him than he'd imagined.

The sea was now in sight. They were off course a little and had to bear to the right to get a line on the little row of cottages where Fallowfield lived.

There was no sign of life in or near any of the buildings, though there were quite a few people on the beach. The sea was absolutely still and there was a soft blue haze on it, drawn up by the sun, like something invented by a Hollywood colour technician. Those bathing in the shallow waters seemed distant, enchanted, their voices and laughter overheard from another world.

There was nothing distant or enchanted about Dalziel's knock on the door.

He paused a second, scarcely long enough for anyone within to recover from the shock, thought Pascoe, and then hammered away again.

There was no sound from inside.

'Have a look along the beach. See if he's there,' ordered Dalziel, making his way round to the little cobbled yard behind the cottages.

Pascoe had only gone about twenty yards, walking awkwardly on the soft sand, when he heard his name called. Turning, he saw Dalziel standing in the open front door of the cottage. Quickly he retraced his steps.

'I got in through the back,' said the fat man, adding sardonically in response to Pascoe's unasked question, 'the door was open.'

He went back into the house. Pascoe followed.

The front door opened into the main living-room, probably a draughty arrangement during the winter gales. But Pascoe's mind dwelt for a split second only on design problems. He blinked at the translation from bright sunlight to the shadowy interior then stared wide-eyed around him.

The place was a shambles.

The floor was covered with torn paper, most of it, as far as he could tell, pages ripped from the books which had once lined the shelves along one side of the fireplace. Mingled with the paper were the innards of cushions, pillows, chairs; flock, feathers and horse-hair lay inches deep in many places. There was a strong smell of spirits, and, lined neatly on the old dresser, Pascoe saw the empty bottles. Someone had carefully poured their contents down on to the general mess below. The walls also had been defaced. Scribbled over them was a variety of obscene drawings, mostly outrageous caricatures of a penis, being attacked by a knife or scissors, with a selection of accompanying slogans, equally simple and direct. Their common burden seemed to be that Fallowfield was a bastard pig who co-habited with his own mother.

No matter how often you saw it, it was always a shock to see a room reduced to this kind of chaos, but Pascoe quickly recovered and stood stock-still, not wanting to disturb anything till he had taken it all in. Dalziel stood quietly by his side.

Impressions began to form.

This shambles was *not* the kind created by a struggle. Indeed far from it, Pascoe decided. This was a very quiet kind of wrecking. So far as he could see, nothing had been broken, no glass anyway. The empty bottles had been put safely down, the small glass-fronted cabinet from which they had probably been taken was intact, as were the glasses it contained. The old plates which lined the big old-fashioned dresser were undisturbed. A grandmother clock stood in a corner. The face had been opened and the hands torn off, but no glass broken. Nowhere had anything large or heavy been overturned.

Dalziel spoke his thoughts.

'They took their time, didn't they? Took their time and did it quietly. You could have come to the door and knocked and not known anyone was in here.'

'Perhaps we did,' suggested Pascoe.

'I hope not,' said Dalziel gloomily. 'Nearly all the buggers likely to have done it were sitting back there watching the cricket.'

'It looks recent, though.'

'I presume it bloody well is recent! It's not the kind of decor you choose to live with for a long time, is it?'

'No, sir.'

'Right. Let's have a good look around. But tread carefully.'

Pascoe felt rather slighted that Dalziel needed to give the instruction. The fat man caught his expression.

'I mean, watch where you tread. Literally. They often crap or piddle all over the place when they make this kind of mess.'

Pascoe trod carefully but it turned out there was no need. The cottage was not large – living-room, kitchen, lavatory, shower, one bedroom and a boxroom. The damage was restricted almost entirely to the living-room. Even those things belonging elsewhere which had been damaged – like the pillows and some clothing from the bedroom – had been taken downstairs first. There was a drawing in the lavatory – rather more care had been taken this time, but the theme was the same as below –

and on the shower floor a tumbler had been shattered, whether by accident or malicious design it was hard to say.

As he stood looking out of the back window, Pascoe saw Halfdane coming over the dunes, making for the beach, with Ellie and Marion Cargo. All three had towels bundled under their arms and were obviously going swimming.

Swiftly he moved downstairs, out of the back door, and intercepted them.

'Hello,' said Halfdane cheerily. 'Well met by sunlight! Come and join us, do.'

'I'd love to,' said Pascoe, smiling at Ellie. 'But duty and modesty forbid. Look, I'm sorry to hold you up, but I just wanted to ask if you'd met anyone making their way back to the college?'

They looked at each other, then shook their heads.

'Sorry,' said Halfdane. 'Anyway we couldn't have been far behind you. Why do you ask?'

'It's not important,' said Pascoe casually. He saw Ellie roll her eyes with exaggerated exasperation, but surprisingly it was Marion Cargo who made the usual complaint.

'If you people never say what it is you really want to know, how do you expect anyone to co-operate?'

'Us people?' said Pascoe looking over his shoulder as though in search of them. 'Oh, you mean *me*? *Never*'s a bit strong to someone you've only met twice, isn't it, Miss Cargo?'

He pulled himself up. It was foolish to let these people get up his nose. These people! There, he was doing it now. It was just that, somehow, a shared background and many shared interests seemed to separate rather than bring them closer. He might have ended up like them if . . . if what? If there hadn't been something in him which made it necessary to be a policeman.

In any case, as a policeman he could be conciliatory and seek information at the same time.

'I'm sorry,' he said with his best smile. 'I just wanted a word with Mr Fallowfield, that's all, and as he's not at home, I wondered if I might have missed him in the dunes. You haven't seen anything of him today, have you?'

Again the exchange of glances and the shaking of heads.

'In that case, I'll go back and wait a bit,' he said. 'Have a nice swim.'

He smiled once more. Ellie rolled her eyes again, but this time in a mock amazement at his performance which invited him to be amused with her. He grinned warmly. Marion remained impassive.

He had only gone a few steps when Halfdane overtook him.

'By the way, Sergeant, I wanted to have a quick word with you.'

'Yes?' said Pascoe, rather brusquely he realized as he saw Halfdane's eyes narrow.

But, Christ! why did he have to be grateful just because people condescended to talk to him?

'It's probably nothing. I would have mentioned it to your superintendent, but his manner's a bit off-putting.'

Suddenly Pascoe was fed up.

'What is it you want to tell me? Sir?'

'There's a lot I could tell you,' said Halfdane ironically, 'but I really wanted to ask you something. In a case like this, a serious case I mean, if some minor breach of the law comes to light incidentally, while you're pursuing the important enquiry, what do you do?'

'I don't follow,' said Pascoe woodenly.

'I think you do.'

'We don't make bargains. And we don't make judgments.'

166

'No? But you pay informants, don't you?'

Pascoe shook his head, not in denial but in sheer impatience.

'Look,' he said. 'If you've got information, it's your civic duty to pass it on, no matter what it is.'

'Get knotted,' said Halfdane, turning back to where the two women waited.

Pascoe did not wait to hear more but set off smartly back to the cottage.

'Well?' said Dalziel.

'They've seen no one.'

'There's none so blind,' said Dalziel. 'I'm beginning to think they're all in a gigantic conspiracy.'

'Perhaps so,' said Pascoe, trying (unsuccessfully he was sure) not to let his chief see his own annoyance at the encounter. 'Still; where's Fallowfield? That's the big question.'

'It's bigger than you think,' said Dalziel. 'Come and see what I've found.'

He led the way into the bedroom where he had obviously done a fairly comprehensive search.

'Look,' he said, pointing into a suitcase which lay open on the bed.

In it were a flowered mini-skirt; some underwear; a pair of sandals.

Pascoe looked at the superintendent who nodded.

'They fit the description,' he said. 'I'd lay good money they're Anita Sewell's.'

Pascoe snapped the case shut.

'I'll check it out,' he said.

'Hold on a minute!' said Dalziel. 'It'll keep. No, you keep on sniffing around here for a bit. See if you can do a bit of detecting for a change. You should be well up on the psychological stuff. Well, tell me what kind of person would tear up a place like this? And what kind of person would have a place like this to tear up?'

167

'All right,' said Pascoe cautiously, uncertain how serious Dalziel was.

He went back downstairs to the living-room. Behind him he heard the bed creak protestingly. Dalziel was a great believer in taking rest when and where you got the chance. Pascoe was always ready to recognize the wisdom of others. He turned the slashed cushion of the deepest armchair upside down, gathered up an armful of paper from the floor and sat down.

Something about the drawings which defaced the walls caught his attention first. Some had been done in some kind of chalk. Bright yellow. There had been no sign of it during the search. He made a mental note to look more closely.

Other drawings and pieces of writing had been done more primitively by scoring the plaster with a sharp-edged object. The brass candlestick on the mantelshelf? He stood up and looked more closely. The corners of the square base were scratched and smeared with powdered plaster.

Perhaps the chalk had just run out. It had been laid on pretty thickly.

He sat down again and began looking at the papers he held. It was a disappointing task at first. The only sheets which were not out of books were typewritten lecture notes, or at least so he assumed from the subject-matter. The books from which the majority of the pages had been ripped were again mainly text-books, easily identifiable as the pages had merely been torn whole from their covers. But here and there he noticed were smaller fragments of pages, some reduced almost to confetti, and he began to fit some of these together to see why they had been given special treatment.

It wasn't an easy task and after a few minutes he chucked the whole lot on the floor in annoyance and began to do what he ought to have done in the first place – look for book covers.

It didn't take long to sort out the odd ones – or rather the non-biological ones, for they were not particularly odd in themselves. Huxley's *The Doors of Perception*, Leary's *Politics of Ecstasy*, Professor Thorndike's *History of Magic and Experimental Science* (only three volumes out of eight), Aleister Crowley's *Magic in Theory and Practice* and the same writer's translation of Eliphas Levi's *The Key of the Mysteries,* Allegro's *The Sacred Mushroom and the Cross* (particularly badly damaged – Pascoe could find no piece of a page larger than a postage stamp), *Eros and Evil* by R. E. Masters; the covers from these and a score of others on related topics Pascoe stacked in the space he cleared on the floor in front of him. He heard the stairs creak and Dalziel appeared in the doorway.

His eyebrows went up when he saw what Pascoe had been doing.

'Pornography?' he said hopefully.

'No, sir,' said Pascoe with a poorly muffled groan.

'No?' said Dalziel, poking around. 'Still, it's odd, isn't it? A bit bent.'

'I've read most of them myself,' said Pascoe challengingly.

'Still, you thought it was worth picking out this lot specially,' said Dalziel mildly. Pascoe found he didn't have a reply.

'Anything else?' Dalziel went on. 'Good. Let's get things moving. First thing is, where's Fallowfield? Failing that, who did this lot? Perhaps *he'll* know where Fallowfield is.'

'Unless it was Fallowfield himself,' suggested Pascoe. Dalziel looked unimpressed.

'To confuse the picture, I mean, while he makes off,' the sergeant added.

'But why make off at all? And he was a bit careless leaving those clothes lying around, wasn't he?'

'I suppose so.'

'Still not happy?' said Dalziel sympathetically.

'Yes. That is, well, I don't know, sir. There's something . . .'

'Perhaps it's the fact that two people did the wrecking that bothers you,' Dalziel went on, the sympathy oozing out now.

Oh God, thought Pascoe. I've missed something. I should have known as soon as he started sounding pleasant!

'You noticed the drawings, of course?'

'Why, yes. You mean some are done in chalk, others scratched?'

'Partly that. But have another look. It's not just the instrument, it's the *style*.'

Pascoe looked. It might be true, though he had reservations. One piece of graffiti looked much like another to him.

'So there were two,' he said neutrally.

'But the question is, lad, *together* or *apart*? Anyway, we mustn't stand around here when there's work to be done. I'll get these clothes back to the college. You have a go at the neighbours, though I doubt they'll be any use.'

'They don't seem to be in,' said Pascoe.

Dalziel looked at him pityingly.

'Of course they're not in. Only fools and policemen are inside on a day like this. Walk down the beach a bit, they're probably not far. And, Sergeant . . .'

'Sir?'

'Don't let all that sunburnt flesh take your mind off the job.'

Even with the jacket of his lightweight suit slung

170

casually over his shoulder, Pascoe felt very much over-dressed as he furrowed his way through the soft sand towards the sea.

He had been right, the people next door were out; but in front of the farthermost of the four cottages he found an old woman who preferred the shade cast by the afternoon sun to its direct beam. She directed him to her family who were interested but unhelpful and in their turn they directed him to Fallowfield's immediate neighbours.

There were a lot of them, three adults, one selfconsciously almost naked teenage girl, an indistinguishable number of children and a dog.

The adults it seemed were Mr and Mrs Plessey and another Mr Plessey, brother to the first.

No, they hadn't seen Mr Fallowfield all day; no, during the brief spells they had spent in their cottage that day, they had heard nothing suspicious, which was hardly surprising, thought Pascoe, listening to the din the children and the dog managed to make even while attending with great interest to what he was saying.

Finally; no, they hadn't seen anyone, suspicious or not, anywhere near the cottage that day.

Pascoe turned to go.

'Except the lady.'

He turned back. It was one of the children, a happy-faced boy of about six years.

'No!' said one of his fellows, a little girl slightly older, who managed to inject considerable scorn into her voice. 'That was at night.'

'Oh bother!' said the boy, smacking his left fist into his right palm with a look of mock-exasperation. 'That's right. Sorry!'

He jumped on top of the dog which didn't seem to mind, and the others followed suit.

With some help from the elder Plesseys, Pascoe brought him to the surface again.

'What's your name?' he asked.

'Davy,' said the lad.

'Which night was it you saw the lady? Can you remember?'

'I dunno. Last night,' he said with great charm but little conviction.

'The night before last,' said the little girl with quiet certainty.

Pascoe turned his attention to her as the more reliable witness, but instantly she became shy and tongue-tied, so he went back to Davy.

'What time was it?'

'Very very late,' he said shooting a sideways glance at his mother.

'How late?'

'Midnight,' he said. 'We were having a midnight feast. It was her idea.'

He spoke very earnestly, pointing at his sister, but spoilt it by starting to grin as his mother looked accusingly at him.

'It was nearly two-o-clock. Dark two-o-clock, I mean, not light two-o-clock.'

'She can tell the time,' said Davy proudly. 'She's got a clock.'

'It's an alarming clock,' said the girl. 'It wakes you up.'

'What about this feast, Julie?' asked Mr Plessey sternly.

'It wasn't really a *feast*,' protested Julie. 'It should have been, but the others wouldn't wake up, only Davy.'

'And the lady?' prompted Pascoe.

The lady whom they had seen going into Fallowfield's house at two o'clock on Friday morning sounded – once Julie had modified Davy's extremely sinister description – very like Anita Sewell.

Happy, Pascoe offered ice-creams all round. He hadn't realized quite how many little Plesseys there were and how much the cost of ice-cream had risen since he was a boy. Perhaps, he thought not very optimistically, Dalziel would let it come out of their informant funds.

Only once more did he pause before leaving the beach. Something distantly observed from the corner of his eye tickled his consciousness. He glanced to the side, did a double-take.

No, he hadn't been mistaken. The figure was some distance away, but quite unmistakable.

What on earth was Miss Disney doing recumbent in all her tweedy glory among the hoi-polloi on this holiday beach?

Dalziel had initiated the hunt for Fallowfield very cautiously. For all he knew, the man was merely spending a week-end with friends somewhere, or perhaps even doing some shopping in one of the neighbouring towns. If so, he would come trotting back to Dalziel of his own accord and the superintendent had no intention of sending him to cover by advertising the eagerness of the police to interview him.

Nevertheless the wheels were set in motion, and what little information they had on the man was disseminated. It was very little indeed; there wasn't even an easily accessible photograph. In fact, the information consisted almost entirely of name, verbal description and car-make and registration number.

This last item produced almost instant results. Within the hour the car was spotted outside a garage only a few miles from the college. Dalziel's satisfaction when this was reported to him was short-lived. Within ten minutes it was established that the car had been left for servicing two days earlier. Fallowfield had not been back to collect it. Going by the book, Dalziel immediately diverted more of his men to checking local car-hire services, but he felt uneasy. Checks at bus and rail stations had already proved fruitless.

Pascoe on his return from the beach had found an attentive audience as he described Fallowfield's night visitor.

'So now you think Anita didn't get killed right after the dancing party split up, but got dressed and later went to keep her appointment with Fallowfield?'

Pascoe was used to being appointed owner of theories until they became certainties, when they returned to his superior.

'It could be,' he said.

'But why did he undress her after killing her?'

'Perhaps she was naked when he killed her?'

Dalziel shrugged.

'What for? They'd never been at it before. Why start now? Or, if they did start, why stop and kill her before things really got underway?'

'Perhaps Fallowfield couldn't get underway. Perhaps that was the trouble. She said something . . .'

'You've been reading those dirty psychological books again,' said Dalziel reprovingly. 'No; if he killed her in the house, then he undressed her and took her out to the dunes. Or took her out to the dunes and undressed her.'

'And brought her clothes back with him?'

'Yes.'

'Odd.'

'It's fairly straightforward compared with the rest of this business. No, the interesting thing is, why did he undress her? Eh, Sergeant?'

'To make it look . : .' began Pascoe slowly.

'To make it look as if she was killed right after the dancing. Which means?'

Pascoe was there already, but diplomatically looked enquiringly at his superior. He overdid it ever so slightly, hoping Dalziel would wonder if he was being condescended to.

'It means,' said Dalziel ignoring the subtleties of

Pascoe's facial expression, 'it means that he *knew* there had been a wild, orgiastic, Bacchanalian rout.'

He brought the phrase out with mock-triumph.

'Hardly Bacchanalian,' Pascoe murmured, but Dalziel ignored him.

'And that could tie up with those books, couldn't it? In Fallowfield's room?'

'It crossed my mind when I found them,' admitted Pascoe.

'Well, lad,' said Dalziel, 'if you want credit for ideas, you'll have to spit them out before I do, won't you? Now, you bugger off out there again. That tedious bloody game's still going on, I think. You can tell by the roar of the excited crowd. Start asking around about friend Fallowfield. I don't want people getting ideas, you understand. Not yet. But find out when he was last seen. Where. Doing what. Anything else you can. Use a bit of charm.'

Someone tapped discreetly at the door.

'Come in, for Godsake!' he bellowed.

'Hammer the bloody wood, will you?' he said to the uniformed constable who entered. 'You're a policeman, not a butler.'

'From HQ, sir,' said the constable handing over an envelope.

'Right,' said Dalziel opening it and glancing quickly at the contents.

Pascoe held the door open so the constable could follow him out. It would be quite pleasant to watch a bit of cricket, especially once the cooling breeze which often blew up in the late afternoon put in an appearance.

'There's one thing you've got to give those Krauts,' said Dalziel. 'They're bloody thorough.'

'Sir?' said Pascoe, stepping back into the room.

'That Austrian fellow you were talking to at vast bloody expense yesterday. You must have interested him.'

It sounded dirty.

'Sir?' said Pascoe.

'He's been doing some more checking round the hotel where Miss Girling always stayed. And he came up with this.'

He waved a sheet of paper in the air.

'Sir?' said Pascoe. This was getting monotonous.

'That year, it seems, according to the old booking charts he unearthed, Miss Girling made an extra booking in October. Her own booking was carried on from year to year, it seems.'

'Oh,' said Pascoe, trying not to sound too supercilious. 'You mean Miss Mayflower? From Doncaster? She's dead.'

'What on earth are you mumbling about, Sergeant? No, this booking was cancelled in December, at the last moment.'

'Someone at the college?' said Pascoe. 'Good lord! You don't mean she was taking Disney!'

'No,' said Dalziel. 'Cargo. Marion Cargo.'

Chapter 13

Profoundness of wisdom will help a man to a name or admiration, but it is eloquence that prevaileth in an active life.

SIR FRANCIS BACON
Op. Cit.

Marion Cargo seemed more relieved than confused when confronted with this new information. Dalziel had half-expected the usual excuses and rationalizations – 'I didn't think it was important,' 'it was all so long ago, I'd forgotten.' In fact, he was half-ready to accept them. It was hard to see how the investigation could be helped by anything Marion could tell them. And when she had finished, he still wasn't sure whether he had been helped or not.

'I should have said something sooner,' she said, only her tightly clasped hands in her lap contradicting her appearance of complete self-possession. 'There's nothing much to tell, mind you. Miss Girling was very – kind to me. I was a favourite, I suppose. She got me working on that statue. It was absurd really. *Youth* it was to be called! It cost a fortune, most of it her own money.'

She paused.

'A favourite?' said Dalziel softly.

'Yes,' she said. 'That was all. Nothing more. At least, I didn't think so. I still don't. But she suggested that I should go on holiday with her that Christmas. My mother had died during the previous summer – I can't remember my father at all – and I was temporarily with a very dull uncle and aunt. It was just a nice, thoughtful gesture. I was delighted.'

177

'What happened?'

'Miss Disney came to my room one evening. Everyone was scared of her then. Not like now, students don't seem to be scared of anyone, but we were all frightened little mice just five or six years ago. Anyway, she started talking about me and Miss Girling, about the holiday. I didn't understand her at first. But I began to get the idea pretty quickly. She made it sound awful, as if somehow *I* was a bad influence on Miss Girling! She got very worked up, not hysterical or anything, but full of indignation, all puffy and red. I didn't know what to think. She implied all kinds of things, even that Miss Girling could lose her job because of me! It was absurd I know, but I was very innocent, naïve I suppose. Disney left finally; I just sat for a bit, then went round to Miss Girling's room. This was the last Sunday of term, I was about the only student left in the place, there was no one of my own age to talk to and in any case, I just had to see her. But all I could do when I saw her was blurt out that I couldn't go to Austria after all, something had come up. I suppose I expected an emotional scene, with tears, explanations, comfortings etc. But she just looked at me and nodded. Then picked up the phone and started cancelling my booking, plane-seat and so on.'

'Did you see her again?' asked Dalziel.

'No. I was as miserable as hell all night and most of the next day, that Monday. Finally I plucked up courage to go and see her again.'

'What time was that?'

'I don't remember. About tea-time. It was dark, but then it got dark even earlier than usual that December with the fog. I tapped on her door. There was someone inside, I could hear voices.'

'Her door? Which door?'

'This one,' said Marion surprised, pointing to the door of Landor's former study.

178

'Of course,' said Dalziel. 'I thought you might have meant her house.'

'Oh, she didn't have a house. The principal's house was only built when Dr Landor came. Miss Girling had a suite of rooms here, through that door and up the stairs.'

She nodded at the room's other door which Dalziel had already tried and found to be locked.

'What happened to the rooms?'

'Oh, they're used for other things now. A library storeroom. The bursar's office. That kind of thing.'

Dalziel tried the door again. Still unsuccessfully.

'Interesting,' he said. 'Whose voices did you hear?'

'When? Oh, you mean after I'd knocked? I don't know. One was Miss Girling's. The other was a man's. There may have been two. They all seemed to be talking very loudly. I don't think anyone even heard my knock, it was so timid. Anyway, it didn't seem a good moment, so I crept away.'

'Did you try again later?'

'I meant to. But as I was walking over about an hour later, her car went belting by me along the drive. It was going very quickly, I lifted my hand, but I doubt if she saw me. I just stood there in the middle of the drive, feeling quite miserable, watching the tail-lights disappear. I think I'd have stood there for ever if another car hadn't come up behind me. I was almost knocked down. I don't think I'd have minded much,' she said with a wry grin.

'Another car?' said Dalziel. 'Whose?'

'I don't know. I jumped out of the way when he blew his horn and he went on up the drive almost as fast as Miss Girling.'

'I see,' said Dalziel thoughtfully. 'And that was all?'

'Yes. I went back to my room, then spent Christmas with my dull relations. I knew nothing about the avalanche till I came back to college in January. It was terrible news. I suppose I should have been relieved I hadn't gone. Disney certainly thought so. She alternated between the tragic bereaved bit and the I-saved-your-life line. I was too numb to take much notice. I just hung on till finals were over in the summer, then got out, rejoicing that I'd never see the place again.'

'And here you are.'

She shrugged.

'Things change after a couple of years. You grow up. I saw the job, it was a good step career-wise, and I was a bit curious to see the old place. It was quite a surprise to be offered the post in fact. I hadn't really banked on it. But I said, why not? and here I am. Disney returned to the attack, but apart from that, it was very pleasant, till Dr Landor decided to move the statue.'

'Miss Disney bothered you again?'

'No, not *bothered*. She started by implying that her influence had got me the job, then began dropping in on me, going all girlish, "isn't it nice that we're colleagues now?" and "let's tell each other secrets and talk about Al," that sort of thing.'

'What happened in the end?'

She laughed.

'It was funny really. The others noticed, of course, and most of them sympathized. But it was only Sam Fallowfield who did anything about it. I suppose in the end I'd have worked my courage up to the point where I'd have told her myself, but I'm not a very bold person, Superintendent. So I was very pleased when Sam took a hand. All he did was join me as soon as Walt came and sat beside me. And he called to see me a couple of times just after she'd arrived. He just sat and smiled at her, nodding sympathetically every time she spoke. After a couple of weeks, she gave up. I was delighted, of course. But she hated Sam. It was obscene to see how pleased she was after this trouble with the girl blew up. She went around saying it was no more than she had expected. I could have killed her.'

'I see,' said Dalziel, wondering if she was speaking purely figuratively.

'You don't think there was any chance she could have put the girl up to it, do you?'

This was obviously a brand-new thought to Marion. She gave it careful consideration.

'I don't think so,' she said slowly. 'She was a nice girl, Anita. I'm not saying she couldn't be influenced, but not by Disney. No, I'm certain of that. It would need a very different kind of influence than a woman like Disney could bring to bear.'

'Good,' said Dalziel, standing up to show that the interview was over. The move was abrupt, but, as Pascoe would have vouched, it passed for courtesy compared with many of his usual modes of dismissing people.

He watched with open pleasure as Marion uncrossed her legs and stood up.

'Thank you for being so frank, Miss Cargo,' he said.

'I'm sorry you had to ask,' she replied. 'It was silly of me.'

'Not at all.' Gallantly he opened the door.

'Just one thing,' he said as she passed through it. 'The other voice you heard when you knocked on Miss Girling's door that night. It was definitely a man? Or men?'

She hesitated, looking back into the study as if somehow projecting herself back in time to the point where she had stood outside this same door vainly waiting to be invited in.

'Yes,' she said. 'Definitely a man.'

'But you didn't recognize it?'

'I'm not sure,' she said slowly. 'It was somehow familiar. But it was so distorted, I couldn't say.'

'Distorted?'

181

'Yes,' she said. 'With anger.'

The cricket match was almost over when Pascoe finally reached it. He had been delayed first of all by the task of getting hold of Marion Cargo and escorting her to Dalziel. She had come without hesitation or protest, almost as if relieved. But Halfdane, still nursing his earlier annoyance, had more than compensated for her easiness. It had only been Marion's own insistence that prevented him from following her into the study.

Pascoe had been tempted to question him very roughly about his last sighting of Fallowfield, but remembering Dalziel's invocation of his charm, decided he would leave it till later and start elsewhere. So, leaving Halfdane striding sentry-like up and down outside the study door, he set off on his delayed journey to the playing-fields.

He had missed the day's main excitement, it seemed. Half-way through the afternoon one of the umpires, an elderly man with a gouty toe which made the time-lag between overs even longer than it usually is, had fallen into a kind of sun-induced trance at square-leg and had to be nursed back to consciousness with iced lemonade in the pavilion. Subsequently he had been weaned on to strawberries and cream and the prognosis seemed good. But his place had been taken by the portly figure of Henry Saltecombe who, determined not to suffer the same fate, protected his bald pate with an incongruous pork-pie hat. The hat was the most interesting thing on the field as far as Pascoe was concerned. It would bear looking into, as the actress said to the conjuror, he thought.

His informant about the affairs of the day was George Dunbar who masochistically was hanging on to the bitter end, despite his expression of distaste for the game.

Perhaps he wants to establish exactly where he is,

thought Pascoe, laughing at his own conditioned sus-
piciousness, but not dismissing the suspicion.

'Mr Fallowfield around?' he asked casually.

'Fallowfield? He's got more bloody sense.'

'Oh. What's he do at week-ends then. Golf?' asked
Pascoe at random.

'No, he hasn't got that much sense. Why're you asking,
eh?' Dunbar glanced keenly at the sergeant who grunted
non-committally.

'If he's wise, he'll be at the quack's,' Dunbar went on.

'Quack's?'

'The doctor's!' said Dunbar exasperatedly. 'Did you
see him yesterday? Man, he looked ill. All this business
must have been a strain. I reckon he's heading for a
crack-up, myself.'

He spoke with some relish.

'So you haven't seen him today?'

'No. Not a sign. Now, why do . . .'

But Pascoe had already moved on.

He stopped trying to be subtle after a while, deciding
that even if he just asked people what time it was, they
would start wondering what this had to do with the
investigation.

Only with the group of students round Franny Roote
and Cockshut did he have any success.

'Yes, I saw him this morning, going towards college,'
said a little square, ugly girl.

'Time? I don't know. About half-nine, wouldn't you
say, hey, Franny?'

'Whatever you say, lovey, whatever you say,' chanted
Roote melodiously, lying on his back still, smiling happily.
Pascoe wondered if he was slightly drunk.

'But you didn't see him later?' he pursued.

'Well played, sir!' cried Roote, clapping his hands, his
eyes fixed rapturously on the sky.

'Christalmighty, you're a detective, go and detect.' It

was Cockshut of course. 'Anyway, why doesn't that fat crud come out and ask his own questions instead of sending the help?'

A shout from the middle of the field and a ripple of applause round the perimeter drew his attention back to the match. The last wicket had fallen and the players were straggling off. Pascoe started heading for the pavilion with the intention of cutting off Saltecombe but someone called his name and he stopped. It was Halfdane.

But surprisingly Halfdane seemed to be in a much more conciliatory mood. He was still far from apologetic, but at least he didn't open with too much aggression.

Not again! he thought with an inward groan. What's he want? A fight?'

'I've been thinking,' he said. 'This business has got to be cleared up. It's stupid for me to withhold information out of pique.'

What's he want? wondered Pascoe. Applause for acknowledging what nobody but a criminal or a moron would deny? Or perhaps he's just clearing the decks so that he can get down to disliking me with a clear conscience.

'Mind you,' said Halfdane, 'what I've got to say is probably irrelevant and I hope you won't want to do anything about it if it is.'

Again Pascoe produced his non-committal grunt.

'Anita Sewell,' said Halfdane, 'was there any evidence that she'd been taking drugs?'

'Why do you ask?' said Pascoe.

'It's just that, well, occasionally I've been to one or two student parties, or parties where there have been students. There's usually pot available at these do's. It's just like another form of booze these days, and no more harmful.'

He looked defiantly at Pascoe who still said nothing. Is

184

this all the poor bastard's got to tell me? he wondered. Confession of an ageing teenager.

'Now, a couple of times I've noticed Anita, and she's been really high. I mean really.'

'And what did you do?'

Halfdane tried to look surprised.

'Do? She was an adult, she was responsible. But I did wonder what she was getting, whether she'd moved on.'

'You mean, whether she had started taking a habit-forming drug which would eventually kill her?' said Pascoe coldly.

'For God's sake!' said the other in anger.

'But I forgot. She was an adult. Who was she with?'

Halfdane's anger subsided.

'That's why I wondered about telling you this. You want names. If it's anything to do with her death, fair enough. But if it isn't . . .'

'Names please, sir.'

'Cockshut. Stuart Cockshut was the main one,' he said reluctantly. 'And Roote and all that gang. But especially Cockshut.'

Pascoe made a note in his pocket-book, more for appearance than necessity. The information wasn't all that helpful. It confirmed what he already suspected. It might explain Roote lying on his back, applauding the sky. But there had been no evidence of any sampling of 'hard' drugs in the autopsy on Anita's body. And the dancing as described by Lapping had seemed to be sex-rather than drug-centred. Of course it depended on the drug. And if these people had access to anything more sophisticated than cannabis, despite any assurances Halfdane might imagine had been given, he and Dalziel were going to be very interested indeed.'

'Right,' he said, closing his book.

'I'd better get back and see if your boss has finished with Marion,' said Halfdane with slightly nervous jocularity.

That's what he's really worried about, that Bruiser Dalziel is going to stick something on his girl. So anything which seems to lead elsewhere he's now happy to give me.

Pascoe didn't know whether the thought made him like Halfdane more or less. But another thought came swiftly and unbidden into his mind.

Poor Ellie!

'Right you are,' he said. 'If we want to talk to you again, we'll let you know.'

He was damned if he was going to thank the man.

He resumed his walk towards the pavilion and Henry Saltecombe.

'And that's all he said?' asked Dalziel sounding as incredulous as stout Cortez looked on stumbling across the Pacific.

I didn't have my Iron Maiden handy, thought Pascoe; but what he said was, 'That's all. Yes, it was his pork-pie hat; no, he hadn't been wandering round the dunes at midnight last Thursday, he'd been sitting up late at home after all his family had gone off to bed so that he could watch a documentary on medieval industry. Anyway, if Anita was going into Fallowfield's cottage a couple of hours later, what does it matter who disturbed the dance?'

'There's a porpoise close behind me and it's treading on my tail,' said Dalziel thoughtfully. 'Of course those kids might have been dreaming. Or for that matter, it might have been some other long-haired beauty that Fallowfield's having it away with. We won't know till we find the man, will we?'

'No, sir.'

'And of course, if the kids *are* right, then everyone's going to need new alibis, aren't they?'

'That's right,' said Pascoe, brightening. 'Including these bloody students.'

Dalziel eyed him sardonically.

'Watch it, Sergeant,' he said. 'Never forget, the country's full of wonderful young people who stand up for pregnant women in buses and run errands for the aged and decrepit. The *Daily Mirror* said so last week. Or was it the *Express*?'

'Then it must be true. What now, sir?'

Dalziel glanced at his watch. It was nearly a quarter to seven. It had been a quick day and he still wasn't sure whether they had advanced or gone back. But first things first.

'Dinner,' he said with satisfaction.

After dinner, Pascoe sat in his room and contemplated the rest of the evening. He felt lonely. His meal had been brought to him on a tray as usual and used though he was to eating by himself, it always seemed a particularly lonely thing to have to do. He supposed no one would have thrown bread-rolls at him if he had appeared in the dining-hall, but he doubted if he would have felt less alone.

He suddenly thought how lonely such a life could be for many of those permanently committed to it. Perhaps it just seemed so on the surface. Perhaps the seeming-lonely like Disney or Scotby really had troops of friends, tribes of loving relations, acres of exciting interests, at their beck and call.

But it wasn't just them. It was people like Marion, and Ellie as well. Halfdane too, even Fallowfield. The unmarried. Those for whom home was – this. He looked around the room. It was at least as comfortable as his own minute flat. And, God knows, he knew what it was to be lonely even in a job which often kept him at it for anything up to twenty hours a day.

Therefore, he said, if all people are lonely some of the time and some people are lonely all of the time, it is not merely self-indulgence to thrust myself at them, it may even be a social service.

The obvious person to thrust at was Ellie. He reached for the phone and dialled.

'Hallo, Ellie.'

'Oh, it's you.'

'Right first time,' he said. 'Look, I've been glancing through your manuscript. Very interesting. But I thought I'd get it back to you before I do something awful with it, like spill coffee all over it or lose it. Is it OK if I come round and return it now?'

There was a pause.

'Yes. No. Look, I'll come and collect it. You're in 28, aren't you?'

'That's right. Worried about the kind of person seen going into your room, are you?' he said with an attempt at lightness.

'Piss off.'

The phone went dead. He wondered if this meant she wasn't coming, but within five minutes there was a tap at the door.

'Hi,' she said. She looked very attractive in a simple white dress with large black buttons right down the front. He couldn't quite decide whether they were functional or merely decorative.

'I enjoyed your book.'

'Liar,' she said calmly. 'You haven't had time to look at it.'

'No,' he protested. 'Some of the characterization helped a great deal in understanding life here at the college. I'm looking forward to reading the finished thing when it's published.'

She sat down, smiling now.

'It's like listening to some sentimental song,' she said. 'Hackneyed tune, meaningless words, but it works on you. Keep talking.'

There was a tap on the door. It was Elizabeth, neat as ever in her nylon overall, come to collect the dishes. It was nice to have such a pretty girl looking after him. She seemed very obliging. In fact earlier he had found her in the room tidying up. Perhaps she fancies me, he thought.

She seemed a little disconcerted to find Ellie there also and let a fork slide on to the carpet.

'Sorry,' she said, bending down. Pascoe automatically stooped also and the heads nearly cracked together. They both rocked back on their haunches, smiling, the girl showing a lot of leg where the overall parted above her knees. Pascoe glanced down involuntarily. On the inside hem of the garment he saw the initials in indian ink E. A.

There wasn't a blinding flash. There rarely was. Just another certainty sliding into place. Fancies me, hell! he mocked himself.

'Tell me,' he said conversationally, 'what time did you get back from the beach on Thursday morning?'

The girl turned pale. Bulls-eye! thought Pascoe.

'Were you asked to keep a close eye on us as well, the superintendent and me?' he went on pressing his advantage.

The girl stood up, leaving the crockery on the floor.

'I don't know what . . .'

'Come off it, love,' said Pascoe. 'You were there. That makes you a witness. You should have come forward, you know. But better late than never. We'll need a statement. And you'll want your bra back.'

'I don't know . . .' she said again, then turned and hurried from the room.

'What the hell are you doing to that poor kid?' demanded Ellie angrily. 'For Christ's sake, I'd never have believed it. You're like the bloody SS. Those sergeant's stripes go all the way through, don't they?'

Pascoe threw up his hands in mock bewilderment.

'That poor kid as you call her was big enough and old

enough to enjoy a moonlight orgy after which a girl got herself killed. She also probably gets high pretty frequently on cannabis and doubtless does a bit of dabbling in the supernatural on the side. I should think she can stand a few straight questions from a policeman.'

'What the hell are you on about? You mean . . .' For a few seconds Ellie was lost for words. For a few seconds.

'Look. OK. What's the difference? If that's the way she likes her sex, what's it to you? It's a lot to her though; these others, students, it's nothing to them, a bit of embarrassment at home if mummy and daddy get to hear of it, but that's all. But it's that girl's *job*. She's not just a skivvy, she's doing a training course in catering. And this kind of thing could easily get her chucked out on her ear.'

Pascoe shrugged.

'I'm sorry. It won't come to that. There's probably nothing she can tell us, no more than the students we've talked to. It's unimportant.'

'Unimportant! You didn't make *her* feel it was unimportant!'

'No. I'm sorry. Excuse me.'

He picked up the phone again and dialled Dalziel's room. There was no reply, so he tried the study.

'Superintendent Dalziel.'

'Pascoe, sir. I thought you'd like to know I've identified the owner of that bra found in the dunes. Elizabeth Andrews, the girl who brings our meals.'

There was a snort at the other end of the line.

'Yes, I know. I saw her leaving Roote's room the other night. Is that all?'

'Well, yes sir. I thought she might have been keeping an eye on us for some reason.'

'You haven't talked to her?'

'Well, yes, I have.'

190

'Oh God,' groaned Dalziel. 'Now I'll probably have my meals brought by some sour-faced harridan.'

The phone was slammed down.

'Well,' said Ellie who had come close enough to hear both sides of the conversation. 'He didn't seem madly impressed. Strange. I should have thought the graduate wonder would always be miles ahead of the non-intellectual bluebottle.'

'He should have told me.'

'Poor sergeant,' laughed Ellie, much mollified by his discomfiture. 'Doesn't the nasty super tell you everything then?'

He grabbed her violently and kissed her till she gasped in pain.

'Let's go and start an orgy in the dunes,' she whispered.

'This will do me fine.'

He kissed her again. Outside a bell began to ring and there was a distant confusion of voices.

'What's that?' he asked lifting his head.

'It's the Union. There's a students' meeting tonight. They summon them like going to church.'

'Why? What's up?'

'Nothing. That's the trouble. They've been organizing protests and boycotts on a small scale all year, but the big issue was going to break loose if she wasn't reinstated. And all hell *was* breaking loose because Fallowfield refused to acknowledge the right of student governors to be present when he was giving evidence. But now Anita's dead, they've lost their cause. No doubt they'll find another.'

'If we don't hurry, I'll lose my cause,' said Pascoe.

'Softly, softly. There's a long night ahead,' said Ellie drawing his head down again.

The big black buttons, he was pleased to find, *were* functional as well as decorative.

* * *

191

'Order, order,' murmured Franny. 'Will the meeting come to order?'

He tapped his gavel gently twice on the table across which he surveyed the assembled members of his Union. There had been a good turn-out, considering the fact that this was a very warm Saturday evening in June, and it would not be necessary for Stuart to use any of the complicated manoeuvres he had devised for overcoming the lack of a quorum.

Cockshut was at present on his feet refusing to give way to a thin, spectacled, crew-cutted youth who was attempting to turn a point of information into a speech. The secretary stood impassive, calculating the feeling of the meeting and watching Franny carefully. He observed the chairman's enjoyment of the situation, his sense of self-parody as he requested order in a voice which even Stuart, who as secretary was positioned at one end of the official table, could hardly hear.

A clown, thought Stuart. A self-centred, amoral, socially non-productive clown. He had known him for three years now and was still unsure how seriously the man took his own claims. He himself had never concealed his own scepticism for all the mumbo-jumbo of seances and magic ritual which Franny delighted in. And his philosophy, if it merited so respectable a title, was a lot of meaningless, anti-social crap. But the man had something; power, charisma, call it what you will. Such men had to be used, though never trusted. It had been wiser to join him rather than oppose him, Stuart reassured himself; politically wiser he meant, of course, uneasily aware at the back of his mind of the whole range of sensual delights the union had procured for him. Nor, he had to admit, had the political education of the college proceeded at quite the speed he had hoped for. The place was still fragmented, divided.

He was in his final year now. There was a career in protest

these days for the dedicated true-believer, which was what he was. They thought highly of him at the International Action Group HQ. But despite all his efforts, little of note in the world of student politics had taken place here. Poor Anita had seemed the best bet, though it had been Franny who masterminded that. In fact in his more pessimistic moments, Stuart sometimes felt that his pretence of lieutenantship was becoming a little too real.

But tonight, if he moved with care, they might get some concerted action at last.

The interrupter sat down and Stuart resumed his speech.

'I think we have been patient long enough; there comes an end to patience. We have delayed action long enough; there comes a time for action. Anita Sewell's death was a terrible thing; but it should not be allowed to obscure the authoritarian, anachronistic and cavalier fashion in which she was treated before her death. And since her death, arising out of it in fact, we have had other instances of the relatively insignificant and subordinate role we are expected to play in this college. At the principal's request, the staff are kept fully informed of the developments of this unpleasant business. But what of us? It's one of *us* who is murdered, it is the rest of *us* who may still be in danger. What danger? you ask. How can I tell you when no one will tell us anything? No; the only approaches made to any of the student body by the police have been high-handed, arrogant, and worse still, they have often revealed a depth of background knowledge about individuals which can only have come from their getting access to so-called confidential files of a type we have been assured does not exist!'

There was very satisfying uproar at this point. Franny and Stuart permitted themselves a brief shared smile, and rumours of the noise were once again borne on the still air to Pascoe's room, but neither of the inmates was in the least disturbed.

Chapter 14

For the mind of man is far from the nature of a clear and equal glass, wherein the beams of things should reflect, according to their true incidence; nay, it is rather like an enchanted glass, full of superstition and imposture if it be not delivered and reduced.

SIR FRANCIS BACON
Op. Cit.

Dalziel was used to being dragged from the black depths of sleep by untimely summonses. But it didn't make him any sweeter when it happened.

Usually it was the telephone. This time it was a sharp double knock at his door. He glanced at his watch as he rolled out from under the solitary sheet that was all the warm night required. It was twelve thirty-five.

'Who's there?' he snarled as he began to pull his trousers over his muscular, tortuously-veined legs. He was expecting to have to go out. He had spent many years training his subordinates – and some superiors – in this if nothing else. Nobody ever woke him up on business not urgent enough to take him out.

'Simeon Landor. May I come in?'

Dalziel paused, surprised by the light, academically-diffident tones where he had expected the official brusqueness of Pascoe or one of the others.

'Wait,' he said, slipping his braces over his bare shoulders. It took him a couple of minutes to find the key which had fallen from beneath his pillow down the back of the bed. He had slept behind locked doors ever since his wife left him. Perhaps before. Perhaps that had been one of the reasons. He had managed to forget everything

194

except the pain and surprise. Nothing ever surprised him now without casting that shadow of pain, even when the surprise was pleasant.

'What's up?' he asked as he opened the door. He felt uneasy. Landor wouldn't come running himself unless it was urgent. On the other hand Landor had never undergone the Dalziel training course. Perhaps he could have stayed in bed.

Landor's first words confirmed his suspicions.

'Sorry to disturb you, Superintendent, but I thought you ought to know, there's a student demonstration going on.'

Dalziel groaned and started back towards the bed.

'You know the rules. I thought people in your position got special training courses for this kind of thing now? If they move off the college campus, or if there's danger to persons or property and you wish to make a complaint, then wake up my sergeant and he'll sort it out.'

He sat on the edge of his bed and began looking for his pipe. Landor took an uneasy step into the room.

'No, there is no damage. Not yet. But they've got into the administration block and are staging a sit-in.'

'Same applies. Watch 'em like hawks when they come out though. They usually steal anything loose, like type-writers, photo-copiers, that kind of thing. What are they after, anyway. Files?'

'I fear so,' said Landor. 'But what I felt you'd want to know is that they've got into the room you're using, my old study. I fear that they are under the misapprehension that I . . .'

But Dalziel heard no more. He was too busy buttoning up his trousers and shirt, pausing only to grab the phone and dial Pascoe's number.

A female voice answered after some delay.

'Dalziel!' bellowed the superintendent. 'Get Cassa-bloody-nova out of bed and down to my room, the old study I mean, right away!'

195

'I'm sure they don't realize,' Landor was still saying as he followed Dalziel's ponderous rush down the stairs and out of the building.

'They soon bloody will.'

There were lights on everywhere, though there was not much noise. At least, not until he entered the Old House.

From behind the large oak door to the study there was noise enough. Dalziel gently tried the handle. It was locked. He beckoned Pascoe who came in through the main door at that moment, still buttoning his shirt.

'I want half a dozen men here in ten minutes,' he said. 'Tell them to come quietly. No sirens, no lights flashing. But I want them quick. Use the pay-phone outside the dining-hall. I suppose they've got hold of the college switchboard?'

Landor nodded.

'Right. Now let's see what sweet reason can do.'

He rapped sharply on the door. Someone inside rapped back and there was a roar of laughter. Encouraged, the humorist cried, 'Come in!'

Dalziel stepped right up to the door and spoke loudly.

'This is the police.'

There was a confusion of noise within, some laughter, a hubbub of chatter, one or two instructions to go away and get sexually assaulted. A cry of outrage near Dalziel's right ear told him that Miss Disney had arrived. Even non-verbally, her tone was quite distinctive.

'This is the police,' he said again. The reaction was not quite so noisy and he repeated the words yet again.

Now there was comparative silence within except when a voice, clearly Franny Roote's, said conversationally, 'I think it might be the police.'

Dalziel spoke again, very slowly, articulating each word with great care.

'The room you are in is no longer part of the administration offices of this college. It is temporarily the police-headquarters of a murder investigation. Any papers, files

196

or other material in this room is not college property and interference with it will make you liable to very serious charges. This is a police matter, not a college matter. The college authorities will not be able to exercise discretion in the matter of prosecution. That will be up to me. And, by God, if there's any damage, I'll prosecute every last one of you!'

Only in the last sentence did his voice deviate from an impersonal official monotone. Pascoe had reappeared. With him was a constable in uniform whom Dalziel recognized as the local man.

'Someone telephoned him,' explained Pascoe. 'I met him on the drive. The others will be here shortly.'

'Telephoned?'

'A Miss Disney, sir,' said the constable.

'I thought our lives were in danger when the noise woke me up,' declared the lady, unrepentant before Landor's reproving glance.

'Fine,' said Dalziel giving unexpected support. 'It's Shattuck, isn't it? Get round into the garden, unobtrusively as you can. Watch the window of this room. Anyone tries to get out of it, grab 'em. Sergeant, wait outside for the others. Let me know when they arrive.'

'Superintendent, you will be careful?' It was Landor, worry deepening the lines of his finely drawn face. 'If they think I've brought a whole gang of police in – well, records of this kind of thing show that when the police have been involved, reactions can be very violent. Panic, anger – not your fault I know, but . . .'

'I'll be discreet as possible, and the main body of students is in the new admin. block, not here, I gather,' said Dalziel. 'But I won't let *any* consideration prevent me from dealing with this lot.'

He nodded fiercely towards the door which at that moment swung quietly open.

'Come in, Superintendent,' said Franny, standing courteously by the door like a butler.

Dalziel stepped forward, Landor and Disney hard on his heels, but the door was closed quietly but firmly in their faces and he found himself alone in the room with about two dozen students. Some he knew: Roote, Cockshut. Others were familiar though he had no names. Some few he had never seen before. The room itself was reasonably tidy. There was no sign of damage; the filing cabinet showed no evidence of any attempt to force it open. He walked over to it, stepping carefully across the bodies of some students – who lay sprawled on the floor and examined it without touching. The same with the desk, ignoring the couple who lay on it, fast in each other's arms, mouths pressed together as though in violent passion, but their eyes open, following his every move.

'Satisfied, fat man?' said Cockshut who was sitting arrogantly in his chair. He had the top of a Thermos flask in his hand; there was other evidence – packets of sandwiches, crisps, blanket-rolls – that they had come prepared for a lengthy stay. Dalziel locked eyes with Cockshut and leaned so close to him he could smell the whisky fumes rising from his plastic cup.

'I will be before I leave,' he said quietly.

'Ah, get stuffed!'

Roote coughed politely behind him.

'I'm sorry, Superintendent. We didn't realize that this was no longer the principal's study. If we had known that the police had taken over the room absolutely, of course we wouldn't have entered.'

Dalziel turned and saw for the first time the long wall facing the window. Across it someone had scribbled his name, misspelling it but managing the accompanying four letter word correctly.

'An odd thing to write if you thought you were occupying Dr Landor's room,' he said with a faint smile.

198

Franny returned the smile apologetically.

'It was done when you started shouting at the door. I'm sorry. I'll send someone in to wash it off.'

'I'd be obliged,' replied Dalziel.

'Fine,' said Franny. 'We'll leave quietly now and go and join the others in the new block. This is purely an internal dispute, of course. I'm extremely sorry you've been fetched from your bed. Right, everybody. Pack up! We're leaving.'

There was a general bustle round the room, everybody moving except Cockshut who sat glowering at the superintendent. Roote walked over to the door, unlocked it and opened it. Landor and Disney were still outside, joined by a group of other members of staff now. Ellie Soper was there, Marion Cargo and Miss Scotby. Also Pascoe who nodded at Dalziel, and received a slight jerk of the head in reply. He turned and went out of the main door.

'Good evening, Dr Landor,' said Franny. 'We're just leaving.'

A look of relief passed over the principal's face, but did not linger long.

'No,' said Dalziel.

Everyone stopped. Everyone looked at him.

'No one's leaving.'

For a second nobody moved, then there was a general surge towards the open door.

'Sergeant!'

Through the main entrance came Pascoe accompanied by half a dozen uniformed policemen. They filled the study doorway in a very solid fashion. There was only one of Constable Shattuck who came and stood outside the window, but seen through a glass darkly, he looked even more stern and unpassable than those within.

Dalziel spoke.

'I am holding everyone in this room on suspicion of illegal entry, of interfering or being accessories to

199

interfering with evidence and statements in an official investigation – '

'But we've touched nothing!' protested Franny.

'I really think,' began Landor nervously, but Dalziel ignored them both.

' – of causing damage to property by defacing a wall and – ' he sniffed the air ' – I think we might add illegal possession of the drug, cannabis. Sergeant. I want the names of everyone here, I want them cautioned individually, I want their statements and I want their fingerprints.'

'He can't do it,' said Cockshut, mockingly. 'The fat bastard's bluffing.'

He lifted the cup to his lips. Dalziel moved swiftly across and took it from his hand, careful not to spill the contents.

'I want this analyzed as well, Sergeant. If, as my sensitive nose tells me, it is Glen Grant that's being debased in this coffee, I think we'll add a charge of theft against Mr Cockshut. Right, now, who's got the keys?'

Again a stunned silence.

'Keys?' said someone tremulously.

'The set of duplicate, or master keys,' said Dalziel patiently. 'The ones you used to get into this room, to unlock my desk and my filing cabinet. Those keys. Oh come on, Mr Roote, you're an intelligent man, I hear. There'll be fingerprints over every bit of paper you touched in there. And over my whisky bottle too I've no doubt.'

'You're mistaken, I assure you,' said Franny, spreading out his hands before him, the picture of injured innocence. 'But I do think if you're going to make this absurd fuss, lovey, we ought to have some legal representation. We're entitled, aren't we?'

He picked up the telephone before anyone could stop him. Obviously someone was sitting at the ready at the other end of the line.

200

'Hello, love,' he said softly. 'Franny here. We're having a bit of trouble with the police down in Simeon's old study. Yes, the police. Just tell the others in case they're worried, there's a dear. And get Mr Pearl, the solicitor, on the line. Ask him to come over. Many thanks.'

He replaced the receiver. Dalziel had made no attempt to interrupt, but his face was hard.

'Dr Landor, these students' names please.'

Landor's face was a mask of misery as he hesitated whether to speak or not, but he was saved from the decision and its attendant obloquy by Miss Disney who pushed forward, majestic in her voluminous, quilted dressing-gown, and said, 'This is outrageous!'

For a second, Dalziel thought she was referring to him. But instantly she followed it up by beginning a recital of the names of those present. Pascoe busily made notes.

Dalziel knew he had to move quickly now. The last thing he wanted was for his investigations to be complicated by a full scale student-police confrontation. While it had seemed possible to isolate this small group, he had been happy to see they got what he firmly believed they deserved. But the moment Roote had been allowed to lift the telephone, he knew that it would require swift thinking to avoid either a retreat or a battle. Personally, he didn't give a damn how unpopular he was; in fact at times he gave the impression of revelling in it. But the job he was here to do was nothing to do with student politics and he had no desire to get involved at that particular moment.

Disney was coming to the end of her recital of names now, oblivious to the abuse which was being directed at her from one or two quarters. Privately, Dalziel appreciated the aptness of many of the epithets, but he was too busy talking to the uniformed men to pay full attention.

'Move away quietly. Wait outside the main gates for half an hour, but don't come back in unless you get a message direct from me. All right? And keep out of sight, eh?'

Roote watched them disappear with an amused smile on his face.

'Finished, Sergeant? Right, Mr Roote, if you and your friends will kindly leave, we'll sort out this matter in the morning.'

'You've changed your tune, blubber-gut,' jeered Cockshut.

'Yes, I have,' said Dalziel quietly. 'But I can start playing another, laddie, that'll make you dance if I have much more of your lip.'

Cockshut looked as if he was going to indulge in another outburst, but Roote silenced him by making for the door.

'Come along, my dears,' he said. 'Let's go and see the others.'

He too knew when to make a diplomatic withdrawal. Dalziel followed them out into the warm night and took a couple of deep breaths. They had been just in time. A large and noisy group of students, some hundred he reckoned, was making its way down the drive from the new admin. block. Franny and the others were greeted with rapturous cheers.

'Shall we get inside?' suggested Pascoe at his shoulder.

'No. There's just a lot of wind in that lot. Get back in. Here's my keys. Check there's nothing missing. I doubt if there will be, they're not quite daft. In fact Roote looked a sight too complacent. I doubt if we'll find a print. Not his anyway, but the others are probably less careful. And check my whisky, eh?'

'Why did they want to do it anyway?' asked Pascoe.

'That'll bear thinking about. Give me a ring if anything turns up. I'm off to my bed. You'd better make yourself a bed up in the study and spend the night there. I doubt if they'll be back, but you never know.'

'Right, sir,' said Pascoe, moving back into the building.

'And, Sergeant, by yourself, mind. You're on duty, and on duty you sleep by yourself.'

On or off duty *you* sleep by yourself, thought Pascoe viciously as he went through the door wondering how many of those in the hall had heard.

Dalziel chuckled to himself as he walked towards the block in which his room was situated. The students saw him and a cry of mockery and abuse went up.

'*Sieg Heil*!' shouted some wit. 'Fascist bastard!'

Roote detached himself from the crowd.

'Is there something else, Superintendent?'

'No, thank you, Mr Roote. I'm just away to my bed.'

'You're not so brave without your bully-boys, are you, Dalziel?' said Cockshut. 'Weren't there enough of them? Have they gone for help?'

'It's provocation that's what it is!' shrieked a hysterical little girl. 'Bloody deliberate provocation.'

She was an ugly little thing, hardly coming up to Dalziel's chest and he felt a pang of pity for her. This was obviously the most exciting experience she had ever had in her life.

'Provocation! Provocation!' Others took up the chant. It only lasted a minute, however, and as it died down Dalziel shouted, using all the projection power of his large lungs, 'Well, if I can provoke all you lot just by myself, I'd better become a pop-singer! Now I'm off to my bed. Good night!'

There was a ripple of laughter, then someone started singing, 'Good night, Dalziel, Good night, Dalziel. Good night, Dalziel, it's time to say goodbye.'

They all took it up and opened up an avenue through their midst.

Feeling relieved, though showing nothing on his face, he began to walk towards the now very attractive sanctuary of the entrance to his block. He had nearly reached it when another sound became audible above the singing, which died away as the students too became aware of it. Dalziel's first reaction was incredulity, followed immediately by anger.

It was the noise of a siren, swiftly approaching, and the glare of strong headlights was already visible at intervals along the main road which swung in a broad curve away to the west.

'The bastards are coming back,' said someone.

'You rotten lying pig.'

'Fat, stinking . . .'

'Liar! Shitting liar!'

'Bugger bugger bugger!'

It was the little ugly girl again. She began to rain futile blows on his chest with little fists clenched like pigs' trotters. The others began to press round and Dalziel felt himself being shoved and pulled with increasing violence. He did not retaliate, concentrated on keeping his balance, mentally promising to do a grievous injury to whoever had brought in this police car with all systems blaring. Disney again? Very probably. Stupid bitch. But at least the men waiting at the main gate would stop it.

But the noise got nearer and he realized it must be in the college grounds now. Fools! he groaned. 'Fools,' he shouted aloud. But someone else was shouting now, a girl's voice, a cry taken up by others.

'It's not the police! It's not the police!'

The headlights swept round the last bend in the long driveway which wound through the college precincts, lighting up the struggling mob of students and dazzling the eyes of those who stared into them. But the vehicle was close enough now to be identified.

It was an ambulance.

The students parted before it and it slowed down almost to a stop. A girl ran out and spoke to the driver. It was Sandra Firth and Dalziel realized it was her voice

204

he had heard before. The ambulance swung off the drive and ploughed across several yards of lawn towards one of the teaching blocks, with Sandra Firth running ahead, a strange unearthly figure in the luminance of the headlights. She disappeared inside, followed by the ambulance men. Dalziel began making his way after her, but his progress was impeded by the press of students, mostly completely oblivious of his presence now. By the time he forced his way to the front, the men were coming out again, carrying someone on a stretcher. The onlookers went quite silent except for an excited voice which said over and over again, 'Who is it? Who is it?'

The ambulance lights touched the face of the figure on the stretcher, but it was not just their brightness which made the skin seem unnaturally white and drawn. The face was like a rubber mask which had slipped awry and no longer clung to the outline of the bones below. But it was still recognizable.

It was Sam Fallowfield and as he was carried swiftly by, Dalziel found himself unable to say whether he was alive or dead.

Sandra Firth came out of the building after the stretcher and Dalziel seized her arm as she went by.

'Did you call the ambulance?' he demanded.

'Yes.'

'Why the hell didn't you tell me?'

'Could you bloody cure him?' she asked scornfully, pulling herself free.

'Where'd you find him? Show me,' he said. The girl hesitated, looking at the ambulance which was now ready to depart.

'You can do nothing there,' he said brutally. 'You can't work miracles either.'

The ambulance moved away, siren wailing once more.

'Now show me.'

Without a word she turned and went back into the

building. Dalziel paused only to speak to Roote who was standing looking after the disappearing vehicle with a concentration of thought so intense that Dalziel had to speak to him twice.

'Get these people out of here,' he said curtly. 'Get them out of the offices. Get them back to bed. There'll be plenty of opportunities for this foolishness. Now isn't the time.'

'Yes,' said Roote distantly. 'Yes. I will. I will.'

Dalziel looked at him doubtfully but now the youth seemed to wake up and before Dalziel had followed Sandra through the door he was already shepherding students towards the dormitory blocks.

Sandra had disappeared when he finally got into the building.

'Miss Firth! Sandra! Where are you?' he shouted up the stairs.

'Up here.'

Here was a small laboratory whose frosted glass door opened on to the long corridor which led away from the landing. An even smaller storeroom-cum-office opened off the laboratory itself and it was here that Sandra took him, pointing to the small desk shoved against the wall beneath the window and the institutional plastic and metal chair which stood beside it.

'He was sprawled over the desk,' the girl said. 'I thought he was asleep. I thought . . .'

For the first time, Dalziel looked closely at the girl and realized just how shocked she was.

'Sit down, for a minute, love,' he said in his best kindly voice, spoiling it a little by snapping, 'no, not there!' as the girl uneasily felt for the chair in the storeroom. He led her back into the lab where the best that could be managed was a rather tall stool. Taking a beaker off a shelf, he sniffed it, rinsed it thoroughly and filled it with water.

'Here, sip that.'

She took it gratefully.

'Now,' he said, 'what the hell were you doing up here anyway?'

She drank the water as though she had a heavy thirst and handed back the beaker.

'More?' he asked. She shook her head.

'I just got fed up,' she said suddenly. 'I was up in the general office. The place was packed, everyone being very jolly, and permissive and just a little bit hysterical. It was like those scenes you sometimes see on the old newsreels during the war – everybody in a shelter, all united and smiling through, you know what I mean. And then there were the organizing ones, hammering away at the typewriters, producing lists and schedules, like the revolution had come or something, instead of just a crummy little demo in a crummy place like this years after everyone else had had theirs. So I just helped myself to a bunch of keys and went for a walk.'

'I see. Why here?'

'Why not?'

'Well,' said Dalziel thoughtfully, 'it's not the first place you'd come to, or the most comfortable, or attractive, I shouldn't have thought.'

'Anyway, what's it matter? I came. It was eerie. I suppose I felt brave, being here all by myself. I came up the stairs in the dark – '

'Was the lab door locked?'

'Yes. But I had a master key for all the rooms in this block. So in I went, this other door was a bit ajar, I peered in. I'd got my night eyes by then and I could see quite clearly. I just took one look and ran outside. There's a phone in the corridor. I knew the girl on the switchboard, so she gave me a line though she wasn't supposed to, not according to the planners. And I asked for an ambulance.'

Dalziel digested the information for a while.

'Was he dead?' he asked finally.

'I don't know. He was very still. And when I touched his hand he felt – funny.'

'You didn't say you touched him.'

'No, that was when I went back in, to see if there was anything I could do. But I couldn't think of anything, and I was scared, so I went and stood in the corridor till I heard the ambulance coming.'

'You've been very brave indeed,' said Dalziel sincerely. 'Would you mind having another look inside?'

'No. Of course not.'

She slid off the stool and followed him back into the room.

'Now you say he was sprawled out over the desk? Good, good,' he said. 'Now, did you touch anything in here?'

'Well, yes. I mean I had to. I touched him, Mr Fallowfield, just once. And I moved the chair back when the ambulance men came. And I touched the light switch.'

'But you didn't remove anything? A piece of paper or anything at all?'

'No!' she said with some indignation.

'I have to ask,' he said. 'If for instance he had tried to kill himself, and left a note it would be wrong of anyone to remove it, even if it was addressed to some specific person. You follow me?'

'I've overtaken you,' she said, recovering her spirits now. 'And I haven't taken anything.'

'Good-oh,' said Dalziel making a minute examination of the room but touching as little as possible. He ended up on his hands and knees peering under and around the desk.

There was a clatter of feet on the stairs and Pascoe came into the laboratory, halting outside the storeroom and looking down at his superior's proffered backside with an impassive face.

Dalziel stood up, dusting his elbows and knees. In his hand he held a broken hypodermic syringe which he wrapped carefully in his handkerchief, ignoring Sandra's questioning gaze.

'What's going on outside?'

'There's still a lot of people standing around, chatting, but the revolutionary spirit seems to have evaporated for the time being.'

He caught Sandra's eye and grinned sympathetically. She looked away.

'Is this where he . . . ?'

'Whatever happened to Mr Fallowfield probably happened here,' said Dalziel carefully. 'I'll want this room sealed off until the lab boys can have a look at it. I'd better have your keys I think, Miss Firth.'

She passed them over without demur and he locked both the storeroom door and the laboratory door behind them. On the stairs they met one of the uniformed men from the car. He looked apologetic.

'I know you said wait, sir, but after the ambulance . . . well, we thought one of us should take a walk down. It might have been for you.'

'Sorry to disappoint you, lad. As you're so keen, you can bloody well stay here. No one gets into this block without my say-so. Right?'

They made their way back towards the old house, ignoring the groups of students and of staff with fine impartiality. Once back in the study, Dalziel gestured towards the phone.

'Is that thing OK?'

Pascoe lifted the receiver and listened.

'Yes. There's an outside line.'

'Get the hospital. Find out what's what.'

Outside the door they heard voices raised in heated

discussion. The door was suddenly opened and a little, balding man strutted in, pushing past Landor.

'Superintendent Dalziel? We met briefly the other day, you'll recall. I'm Douglas Pearl and I'm here to represent . . .'

'Pearl?' bellowed Dalziel, successfully bringing the little man to order; then more quietly, 'Pearl. Well, Mr Pearl, the swine you wish to cast yourself before have rushed off elsewhere.'

'Mr Dalziel! I must protest . . .'

'So must I. You weren't asked in here. Well, what is it, Pascoe? Spit it out, man.'

'He's dead,' said Pascoe slowly, replacing the receiver. 'Fallowfield's dead. On arrival.'

The words engendered a silence which spread through the room and out into the hallway beyond.

'How?' asked Dalziel, no respecter of respect.

'It's early to say with certainty,' replied Pascoe. 'But they're pretty sure it's a massive overdose of heroin.'

Chapter 15

There is no greater impediment of action than an over-curious observance of decency.

SIR FRANCIS BACON
Op. Cit.

Sunday morning dawned fine; had been dawning fine before most people in the college got to bed. The scent of the sea was in the air, evocative, invigorating; but it was obviously going to become over-warm later.

Pascoe thought he was probably the first person out of bed, but he gave all the credit for this to the makeshift arrangement of blankets and narrow mattress on which he had finally slept in the study. It was an unnecessary precaution, he was sure, but Dalziel had been adamant. Sheer jealousy, thought Pascoe gloomily.

He decided no harm could be done by having a quick shower and shave. He felt disagreeably grubby and dull-witted.

When he returned, he saw that he was no longer alone in the world. Ellie was standing outside the main door of the old house and he felt a gush of pleasure that she had come so early to see him. Then he saw that she was pinning something to the door. A notice. He came up behind her without being observed and coughed gently. She jumped very satisfactorily.

'Oh,' she said. 'It's you.'

'Good morning,' he said reading the notice. It was typewritten and had obviously been run off from a stencil on a duplicating machine.

> We the undersigned members of staff
> dissociate ourselves completely

from the high-handed and provocative
actions of the police force last night

It was dated and signed by about ten people. Some of them were only names to Pascoe, but others he recognized. Halfdane; Marion Cargo; and Ellie herself.

'That's a bit unnecessary, isn't it?' he said.

Ellie shrugged.

'Halfdane's idea, I've no doubt. You must have got even less sleep than I did.'

'It had to be done quickly. We thought if the notices were there for the students to see first thing this morning, it might help to cool things down.'

Pascoe laughed without humour.

'Cool things down! You've got to be joking! People like Cockshut will be delighted when they see this. It's *carte blanche* for anarchy.'

'Piddle diddle,' said Ellie lightly. 'You are an old reactionary now, aren't you? You've forgotten what it's like to be young.'

He looked at her coldly.

'Don't try to kid me, Ellie,' he said. 'You're no political animal. You'd better watch yourself. It's very easy for single women in places like this to mistake sentimental maternalism for radical idealism. But I don't think you're as far gone as that, though there's always the danger. Then what is it you're after? Pretty boy Halfdane's approval?'

She slapped his face, almost dispassionately.

'You can go to jail for that,' said Dalziel's voice behind them. The fat man shouldered his way between them and read the notice.

'Bloody cloud-cuckoo-land,' he said. 'You all live in bloody cloud-cuckoo-land. Come on in, Sergeant. We've got a *real* job to do.'

Jesus wept! thought Pascoe as he went inside, not

212

looking back at Ellie, what strange allies we find ourselves lined up with! Dalziel, Disney, Dunbar, Scotby, all the oldies, all the wrong reasons, but facing in the same direction.

'Bloody students,' groaned Dalziel, once they got inside. 'All social reform and young idealism on the surface, but give 'em half a chance and they're just young criminals.'

'Protest is hardly criminal,' said Pascoe mildly.

'Not protest, no. But I've just been talking to Landor. The stuff that's missing from the admin. block! I warned 'em. Mostly small stuff, but a typewriter's gone. And some bright spark broke open all three college posting boxes last night and tore up half the mail. Isn't that criminal? And the kind of thing they've scribbled around the place and left in typewriters for sixteen-year-old typists to find doesn't bear repeating.'

He shook his head in what seemed like genuine bewilderment. Pascoe felt an impulse to cluck sympathetically but checked it. Dalziel's gloom changed into a huge yawn.

'To hell with 'em,' he yawned. 'Landor doesn't want us officially, so we'll just stick to our brief. Now, the question is, do we still have a case to investigate or don't we?'

'Pardon?'

'A good suspect for one, possibly two murders goes and gets himself killed. Very convenient, saves the state a lot of money, us a lot of bother. I want to be convinced he did at least one of 'em, preferably both. So convince me, Sergeant.'

He settled himself comfortably in his chair, picked up the phone, dialled, and said, 'Superintendent Dalziel, love. Breakfast for two in the old study. Kippers are fine. 'Bye.'

'The only thing we've got that connects Fallowfield with Miss Girling,' said Pascoe, 'is the coincidence that

213

he was interviewed on the nineteenth of December. Presumably he was offered the job on the spot, accepted, shook hands all round, collected his gear and headed for the station.'

'Or he might have had a car?'

'That makes it worse. If he did knock old Girling on the head while he was here, presumably he drove her car a hundred miles to the airport leaving his own here. How did he pick it up without being noticed?'

'Good point. Check with whoever keeps details of expenses paid. They might still have a record of whether he got his train fare or a car allowance.'

'In any case, why? As far as we know, he had no previous acquaintance with the woman. How do you work up a motive in a few hours, especially to kill a woman who's just offered you a job? No, I think he's a non-starter there, sir. It's the mouldy-oldies who were here at the time who are our best bet.'

'You're not helping much, lad,' said Dalziel sadly. 'We'll have to stick with it. The other one looks better though.'

'Yes, sir. But it still puzzles me why he would publicly accept her allegations that he had seduced her when he patently hadn't.'

'But he obviously wasn't going to agree he had fiddled her marks to get her out of the place.'

'No,' said Pascoe thoughtfully. 'There might be a motive there. He didn't give a damn about his reputation, but he wasn't going to lose his career so easily.'

'Still, why did she send him that note? And why above all did he never deny they had been lovers?'

'And who wrecked his flat? And why?'

They were silent for a moment.

'That's the trouble with you bloody intellectuals,' said Dalziel finally. 'I want answers, and all you give is a lot of bloody questions.'

'Henry Saltecombe took Anita's note to Fallowfield,' said Pascoe inconsequentially. 'And he's got a pork-pie hat.'

'That'll really make them sit up in court,' said Dalziel. 'Come in!'

It was breakfast, brought, to Pascoe's surprise, by Elizabeth Andrews.

'Hello, love,' said Dalziel. 'Kippers, eh? The fairest fruit of the sea.'

Obviously encouraged by his tone and studiously avoiding Pascoe's eyes, the girl planted the tray on the desk and said in a low voice, 'Please, what happened the other night, the dancing I mean, will anyone have to know about it? Like the bursar – or my parents. I wouldn't like . . .'

'I don't see why, love,' said Dalziel, slitting open a kipper. 'Not as long as you keep on bringing me food like this. What made you decide to be a witch, love?'

The girl's hand went to her mouth, a completely natural example of a classic gesture.

'Oh, I didn't want . . . I'm not a witch . . . not really, I don't believe . . .'

'It was just exciting, was it? And of course, Mr Roote's very nice, isn't he?'

She blushed deeply.

'Yes, yes. I think so. I just went because of him. I'd only been once before and then he . . . went with me. And I thought it'd be the same. I'd rather there'd been just the two of us. But it was dark, and it didn't seem to matter. But this time, last Thursday, it wasn't me. He explained. It was a special one, midsummer or something . . .'

Pascoe and Dalziel exchanged glances and Pascoe began consulting his pocket diary.

'. . . and he had to have someone who . . . *hadn't*

before. You see. It was the ceremony, that was all, he'd rather have been with me.'

'My God!' said Pascoe.

'So it was Anita, instead,' said Dalziel quietly.

'Yes. It should have been. I didn't want to stay, but I thought if I went . . . anyway, I was glad when someone came, before . . . anything really happened.'

'You all ran?'

'Oh yes. I grabbed my clothes and ran as fast as I could. It wasn't until later I found I'd left my bra and I wasn't going back for it then.'

She managed a bit of a smile which Dalziel returned.

'I don't blame you. We'll let you have it back. You didn't happen to see who it was who disturbed you all?'

'No. I'm sorry. She was too far, just a shape – '

'*She?*'

'Oh yes. I could tell it was a woman, from the outline of the skirts, I mean. But I didn't wait to look closer.'

'Well, thank you very much, my dear. If there's anything else you remember, just have a chat with me, eh? And remember, mum's the word.'

He placed a stumpy finger across his lips and winked ludicrously. With a look of great relief on her face the girl left the room, still ignoring Pascoe.

'So much for Henry,' said Dalziel through a mouthful of kipper. 'Unless he was wearing a kilt. Your breakfast's getting cold.'

'I'll just have coffee and a bit of toast.'

'Please yourself. In that case – ' Dalziel transferred Pascoe's kippers to his own plate.

'Midsummer's eve,' said Pascoe.

'Is that special?' asked Dalziel.

'Yes, in a way,' said Pascoe slowly. 'It's not one of the great witches' nights like *Walpurgisnacht*, April the thirtieth, or Hallowe'en. But it's pretty important. The eve of St John the Baptist as well.'

'Dancing girls and heads on platters,' offered Dalziel starting on his third kipper. 'Look, Sergeant, you're not really taking this witchcraft bit seriously? It's just an ingenious method of getting lots of gravy! Adds a bit of spice too. Like playing sardines at a party. No one says, let's all lie on the floor together and grope each other. No, you have an acceptable structure, a game. And you all end up lying on the floor groping each other. Remember? This boy Roote's just a bit more ingenious.'

'Yes. Isn't he? And the virgin?'

'Variety is the spice. Imagine him telling that nice kid from the kitchen that he'd prefer her but the ceremony required he got stuck into someone else! What a nerve!'

'But she was a virgin.'

Dalziel pushed his plate away and burped.

'So were they all. Once. It's not an uncommon state even in this bloody randy age.'

'Yes, but still . . .'

'Drink your coffee, lad.'

Pascoe supped the lukewarm liquid thoughtfully.

'How about this,' he said. 'Roote gets back from the dunes with the others, who were they? Oh yes, Cockshut and the girl Firth. Then he gets to thinking about what he's missed that night, to wit, Anita. He broods on it a while, and finally sets out to get what he considers his due, ceremony or none.'

'A year's a long time to wait,' agreed Dalziel.

'But she's not there. Perhaps he sees her making off. He follows her to Fallowfield's cottage. Waits till she comes out and is making her way back – '

' – then jumps on her and kills her. Why?'

'If I knew that we'd have him in here with us,' said Pascoe.

'All right. Talk's over,' said Dalziel leaping up energetically. 'They're not going to let us stay here for ever, you know. Let's do some work.'

The morning went by quickly. Checks on the files and papers locked up in the study revealed no signs of interference. (Why should they be interested in interfering anyway? Pascoe asked himself. Unless –) But the bottle of Glen Grant in the filing cabinet had a couple of prints which matched those on the plastic cup Dalziel had taken from Cockshut. The superintendent seemed uninterested now. 'Who wants Cockshut?' he asked. 'It would just make him feel important.' An examination of the room in which Fallowfield had been found was even less productive. The key to the locked lab door was found in his pocket. The heroin had almost certainly been self-administered. Only the absence of a note bothered Dalziel.

'I've a feeling he was the kind of man who would like to have explained himself in the end,' he said.

One of the college gardeners dimly recollected having seen Fallowfield enter the science block about lunch time. This fitted in quite well with the medical report. While the two policemen had been so eagerly enquiring after him, he had been sitting alone in a dingy little storeroom, dying. It was illogical, but somehow the thought made Pascoe feel guilty.

'Perhaps he did do the damage in his cottage himself,' he suggested again. 'Like Prospero, burning his books.'

'What did we do him for?' asked Dalziel, interested.

The memory of those books, recalled another chain of thought which his mind had set aside, incomplete, till they could get hold of Fallowfield. Now Fallowfield was beyond any contact the police could hope for, whatever he himself may have believed. But the links of information might still be obtained elsewhere. He thought a while, then went in search of Sandra Firth.

She was not in her room. As it was shortly after twelve, he started to make his way towards the bar where it seemed likely she might be found. But as he came out into the bright and by now very hot sunlight he saw her standing beneath the beech trees which grew in the patch of ground which lay within the broad sweeping U-bend of the drive. She was talking with considerable animation to someone – in fact, they both seemed to be talking at the same time – and Pascoe felt a tremor of excitement as he looked at the other person. It was Miss Disney, obviously returning from morning service. A prayer-book (he guessed) was clutched in one black-gloved hand while the other held a large crocodile-skin handbag. But the article of attire which had caught Pascoe's eye was her hat. It was absurd. On another woman it might have been forgiven as frivolous. But on Disney – ! It was light blue and dark orange with an artificial red geranium pinned rakishly on one side. And in outline it had the shape of a man's pork-pie.

Pascoe approached.

'Now that evil man is gone,' Disney was saying, 'I had hoped that some of you, that you above all, Sandra, might have been at the service this morning. The vicar cannot understand; it's not my fault I have told him; nonetheless in a small village, such things are noticed.

'*Please*, Miss Disney,' said Sandra desperately. 'I just don't want to talk about it. Not *now*.'

She turned away, but Miss Disney grabbed her arm at the expense of her handbag.

'For your own *good*, Sandra . . .'

'Oh, for God's sake!'

'You've dropped your handbag, Miss Disney,' said Pascoe, picking it up. He flicked the catch with his thumb as he did so and the bag fell open revealing a surprisingly feminine complexity of articles. But one was less common there than the rest. A thick stick of yellow chalk.

'The good teacher is never without,' said Pascoe, removing it.

'How dare you!' said Disney, beginning to swell. She

looked tremendously fearsome, but taking his courage in both hands Pascoe leaned close to her and gently said three words. Her face froze, like a hen with the gapes. Sandra gasped in amazement at hearing such words uttered in such company.

But Disney had said nothing; there was no outburst, no protest, and Pascoe, much relieved, knew he had been right.

'On Mr Fallowfield's wall,' he said. 'That's what you wrote, wasn't it? After you tore up the books.'

She took a deep breath and steadied herself.

'Not in front of the child,' she said. 'She wouldn't understand.'

'Wait,' said Pascoe to 'the child' who while she may not have understood was obviously agog for instruction.

He led Disney gently some yards away.

'Now,' he said. 'The truth.'

'I am not in the habit of lying,' she said scornfully. 'What I tell you may not redound to my credit, not all of it; but it shall be the truth, be certain of that.'

He almost admired her then.

Almost.

There was a ramshackle seat round the bole of one of the trees and they seated themselves, not without some trepidation on Pascoe's part.

'It does not become a woman of my beliefs to hate a fellow being,' she began, 'but we are exhorted in the Bible to hate evil and the man Fallowfield was evil.'

She nodded emphatically as though defying contradiction.

'How was he evil, Miss Disney?'

'In the worst possible way. He corrupted the young. Since he came here, I have noticed a steady decline of interest in the Christian societies I run, a growing scepticism and cynicism in seminar discussions I have with students.'

'But surely that's symptomatic of the age?' said Pascoe.

'If it is, it is people like Fallowfield who are responsible for it. Girls who would have looked to me as a friend and counsellor have turned away; even among the staff, among my own colleagues, he has mocked me unre-proved. And when he debauched that poor girl, Anita Sewell, and finally brought about her death . . .'

'We have positive evidence that he never debauched her,' said Pascoe mildly, 'and there's no evidence that he had anything to do with her death. Is there?'

'She was there! She was there that night! I saw them! That was his doing. Isn't *that* evidence?'

'You mean last Wednesday night out in the dunes? You saw them dancing without their clothes?'

Disney covered up her eyes and groaned. Pascoe was not in the least tempted to admire her now and pressed on relentlessly.

'What did you do when you saw them, Miss Disney? Did you shout, cry out? Or did you just stand and watch till you were seen?'

'I feel faint,' she said suddenly. 'I want to go to my room.'

'Soon. Tell me what happened.'

'They all ran away. At least I did that. I stopped it before . . . I couldn't sleep that night. I couldn't get the sight out of my mind.'

'You went there deliberately? You knew what was going on?'

'Yes. I suspected. I had overheard some young men talking.'

'And yesterday, did you go to Mr Fallowfield's cottage deliberately?'

'Yes. It had all been too much. Miss Girling, Anita, the dancing. All that man's fault, all . . . so I went to confront him, to challenge him. He wasn't there, but the door opened when I pushed it. I went in. The place was

221

in a mess, things all over the floor. At first I went next door to call for help, but there was no one in. Everybody was on the beach. I went back inside and started gathering things up. Then I saw what kind of books he had. Evil ideas. *Evil ideas*. Worse than the flesh. I began to tear them. I tore and tore and tore. And then I wrote on the walls, just what was up there already. The words, the drawings, applied to him, didn't seem wrong, you understand? It was as if some force had come out of me already and begun the damage. Just like when I heard he was dead last night, I knew that I had helped somehow. And I am glad. It is a good thing, a good thing. There may be some hope for all our salvations now.'

Pascoe did not speak but instinctively stood up, disliking their proximity. She looked up at him coldly.

'I fear you too are one of the new generation, young man. If you wish me to make a written statement, I shall be in my room. I have done nothing I am not proud of.'

She strode energetically away between the trees, across the grass.

'What was all that about?' asked Sandra, fully recovered from her emotional scene, and very interested.

'Mainly about Mr Fallowfield. Look, Sandra, he's dead now. He can't be harmed, except by people like Miss Disney who'll be sniping at his memory for ever. What do you know about him? She, Disney, says he was an evil influence. Was he? Or any kind of influence?'

She shook her head thoughtfully.

'I don't know much. This is just my first year, you see. When I first came, I was all dewy-eyed, innocent. A habitual church-goer, you know, the social thing. That's how I got in good with Disney to start with. Then I started getting involved a bit with Franny and his lot.'

She glanced at Pascoe under lowered eyelids.

'This is confidential, is it? I wouldn't like . . .'

222

'Absolutely,' said Pascoe. A policeman's fingers are always crossed, he thought.

'Well, they were – are – fun. Sometimes a bit weird. And sometimes . . . well, we did the usual thing, you know. Drank a bit, smoked a bit of pot; there was one night when we got hold of some acid. It seemed fantastic to me. And I had this thing about Franny. Still have, I suppose.'

She spoke so lowly, Pascoe had to strain to hear her. But he did not interrupt.

'You asked about Mr Fallowfield. Well, I got the impression that he had once been pretty close to the group in some way, I don't know. A kind of socratic figure, I suppose, showing the light. But he wasn't any longer. And all this business about him and Anita was somehow mixed up with this, I don't know how. That was one of the sacred mysteries of the group, reserved for members of the inner sanctum only.'

She laughed as she said this, but with a slight trace of bitterness.

'You never made the inner sanctum?'

'Me? No. Newly-come, that was me. Good for the preliminary lay, but not yet ready for the full initiation. And Franny'll be gone next year . . . hell, this place will be dead without him!'

She looked around desperately. What's the man's secret? asked Pascoe enviously. Disney should think herself lucky he didn't fancy *her*!

He began sorting out some words of kind reassurance to offer Sandra, but she prevented them by glancing at her watch.

'Hell. Nearly lunch time. They're dead traditional here. Roast and two veg. whatever the weather. Phew!'

She wiped her brow with the back of her hand.

'Remember. Confidential, eh? See you.'

'See you,' said Pascoe. That's how I lose all my witnesses, he thought. I start being kind and they just bugger off.

After a working lunch with Dalziel (Sandra had been right – roast beef, carrots and peas) during which he gave the superintendent an account of his talks with Disney and the girl, Pascoe finally managed to track down the senior administrative officer, a long, lugubrious individual called Spinx, whose office contained all the expense records for the college. Grumbling constantly about the interruption to his day of rest and assuring Pascoe that there wasn't a hope of such a record being kept for such a time, he unlocked a large store cupboard and began to dig around among a mound of dusty files and folders. Pascoe left him to it.

Fifteen minutes later there was a knock at the study door and Spinx, now very dusty, stood there looking very disappointed.

'Sorry,' he said.

'That's all right,' began Pascoe.

'I was wrong. Here you are. Is that what you wanted?'

'Yes. Why yes,' said Pascoe taking the dog-eared, stained sheet of paper from his hand and looking at it. 'Thank you very much.'

'Pleasure. That all? Right.'

Pascoe was reading the sheet before the man had closed the door behind him.

A car allowance had been paid based on the mileage between the college and Chester. He glanced at the copy of Fallowfield's *curriculum vitae* which along with those of the rest of the staff he had obtained a couple of days before. Fallowfield had been the senior biology master at Coltsfoot College near Chester which Pascoe knew as one of the modern, reputedly progressive, public schools. The route to Chester would pass, or could be made to pass, conveniently close to south Manchester, to the airport. Somehow Alison Girling's car had got there, had left the college that foggy night in December and made its way slowly, crawlingly, across the Pennines, while Miss Girling herself almost certainly lay in a thin cocoon of earth in the hole in the college garden.

But if Fallowfield were at the wheel, then how did he get his own car to Chester? He couldn't just have left it parked at the college. Even in the holidays there would be a sufficient number of staff, academic, administrative and maintenance, on the premises to notice it. Perhaps someone had. He hadn't asked. But no; it would have been too wild a risk to take anyway.

And above all, why should Fallowfield have wanted to kill this woman he had just met for the first time? As far as they knew.

It's all wrong, thought Pascoe gloomily, I'm like Dalziel. It would be pleasant for once to find everything nice and neat. Two murders, one killer, who commits suicide. Bingo! then we could get back to reality and start catching some thieves.

He took the expense sheet out to show Dalziel who had abandoned the shade of the study and taken a couple of chairs and a small folding table out on to the lawn where he sat with deliberate irony about four feet from the hole, now boarded over, in which Miss Girling had been found.

'Let the buggers see we're still here,' he had said. 'I reckon there's some here as are dying to see the back of us.'

Now he looked at the expense sheet, shading his eyes from the sun.

'That doesn't help,' he said as if it was Pascoe's own personal fault.

'No, sir.'

'He stopped three nights?'

225

'I noticed that.'

'And he should only have stopped one.'

Whoever it was who had checked the expense sheet had with exquisite parsimony deducted fifteen shillings from the total payable. This was itemized at two nights' stay in the college, at seven and six per night, which were not chargeable to expenses.

'Cheap,' said Pascoe. 'Is that what we pay?'

Dalziel ignored him.

'It means he came, unnecessarily in the eyes of the office staff, on the Friday. I wonder why?'

'Is it important, without a motive?'

'You've changed your tune, lad.'

Pascoe shrugged.

'I've given him up for Girling. But I think he's a strong runner for Anita.'

'And no connection between the two?'

'No, sir. Coincidence. Or perhaps the connection is merely that the discovery of the body under the statue put the idea of murder before everybody. You could get away with it well, nearly. The body had lain there all those years and might have lain there for ever if it hadn't been for a turn of fate.'

Dalziel yawned mightily, sunlight glistening off his fillings.

'You're probably right,' he said. 'You know, I'm sick of this place and most of the people in it. I don't understand it, that's my trouble. My generation, most of 'em, worked bloody hard, and accepted deprivation, and fought a bloody war, and put our trust in politicians, so our kids could have the right to come to places like this. And after a few days here, I wonder if it was bloody well worth it.'

He was silent. Pascoe felt obliged to say something.

'These places don't just *train* people, you know. They

help them to grow up in the right kind of mental environment.'

Dalziel looked at him more coldly than ever before.

'I bet you grew up more in your first six months with the force than in the twenty years before.'

Pascoe shrugged again. There were arguments, he knew; but he couldn't be bothered, didn't have the energy or inclination, to use them now.

'To get back to the case,' he said, 'what now?'

'Me,' said Dalziel, 'I'm going to sit here, and see who comes to talk to me. Then I'm going to drive into Headquarters just to liven things up there. As for you, well, there're just two or three things that bother me still about Fallowfield. Why no note? Who had a go at his cottage before Disney? And why did he come all the way to college before killing himself? Let me know the answers before supper. And then I'll tell you who killed everybody.'

He closed his eyes and began snoring so realistically that it was hard to tell whether he was really asleep or not.

Some hope, thought Pascoe. This is one that won't be solved before Christmas. Girling's perhaps never.

One of Dalziel's questions kept running through his head. Why did Fallowfield come all the way to college to kill himself? I know the answer to that, he thought. But if he did, he wasn't telling himself.

Stuff it, he thought and snatched half an hour to read the Sunday papers. There was nothing about the previous night's events. Too late perhaps. The murders themselves got a bit of space though the dailies had picked most of the meat from the bones. Dalziel was mentioned. They made him sound quite good. I suppose he is quite good, thought Pascoe reluctantly.

Out of the window he saw the fat man stir and stretch

himself. It was time, he decided, that he should do the same.

The rest of the afternoon he wasted, talking first to Disney, then to Sandra. Both denied absolutely removing any suicide note. Disney was back in her old form. A couple of hours' meditation had rinsed any vistigial traces of guilt from her lily-white soul. Pascoe could have gladly pushed her teeth down her throat, but he had to admit he was convinced by the time he left her. An after-effect of the Disney treatment was that he was twice as rough with Sandra as he might else have been, bringing her close to tears, but again coming away convinced she had been telling the truth.

He then spent more than an hour searching and researching the cottage and, after that, the laboratory. Both searches were doomed to failure, he knew before he started. But something in himself demanded that they should be done again.

When he returned to the study, it was fast approaching dinner time and Dalziel, red as a Victoria plum, had just come back from town. He noted Pascoe's frame of mind and for once exercised some tact. From somewhere he had obtained a jugful of ice-cubes and a soda syphon. He splashed an ounce of Glen Grant into a glass, followed it with a handful of ice and a jet of soda, and handed it silently to his sergeant.

'No luck?' he said.

'No.'

'Me neither. You'd think I had the plague. Every bugger at HQ thinks I'm having the time of my life.'

He emptied his glass and said diffidently, 'They'll have looked in his clothes, of course.'

'I should think so.'

Pascoe too finished his drink, taking an ice-cube into his mouth and crushing it between his teeth.

'But I'll go and see.'

228

'As you will. You could phone.'

'No. I'll look for myself. It's absurd. There's something, I'll swear. Perhaps when I've cleared away all these impossible possibilities . . . And I'll check with the ambulance men just in case.'

'You think this note's important.'

Pascoe stared at his superior.

'You said he seemed the kind of man who would want to explain himself.'

'Did I? Then it must be true.'

After Pascoe had left, the fat man hefted thoughtfully in his hand the set of master keys he had taken from Sandra Firth.

'Me,' he murmured to himself, 'I'll just have my dinner and do a bit of pedigree checking.'

Dinner was particularly good and he washed it down with the rest of his Glen Grant, which in its turn brought on the need to rest. It was almost nine o'clock when he finally let himself stealthily into the admin. block.

After all, he told himself, as he gently eased open a filing cabinet drawer in the registrar's office, half the bloody students in the place have seen them, so why not me?

Them were the staffs' confidential files. He skipped lightly through them, pausing here and there, till he came to Fallowfield's. Now he lit a cigarette, sat back at his ease and began to read slowly and thoroughly.

His academic qualifications he had already seen on the *curriculum vitae*. They were excellent, a very good first degree and a couple of high post-graduate qualifications. But it was in the comments made by those who taught and employed him that Dalziel was most interested. He read the letter from the headmaster of Coltsfoot College twice. It was couched in terms of high praise. Great stress was laid on Fallowfield's ability to influence thought, his progressive thinking and his pre-eminent suitability to

229

work with older students. Almost too much stress, thought Dalziel. He had many years' experience of reading and hearing between the lines.

On an impulse he picked up the phone and when he got the operator, gave her the number of Coltsfoot College. You never knew your luck.

While she was trying to establish a connection, he helped himself to a few select student files and began to read them. He didn't know his luck.

Pascoe knew his luck. It was rotten. The clothes had contained nothing helpful, the doctor who had examined Fallowfield could offer no useful contribution other than reiterating the cause and probable time of death; and the ambulance men, who were off-duty and had to be tracked to their homes, were no help either and in fact took umbrage at the suggestion that something other than the body might have been removed from the lab.

Pascoe realized he had not been as diplomatic as was his wont and after looking in at Headquarters where the heavy ironies of his mock-envious colleagues did not help, he went round to his flat for a change of clothing and a bite to eat. There was a stack of mail, mostly circulars, and he tossed them on the table beside the telephone. He made himself a cup of tea and a cheese sandwich and sat down in the ancient but extremely comfortable armchair which stood beneath the open window.

An hour later he woke with the cup of cold tea miraculously unspilt on the arm of the chair and the sandwich, one bite missing, still clutched in his right hand. He saw the time, groaned and pushed himself unsteadily out of the chair, knocking the teacup on to the floor. Cursing now he mopped up the mess with an antimacassar and pulled the phone towards him. This time it was his mail which fell to the carpet.

He swore again, looking down at the colourful display.

Threepence off this; half-price subscription to that; win half a million for a farthing. (*Could* you legally wager a non-legal coin?) It wouldn't be so bad if he ever got any of the sexy stuff people were always complaining about. Still, he supposed it all brought revenue to the Post Office.

It was time he reported in. Not that he had anything to report. He might as well send a letter.

It came to him as he lifted the phone. He *had* known the answer all along. The mail! Fallowfield had gone to the college to post his note. Not for him the last letter confiscated by the police and read by the coroner. No, this was one note which was going to reach the addressee.

And with the thought came another, almost instantaneously. Someone else had been a lot cleverer than he was. A lot cleverer and a lot quicker. Someone had broken into the college posting boxes last night. But whoever it was wasn't just quick. Breaking into the boxes, looking for a letter in Fallowfield's hand (he'd bet that all the letters opened had typed envelopes), this meant, could mean, probably meant, he knew that there was no letter in the cottage and no letter in the lab. How? The first was easy; the person who wrecked the house before Disney would have known, been fairly sure. But the lab? Sandra – it had to be Sandra. She must have gone through the sequence of events with any number of people, students and staff, before going to bed. Damn!

So much for the letter then. If it had been in one of the boxes, then it was gone for ever. Anyone who was so keen to get it would surely have destroyed it instantly.

'But was it in one of the boxes?' asked Pascoe aloud. Three had been opened. Fallowfield would certainly have used the one nearest the lab block which was the one outside the bar. Or if not wishing to be seen, and it must have been after opening hours when he arrived at college, he would use the one by the side of the Old House. But he would never have bothered to walk over to the Students' Union. So why all three? A blind perhaps. Or perhaps desperation; it wasn't in the first, or the second; could it be in the third? And if it wasn't, then perhaps there was no need to wish it goodbye. Perhaps it still did lie somewhere, waiting to be picked up . . . waiting . . .

'It might just be!' said Pascoe and dialled the telephone so rapidly he made a mistake and had to do it again.

If he wanted Superintendent Dalziel, the college switchboard girl told him, he wasn't in the study, he was in the registrar's office (though what he was doing there, *she* didn't know, the voice implied) and she would put him through there.

'Where the hell have you been?' snarled Dalziel.

Pascoe didn't waste time on apologies but tumbled out his theory as rapidly as he could.

'And,' he concluded, 'I reckon it might still be there somewhere. It's so obvious, perhaps he missed it. The staff must have somewhere they collect mail, pigeonholes or something.'

'Yes, they do. In the Senior Common Room. I remember seeing them.'

'Well, perhaps that's what Fallowfield did. Put it straight into someone's pigeon-hole. It could still be there.'

'Right. I'll look. You get yourself back over here as quickly as possible. And here's something to chew on while you're coming.'

'Sir?'

'Franny Roote is an old boy of guess where? Coltsfoot College. And he was interviewed for entry to this college on the Friday before the Monday when Girling died.'

The phone went dead. It was nearly thirty miles to the college but Pascoe did it in just over twenty minutes. Even then he was nearly too late.

Chapter 16

... as the fable goeth of the basilisk, that if he see you first, you die for it; but if you see him first, he dieth ...
SIR FRANCIS BACON
Op. Cit.

The headmaster of Coltsfoot College had been most helpful once he had made clear his displeasure at being removed from a bid of seven diamonds at the bridge table.

He had been very cautious at first until Dalziel had told him of Fallowfield's death.

'The poor man! Why did he – ? I never thought – he seemed stable enough, very much so, but in that kind of person – '

'What kind of person?' Dalziel had asked.

'He was a giver, involved, you know. Dedicated to teaching and to learning. And not just his subject.'

'No,' said Dalziel drily. 'He seems to have had very wide interests. We found books on witchcraft, magic – '

'Oh yes. Of course, he didn't *believe*, you understand. But he saw all these things as explorations of the human spirit, its heights, its depths, its potentials. Anything which extended the boundaries of our self-knowledge caught his interest.'

'Like taking drugs?'

'I have often heard him put a case *for* the licit use of certain drugs,' said the headmaster cautiously. 'But as for taking them himself, I have no reason to suspect – '

'No,' said Dalziel. 'Why did he leave you?'

'For a new post. Career advancement. You know.'

233

'No, I don't. Was that *all*? Nothing more?'

There was a moment's pause as though the man at the other end of the line was balancing conflicting ideas in his mind.

'This is a serious matter,' reminded Dalziel in his best conscientious official voice.

'Of course. There was no *real* reason for Fallowfield to leave us. No quarrel or anything like that. We're a progressive school and the freedom we try to give the boys extends as far as the staff-room. Which is not always the case in modern education. But the situation did have its tensions. It's like in politics, or even in your line of country, Superintendent, I dare say; what really irritates the radical is not the reactionary; no, it's the man who is still *more* radical and insists on treating the first radical as a conservative stick-in-the-mud.'

'And that's how Fallowfield reacted on your staff.'

'To some extent. I've oversimplified, of course. A school like mine requires a unified team to run it, with no sacrifice of individuality, of course. But Fallowfield was a loner. And . . .'

'Yes?'

'I felt that many of our boys, even the eldest, were still too young, too naïve if you like, properly to assimilate all the ideas that Fallowfield loved to play with. He was a stimulating man, a man gifted in dealing with the young. But I did begin to feel that the young had to be specially gifted to deal with *him*. I felt that the *older* young, if you take my meaning, students rather than pupils, would provide him with something more – er – suitable to get his teeth into.'

'I see,' said Dalziel, noting the turn of phrase. 'Was he homosexual?'

The progressive headmaster answered very quickly so that there would be no pause to be mistaken for shocked silence. At least, so Dalziel read the situation.

'No more so than the rest of us in the profession. We're all a bit queer I suppose,' he said with an arch chuckle as though to prove the point. 'I suppose all policemen in the same way are just a bit criminal. But whether he was a practising homosexual, I really couldn't say.'

'He didn't practise with any of the boys then?' said Dalziel, still hoping to pierce the man's liberal carapace.

'No! Of course not.' Very emphatic.

'I see. What can you tell me about a boy called Roote?'

'Francis Roote? Of course! He's up there as well. A charming boy, but a *real individual*, an all-rounder. I think we achieved our aim of educating the *whole man* there.'

The headmaster went on enthusiastically. Dalziel was interested to note how the old phrases like 'all-rounder' managed to survive in the ranks of the new vocabulary. But at the same time he extracted all that was relevant and useful from the man's song of praise.

Roote, it seemed, had risen to the dizzy heights of school-captain (this was Dalziel's translation of Co-First-man in the School Council) and had been universally loved. Except, Dalziel got a hint, by his fairly wealthy parents who kept him plentifully supplied with funds, but did not care overmuch if he spent most of the holidays elsewhere. The Head saw this as a conscious effort to let him develop his social potential. There seemed to have been no shortage of 'elsewhere'. His decision to apply for admission to the Holm Coultram College had come as a slight surprise. It was of course then an all-female college for training teachers and it was for a place among the pioneer group of men to start the following autumn that Roote had applied. This, the headmaster suggested, was probably one of the place's attractions for Francis. Breaking new ground.

Oh yes, thought Dalziel coarsely, virgin territory.

235

Had Fallowfield's application for a post there influenced him in any way? He couldn't really say. Perhaps. He was a great admirer of Fallowfield's, certainly, and this was one of the cases where Fallowfield's influence had produced nothing but good. As for their travelling to Yorkshire together, he had no idea. The school term ended early in December and the interviews were well on in the vacation, weren't they? Surely Roote himself could tell?

Curiously enough, the man concluded, the mere prospect of the new job seemed to work a change in Fallowfield. During his final two terms at Coltsfoot he had been unusually subdued, much less contentious than before, so much so that there had been some concern about his health. Roote? Oh no, Francis had been just the same as ever. A nice boy, an interesting boy. Give him all our good wishes, won't you?

Indeed I'll do that, thought Dalziel after the headmaster had gone back to his bridge. But first he looked again at Roote's file which had given him the hint of a connection in the first place. He was curious to learn why the man was still here at the end of nearly four years. It appeared that as the courses available at the college proliferated under the energetic leadership of Landor, Roote had decided that he would rather not commit himself to being a teacher and had changed horses in mid-stream, necessitating an extra year's study.

He's twenty-three! thought Dalziel. Christ, when I was twenty-three I had . . . but he didn't have time to think of all the magnificent things he had done by this tender age as the phone had rung at that precise moment and he had concentrated his mind on shouting at Pascoe.

Clever bugger, he thought after he put the receiver down. But not so clever; why couldn't he have thought that lot out this morning? For that matter, why couldn't I? It's obvious enough, if there's anything in it. Still, it leaves a chance that no one else thought of it either. But they might have done, in which case it'll have gone. Or whoever it was addressed to might have picked it up and be saying nowt. Or Fallowfield might have sent it via the post office in which case it'll turn up tomorrow.

Or perhaps the stupid bastard didn't write one at all. Unlikely, he thought scornfully. Bloody words were all these fairy intellectuals were good for. Pascoe, thank God, had learned the art of silence, sometimes the hard way. And there was nothing puffy about Pascoe, lots of lead in his pencil. Randy young bastard, thought Dalziel, surprised to find himself feeling almost affectionate. A good-looking woman, that Ellie Soper. Something there to grapple with. Not many of those in a pound.

His train of thought had carried him almost unconsciously out of the admin. block into the fresh air of another glorious evening. He glanced at his watch. Twenty past nine. The shadows were very long now. There were still no clouds in the sky but the sun had almost disappeared. The air-staining grime of the industrial North lay all to the west here and the whole horizon was breaking out in a multi-coloured rash.

Nice, thought Dalziel automatically. He had been brought up to think that sunsets, along with the Royal Family and the Liberal Party, were nice. It was difficult to lose all your conditioning.

Now for the senior common room, probably a wild-goose chase. But a necessary diversion first, it being Sunday and the police being what they were about licensing hours.

The bar was packed. It was the first time he had been in here, he realized with surprise. (I've been working too hard, he told himself.) They did themselves well too. None of your spit and sawdust; plush, well-padded comfort. But some of these bloody students – talk about out of place! They looked more suitable for a Sally Army doss-house than these comfortable, middle-class lounge-bar surroundings. And some of the staff he could see dotted around didn't look that much different. At least the students stared honestly.

'A bottle of scotch, malt if you've got it,' he said to the barman.

'I'm sorry, sir,' said the man, 'but have you been signed in?'

'What? Oh, no.' Of course, it was a club.

'Then you can't buy drink, can you?' said Cockshut's voice just behind him.

'That's right, Mr Cockshut,' said Dalziel calmly. 'I'm glad to see you've got some grasp of the law.'

The student secretary was obviously well on the way to being drunk. This could be unpleasant. But Dalziel had never bothered to avoid unpleasantness.

'That's all right, Bert,' said another familiar voice. It was Roote talking to the barman. 'I've signed the superintendent in.'

Bert's eyes widened at the title. He wouldn't have had the nerve to refuse me if he'd known, thought Dalziel. Cockshut would have been on to that.

'What would you like, Super?' said Franny with a smile. 'Pint?'

'No thanks. I just wanted a bottle of scotch to take out. Can you manage that?'

Franny spoke quietly to the barman who bent down and surfaced with a bottle of Glen Grant.

'That's your brand, isn't it?' asked Franny politely.

'That's right.'

'Nice drop of stuff that,' leered Cockshut.

'To those who are mature enough to appreciate it. That right?' he said counting out some money on to the bar. 'Thank you, Mr Roote. Good night.'

He turned to go and almost bumped into Marion Cargo who smiled. Behind her was Landor who looked worried.

'I'm glad I've found you, Superintendent. Our switch-board operator – she's one of our secretaries really, they take turns at week-ends – told me you were in the registrar's office. I wondered what . . .'

'Just prowling,' said Dalziel blithely. 'The door was open. Bad security that after last night.'

'Oh dear,' said Landor. 'I see. Well, could we talk for a moment?'

'Fifteen minutes suit you? In the study. I just have something to do. I want to pop into the SCR. Is that all right?'

He kept his voice down, conscious of the crush of people around them.

'Yes. Of course. But you won't be able to get in. No one uses it on a Sunday, well very rarely, and after last night, I've had it locked all day. It was rather badly damaged once before in a rag of some kind. So the locks were changed and I took the precaution of limiting the number of keys. Here you are.'

He undid a key from his key-ring and handed it over.

'Shall I come up with you perhaps,' he suggested diffidently.

'Oh no. Not necessary. I'll lock up. Fifteen minutes then in the study?'

He glanced at his watch. It was nearly half past nine.

The block in which the SCR was situated was quite deserted. It was the block in which the main lecture rooms were to be found. Presumably the common room had been placed there for maximum convenience during the working day.

The outer door was locked, but once again the bunch of keys he had taken from Sandra came in useful. But it was fortunate he had met Landor as the lock on the common room door was quite different from any of the others.

Protect your comfort. It's the only thing the bloody

239

state won't replace immediately, thought Dalziel. But at least it probably meant it would have been difficult for anyone to get in here during the day.

Anyway it was three floors up and there was no lift. No wonder people kept away on Sunday, he thought puffily.

The room faced east and it was quite dark inside. He put his bottle of whisky down on a table by the door and looked for a light switch. There was a block of half a dozen in the wall. He flicked one down at random and a light went on in the far corner. That would do. It was silly to draw attention to his presence here. He felt strangely uneasy.

There seemed to be a good deal of mail in the pigeon-holes. Of course it was a large staff, over eighty, and many of them would not have been near the place since Friday. He had no idea who Fallowfield would have been most likely to write to. In any case, it was best to be systematic. He started at A and began to work his way along. In his pocket was a page from Fallowfield's letter of application to the college which he had removed from his file. All handwritten envelopes he checked against this. Typewritten ones he examined more closely, occasionally cutting open a small flap with a razor-edge penknife to check on the contents. From time to time, he halted all movement and listened carefully. This was an invasion of privacy after all and he had no desire to be caught at it. There would have been other ways, but not without delay and letting everybody know what he was at. In any case, he decided, replacing the R letters back in their hole, it was probably going to be a waste of time.

The top letter in the S pigeon-hole changed his mind. The handwriting was unmistakable. He compared it carefully with Fallowfield's letter, checking and rechecking. There was no doubt. This was it.

It was addressed to Henry Saltecombe.

Dalziel stood for a moment, uncertain now what to do.

The proper course was to contact Saltecombe and ask him to open the letter in his presence. It was his letter after all. It was only theory that it had any importance whatsoever to the police.

On the other hand it might be of vital importance.

Still uncertain, Dalziel bent forward to replace the other letters. And the blow aimed at his skull crashed with great violence on to the bunched muscles of his powerful shoulders just below his neck. He pitched forward, his mind registering with horror the feel of a thin but rapid flow of dampness running over his head, around his ear, finally dripping to the carpet from his brow.

Pascoe slowed to fifty to turn into the college gates. Why he had driven so fast he did not know. But once out of the town streets he had put his foot on the accelerator and kept it there. Now as he slackened speed still more to navigate the sweeping bend in the college driveway, he felt his whole body relax comfortably, in an almost post-coital languour.

New kicks for jaded appetites, he thought. Only his appetite wasn't at all jaded. He wondered whether Ellie would still be available after this morning's row. He doubted it. Which was a pity. Still there must be any amount of enthusiastic crumpet available in a place like this for the true believer.

But Dalziel first, not the most aphrodisiac of thoughts.

The study was empty. He went outside again and glanced up towards the SCR block. A dim light glowed in one of the upstairs windows. Perhaps the fat man was still up there. Perhaps he had found something.

He went through the main entrance, pushing the heavy door to behind him. It crashed shut as he began to climb the stairs. The noise reverberated up the stair-well for a moment. He stood and looked up the uninviting flights of stairs.

'Are you up there, sir?' he called.

The answer came as though cued on a television thriller. A woman's scream.

Pascoe set off up the stairs three at a time. Each landing had a corridor leading off it, a grey tube leading to an identical landing at the other end and another flight of stairs. On the second landing, Pascoe caught a brief glimpse of movement at the other end of the corridor. He paused for a moment. Distantly he heard footsteps, pattering desperately down the stairs. He was undecided whether to pursue or go on up.

'Oh help, please help!' It was the woman's voice again. That decided him. Up to the next floor, down the corridor a little way, through the open door which let a feeble rectangle of light fall out of it.

The first thing that struck him was the smell. It was like the aftermath of a distillers' orgy. The place reeked of whisky.

Squatting on the floor looking desperately up at him was Marion Cargo. And in her lap she cradled Dalziel's head.

'Thank God!' said Marion. 'Help me please. We must get a doctor.'

Pascoe knelt beside her and took Dalziel's weight. He seemed to be the main source of the whisky fumes, his shoulders were soaked and the floor was strewn with broken glass.

'Sir!' he said anxiously. 'Sir!'

Dalziel opened his eyes and groaned. The groan turned into a sniff. He put a hand up to his face, looked at it, then licked his fingers.

'Oh my God,' he said weakly. 'I thought it was blood.'

He tried to stagger to his feet and Pascoe pushed him without much resistance into a chair. He leaned back, then yelped with pain and bent forward again.

'The bastard!' he said. 'Oh, the bastard. He's broken my whisky.'

'Does it hurt much?' asked Pascoe anxiously.

'Aye, man. Mentally and physically. The letter, has he got the letter?'

'Where? You found it then?'

'On top of the pigeon-holes there.'

The letter was gone.

Pascoe turned to Marion.

'What happened?' he snapped.

'I don't know. I came across to get a briefcase I'd left in here on Friday. The place was locked before because of the trouble last night I think. But I heard Mr Dalziel say he was coming up.'

'You *heard*? When? Where?'

'Why, in the bar a few moments ago.'

'Anybody else there?'

'Nearly everybody,' she said, puzzled. 'Anyway, I finished my drink, came out, saw the light so thought I'd just pop up.'

'Did you see anybody else come in?'

'No. But when I got to the landing of this floor, I heard a crash from inside the common room and as I reached the door, someone came running out and knocked me down.'

She rubbed her left buttock expressively.

'And then?'

'I screamed. Then I came in here and found the superintendent. Next thing I heard you running up the stairs so I shouted for help. Don't you think we should get a doctor?'

'Yes. We will. Look, did you see who it was?'

'No. I'm afraid not. It all happened so quickly and I was dazed for a minute. Mind you,' she added slowly, 'there was something familiar about him. I'm sure it was someone I know.'

'Roote,' said Dalziel, groaning as he tried to straighten up.

'What? Are you sure?' said Pascoe.

'It has to be. Anyway I saw his shoes, those fancy tennis shoes he wears. Between my bloody legs I saw them.'

'Are you sure?' repeated Pascoe. Marion looked amazed.

'For Christ's sake, go and get him!'

'Yes, but you . . .'

'We need that letter. We've bugger all else. Go and get him!' snarled Dalziel. His face was recovering a bit of colour, though it still looked grey. 'You'll be able to smell him. Glen Grant. My God!'

'Miss Cargo, get on the telephone will you?' began Pascoe.

'Go!' screamed the fat man.

Pascoe went. Dalziel was right, of course. Speed was of the essence. The letter itself would only take a minute to dispose of. He had little hope there. But at least if they got Roote straightaway they'd be able to check for certain if he was the attacker. He could hardly have avoided whisky stains and minute fragments of glass getting on to his clothes.

But the man was no fool. He would realize this too. His mind worked fast and it was matched with ice-cold nerves. He must have overheard Dalziel talking in the bar, had the same flash of realization that he, Pascoe, had had an hour earlier and instantly set out to thwart the fat man. He probably stood at the SCR door, absolutely still, watching the search, content to fade away quietly if nothing turned up, but moving instantly Dalziel's demeanour revealed he had found something. Into the room, picking up the bottle of scotch on the way, bring it down club-like on to the detective's back, then away with the letter. Perhaps he had meant to do more. The bottle

244

had shattered on the superintendent's shoulders. If it had caught him on the head . . . Perhaps Marion Cargo's arrival had stopped another killing.

With this thought in mind, he went into Franny's room in the best film-detective fashion, fast and low, crouched ready to ward off attack.

The place was empty, but bore the signs of a recent and hurried visit. The wardrobe door was ajar, a couple of drawers in the chest were pulled out. Pascoe looked around longingly. It might be well worthwhile searching the place.

But not now. If he read the signs aright, Roote had been as quick as he suspected, and realizing that his clothes were a possible giveaway, had got back quickly for a change, but was too clever to do it here. Where then? Someone else's room? Possibly.

Pascoe ran lightly down the corridor, pushing open doors. Most of the rooms were empty. In one an unfamiliar youth was leaning out of his open window smoking a pipe which was far too old for his placid, child-like face. He looked round in surprise.

'Roote?' said Pascoe, retreating as he spoke.

'Franny? I've just seen him heading out towards the beach. He must be going for a swim. I think he had his things.'

He gestured largely with his pipe out of the window. Pascoe went into the room and peered out towards the invisible sea.

'When?'

'About a minute. Less.'

Pausing only to check on a possible bluff by opening the youth's wardrobe, much to his surprise, Pascoe hurried from the building and set off at a gentle trot towards the dunes. His hopes were fading as fast as the light. Roote would know this stretch of coastline like the back of his hand. It had been a good move not to stop in the

245

building. Clothing was always difficult to get rid of indoors. Whereas . . .

Whereas if I were Roote thought Pascoe, I'd get down to the beach, strip off, make sacks out of my trousers and shirt, fill them with stones, swim out as far as I could and let them go. Then gently back, having given myself a thorough washing in the process, and up the beach to where I have left my new gear. The letter could go too if it hadn't been disposed of already. What the hell had Fallowfield said that was so damning? Was it about Girling? It still seemed unlikely. Anita? Or even both?

He doubted if they would ever know now. But if he played his hunch for once and made straight for the beach instead of scouting around the dunes, they might still get enough to make things very difficult for Roote.

He increased his pace to a run, stopping only when he breasted the last line of sand hills and stood overlooking the sea.

It was like a scientist putting his hypothesis to the practical test and finding it worked out perfectly in every particular.

Below him, about thirty yards to the right Franny was kneeling, dressed only in his trousers, thrusting stones into a bag made from his light cotton shirt. The rest of the beach was completely empty, the tide was out and the sea was a mere line of brightness in the hazy distance.

'It's a long walk for a swim,' said Pascoe conversationally. He had moved unobserved along the ridge of the dune till he stood right over the youth.

Franny looked round. His voice when he spoke was the same as ever, but there was a tightness round his face which should have been a warning.

'Hello, lovey,' he said. 'Fancy a dip, do you?'

'No thanks,' said Pascoe, leaping lightly down. At least he meant to leap lightly, but his feet slithered in the soft loose sand and he was thrown off balance. Franny came

246

to his feet and in one smooth movement brought up the shirt with its burden of stones full into Pascoe's chest. The sergeant went down, clutching the shirt, rolled over to the left as fast as he could and rose into the crouch to withstand the next onslaught, feeling as though his ribs were crushed in.

Franny had not moved, but stood facing him, only his eyes moving in his impassive face.

He's thinking, thought Pascoe gasping for breath. He's working it out. Three things – to run, to surrender, or to fight. There's nowhere to run, he knows that. Surrender and bluff it out? What after all have we got on him? An attack on a police-officer. Serious, but without the letter . . . what the hell *was* in that letter? But it was gone now. Wasn't it? Wasn't it?

Was it?

That's why he can't just give up and talk his way out of it! He's still got the letter. All right. Why not run now, give yourself enough start to dump it? With me in this condition, it shouldn't be difficult.

Unless, of course, he no longer has it. In which case . . . Pascoe looked down at the bundle in his arms and slowly began to smile.

I have it!

It's in here, ready for sinking in the sea.

He looked up again, opened his mouth, and received a handful of fine silver sand full in his face. The bundle was torn from his grasp. He flung himself forward, still blinded by the sand, and grappled with Roote's knees. One of them came up violently, crashing into his mouth and he went over backwards. Blinking desperately, he got a little bit of vision back, enough to roll out of the way of the clubbing punch aimed at his head. Enough also to see the young man's face and realize that he was no longer fighting just for the letter, he was fighting for his life.

He pushed himself up off his backside and tried to

scrabble backwards up the sand dune, hoping to get the advantage of height. But the softness of the sand thwarted him and he slid back into the relentless volley of punches that was being hurled at him. Many of them he was able to ward off with his hands and forearms, but he had little strength to retaliate. In the cinema, western heroes, and even policemen occasionally, could give and receive enormous blows for any amount of time. But for mere unscripted mortals like himself, things were different.

The onslaught suddenly slackened, but not out of charity or even fatigue, he realized. Roote was merely casting around for a more satisfactory (meaning, lethal) weapon than his bare fists. He stooped and came up with a large ovoid stone in his hand.

The time had come, Pascoe decided, to admit the boot was on the other foot and run.

His initial burst of energy at the decision almost carried him up the sand dune this time but his foot was seized and he was dragged down into the hollow again.

He took the first blow from the stone on his elbow. It hurt like hell, but it was better than his face. And this time he managed to get in a damaging counter-blow with his knee to Roote's groin. Momentarily the man staggered back, but Pascoe had no romantic illusions about snatching victory from the jaws of defeat. He wanted reinforcements and quick. This time he didn't waste his energy by trying to climb but set off along the beach, parallel with the dunes; a clumsy sideways kind of run, he thought, but in the circumstances who could expect style?

Amazingly when he glanced back after about thirty yards, he wasn't being pursued. He didn't question why, but just felt thankful. It was time to move inland and seek help. His fuddled mind was trying to work out where the nearest point of human contact was. The golf club perhaps? Or that row of cottages in which poor Fallowfield had lived. Poor Fallowfield indeed! God knows what the bastard was responsible for, including this!

248

The dunes looked less precipitous here. He turned inland and began once more to climb up.

As he pulled himself over the top, clutching at the long, tough sea-grass, he realized why Roote had not pursued him down the beach.

He was here instead, standing over him expectantly, stone still held high in his hand. As it came down, Pascoe pushed himself backwards in a last desperate attempt to escape. As he fell, he saw Roote looming over him, dark against the sky, then the youth's body came crashing on top of him, knocking all his breath out.

It took him some seconds to realize that the body was moving even less energetically than his own, that he could push it off him quite easily.

He did so. Another figure now stood menacingly against the skyline. Perhaps not so menacingly after all. The walking-stick with which he had clubbed Franny was still held aloft, it was true. But the bright blue eyes, the old, weather-wrinkled face, the happy smile, the old binoculars dangling free from the scrawny neck, none of these seemed to contain much menace.

'Ee, lad,' said Harold Lapping with a contented laugh, 'you do see some funny goings-on just walking round these dunes of an evening.'

It was a few moments before Pascoe could gasp his thanks. Lapping slid down beside him and helped him to stand up. Franny was still lying in the sand, but his eyes were open.

'Watch him,' gasped Pascoe. 'If he moves an inch, hit him with your stick.'

The old man grinned.

Pascoe walked unsteadily down the beach to where he had first encountered Roote. He picked up the shirt-bundle and carried it back. Anything that might be evidence it was as well to find in front of a witness. Silently he tipped out the stones so that they fell a couple

249

of feet from Roote's staring eyes. Among them was a crumpled envelope. He picked it up and smoothed it out, realizing he had no idea who it might be addressed to.

'Saltecombe,' he said. He noticed with surprise that the envelope was still sealed.

'You haven't read it? Short of time?' he asked, then added, 'No. You weren't even *going* to read it, were you? It was ready for disposal. Why not?'

Roote sat up slowly, his eyes on Lapping's stick. He rubbed the back of his head.

'I don't like sticking my nose into other people's mail,' he said. 'That's constabulary business.'

'Oh no,' said Pascoe staring hard at the youth. 'You were frightened, weren't you? It worried you what a dying man might say about you. Not just because it might incriminate you, in the sight of the law, but because it might condemn you to yourself.'

'Oh, piss off,' said Franny.

Pascoe looked at the letter, faced with Dalziel's dilemma when he had found it. Should he open it now or not?

'Open it for me,' said Franny as though reading his thoughts. 'I've got nothing to worry about.'

He managed to sound quite confident. Pascoe shoved his bruised and bleeding face close to the youth's and pointed to it.

'What do you think did this? Moths?' he asked. He reached down and undid Roote's belt and the top two buttons of his flies.

'Put your hands in your pockets,' he said. 'Hold 'em up. Come on.'

They made an odd trio as they picked their way over the dunes and through the woodland back to the college. The letter was safely in Pascoe's pocket. It would keep till they got back to Dalziel. That small part of Pascoe's mind which wasn't concerned with watching Roote or exploring the pain round his ribs and face kept on sniffing around the case. He ought to have felt happy. Franny's actions demonstrated his guilt, the letter in his pocket would probably give some detailed indication of exactly what had happened. But what in fact was the man guilty of? Ever since he'd talked to Dalziel on the phone he'd been trying to construct models of motive and opportunity which would fit Fallowfield and Roote and the known facts together. So far nothing. It had all happened too quickly. A few hours ago he hadn't been able to foresee an end to this business in six months. Now they had . . .

Well, what *did* they have?

They found Dalziel in the college sick-bay having his back treated by a little Irish matron with Marion acting as dogsbody. Landor was there too, still looking anxious, and Halfdane who did not look over-worried at the sight of Dalziel's discomfiture. Even Miss Disney had somehow realized that something was going on, and only her sense of the impropriety of being in the same room as a half-naked superintendent kept her hovering in the doorway.

The arrival of Pascoe and Roote caused quite a stir. Roote looked round the room with a lop-sided grin and shrugged his shoulders as though in resignation. The matron came across to Pascoe and looked at his bloody face. He caught a glimpse of himself in a wall-mirror and realized how horrific he looked.

Dalziel swung down from the couch on which he was lying for treatment. The top of his back was very nastily bruised and he held his head thrust forward in a rather becomingly aggressive pose. He began pulling on his shirt, despite the matron's protests.

'I'll see the quack when he condescends to come,' he said. 'You too, Sergeant. Meanwhile we need a bit of privacy to talk with Mr Roote here.'

'There seem to be quite a lot of students outside,' said

Landor diffidently. Miss Scotby who had just arrived nodded in confirmation of this.

'The boy, Cockshut, is there,' she said in her precise tones, as though that explained everything. 'Shall I go and disperse them, Simeon?'

She probably would too, thought Pascoe. And it's 'Simeon' now, is it? If she's out to supplant Mrs Landor, please God let her do it by legitimate means.

'That's unnecessary,' said Dalziel. 'Your office will do, if we may, Matron.'

She nodded and led the way into a small room opening off the sick-bay.

Roote sat down uninvited and smiled up at them. He seemed quite recovered from his knock and mentally unperturbed.

'If you beat me, I shall scream,' he said with a grin.

'I think I can promise you that,' said Dalziel softly. Pascoe, who was sponging blood off his face at the small wash-basin in the corner, suddenly felt happy to be himself despite his aches and pains.

Roote had stopped smiling and was fingering the lump on the back of his head where Lapping had hit him. Pascoe caught Dalziel's eye and nodded at the youth's head, making a chopping motion. Dalziel's eyes gave a flicker of understanding. Solicitors made a lot of fuss about their clients being questioned while suffering from untreated injuries, and the courts didn't like it much either.

Now Pascoe brought the letter from his pocket and held it up for Dalziel to see. The fat man's eyes rounded and he began to look pleased. He obviously had not expected to see it again. Pascoe hoped it was going to be worth all the trouble.

Dalziel picked up the telephone on the desk and after a moment spoke to the operator.

'Get me Mr Saltecombe at his home please. Ask him if

he would come to see me as soon as possible. Yes, I'm in the matron's office.'

It was almost possible to sense the switchboard girl's disapproval of Dalziel's free movement round the college.

He replaced the receiver and looked solicitously at Franny.

'Now, Mr Roote, we've got a doctor coming to have a look at that bump on your head. Is there anything you'd like to say before he turns up?'

Pascoe expected some flip obscenity, but strangely the youth seemed to be considering the suggestion carefully.

'I could have got rid of the letter,' he said inconsequentially. 'I didn't think you'd be so quick.'

'We're lightning when roused,' said Dalziel.

'I wish I'd read it now. Then I'd know what – not that it matters. I'm rather tired of it all. It's about time I went off on a new tack. And Sam's probably said it all.' He laughed. 'He was a great one for words, Sam. Ideas. But not so hot on action.'

'Perhaps you should try words for a change.'

'You may be right, lovey. Anyway, what the hell. We'll see. There's an old police proverb, isn't there? He who talks last serves longest? I'll tell you what, Superintendent. You'd better get used to me as a picture of misguided innocence. I'll bring character witnesses.'

He's nervous, thought Pascoe. Somewhere deep down inside him there's a little bit of fear fluttering. He doesn't like to sit and wait. He likes to be doing, doing, doing. He likes to feel the initiative to action lies with him.

Dalziel obviously caught this feeling too. He looked uninterested, glanced at his watch.

'Well, we'll just get the doctor to look at you. Then we can talk later at the station.'

He opened the door and stepped into the sick-room.

'Any sign of that doctor?'

From the window the matron said, 'I think that his car

253

is coming down the drive now. Come along, everybody. I can't have you all hanging around here. What will the doctor think?'

They began to move reluctantly, Halfdane sticking close to Marion Cargo, Landor patting Miss Scotby's elbow reassuringly, Disney walking backwards as though from a royal presence.

'Superintendent.'

The voice stopped them all. It was Franny standing at the office door. Behind him Pascoe hovered, ready to pounce.

'Murderer!' hissed Disney magnificently.

'Mr Dalziel. When Mr Saltecombe comes, may I be there when he opens his letter? I'd like to see it.'

Something about his intonation bothered Pascoe.

'I bet you would,' said Dalziel. 'Don't worry. You'll find out what's in it soon enough.'

Disney snorted and left. Marion, looking ill after the strain of the evening, went out with Halfdane's arm supporting her waist, followed by Scotby and Landor.

Pascoe watched them all go, vaguely disturbed. Roote had sat down again and was whistling softly to himself. Pascoe looked at him with great dislike.

When the doctor arrived he was accompanied by Constable Shattuck. Pascoe turned over his supervisory duties to him and went and joined Dalziel at the sick-bay window, looking down at a sizeable group of students hanging round the entrance to the block.

'Landor's talking to them. Not very successfully,' grunted Dalziel.

A car coming up the drive had to bleep its horn to clear a path through the students. It was a silver-grey Capri.

'Halfdane,' said Dalziel. Pascoe wondered how he knew. 'Vulgar bloody cars.'

They watched it out of sight through the main gates.

'Get the doc. to have a look at you,' said Dalziel and obediently the sergeant went through into the other room. Behind him he heard Dalziel picking up the telephone.

Roote had been pronounced perfectly fit, Pascoe's rib had been strapped, though the doctor didn't think there was a break, and Dalziel was just putting his shirt back on for the second time when Henry Saltecombe turned up.

'I couldn't believe it when they told me this morning. Sam! I've been just walking up and down the beach all day.'

He seemed genuinely upset.

'There's a letter for you here, Mr Saltecombe,' said Dalziel sympathetically. 'We have reason to believe Mr Fallowfield wrote it. I would like you to open it in my presence, read it, and then permit me to read it. It may be relevant to my enquiries and the coroner too will want sight of it.'

Henry seemed to turn even paler.

'From Sam?'

'Yes. Sergeant, just hold that door firmly closed, will you?'

Pascoe took a tight hold of the handle of the office door behind which Constable Shattuck was watching over Roote.

Henry unsealed the envelope awkwardly, tearing it diagonally across the face. There were three handwritten sheets inside. He read them silently, once, twice.

'Here,' he said handing them to Dalziel and turning away. Dalziel read slowly and methodically, then passed them over to Pascoe.

'Mr Saltecombe,' he said. 'A word in your ear.'

They muttered in a corner as Pascoe read the letter.

'Well, that's that,' he said to Dalziel who shook his head warningly.

'Fetch Roote through,' said the fat man.

Pascoe tapped on the door and Shattuck opened it.

'Bring him out,' he said to the constable.

Franny stood framed in the doorway.

Henry took a step forward from his corner.

'You bastard,' he said. 'You slimy bastard! I hope they jail you for ever.'

Franny did not seem taken aback.

'So you've read it,' he said, looking at Dalziel who held the letter in his hand.

'Francis Roote,' he said. 'You will be taken to the Central Police Station where you will be charged with the murders of Alison Girling and Anita Sewell. You are not required to say anything now, but anything you do say will be taken down and may be used in evidence. At the station you will be given an opportunity to contact your legal adviser.'

'The *murders*?' said Franny disbelievingly. 'But you can't do that. Not . . . look, he must say . . . what *does* he say?'

He stepped forward to make a grab at the letter. Shattuck's arms enfolded him from behind in a comfortable embrace.

'He just mentions *you*, Franny,' said Dalziel softly. 'There's a lot about you.'

'*Me*? Just *me*? The fool! The bastard! What did he . . . why . . .'

'Why not, Franny?' asked Dalziel. 'Why not?'

'Is it a bluff?' he asked. 'Is it? What's it matter anyway? Now. Just sit down and listen to this.'

He began talking rapidly. After a couple of minutes Pascoe jumped up, looked at Dalziel and motioned to the telephone. Dalziel standing by the window shook his head and pointed out.

Down the drive moving very sedately came a silver-grey Capri. Behind it was a police-car.

Franny was still talking when the door burst open and Halfdane rushed in.

'What the hell's all this?' he snarled. 'You're in trouble, real trouble, Superintendent. You've never known trouble like it . . .'

Dalziel ignored him completely. Holding Fallowfield's letter before him like a cross held out to a vampire he went towards the pale slight figure standing between two policemen in the doorway.

'Marion Cargo,' he said. 'I am arresting you on suspicion of complicity in the murders of . . .'

He didn't finish. She fainted beautifully into the arms of the policemen.

Only the ironic applause from Roote disturbed the beauty of the performance.

Chapter 17

. . . the unlearned man knows not what it is to descend into himself or call himself to account.

SIR FRANCIS BACON
Op. Cit.

It took them forty-eight hours to even begin to tie the loose ends together. But by the end of that time they had done all that was necessary to do in the college. There had been little time to talk to anyone in the college about events and Cockshut was desperately trying to find some aspect of things which would give him another excuse for action. Pascoe was pleasantly relieved that they were going to get away before this blew up. He glanced at his watch now. He had promised Ellie that he would call in before he went. But Landor had come into the study while they were packing up and Dalziel seemed to be in the mood to offer explanations and assessments.

'The letter!' said Dalziel. 'Everybody sweating on the letter and a lot of bloody use it turned out to be.'

'It wasn't intended to be useful,' said Simeon Landor gently. 'It's just a record of a man's uncertainty and unhappiness.'

'It would have made me a lot happier if it had mentioned a few names,' said Dalziel gloomily.

There was a photostat of the letter on the study desk in front of Pascoe. He looked down at it again and read it for the hundredth time, still with a sense of emptiness, of loss.

Dear Henry,
   This is a strange letter to have to write, and a stranger way

you might think to repay friendship. I am truly sorry if it is painful for you to read this. But pain is a risk we take in becoming fond of people, isn't it? As I have found out to my cost.

I have decided to take my life, not out of despair or anything so religious as that. But merely out of confusion. These past few years have been troubled ones for me, troubled not in the way I have always felt troubled by the problems of life and humanity, but troubled by problems of mere living. I have had secrets to hide which I did not wish to know in the first place; I found that quite unbeknown to me I had become a leader and, as a leader, had to be deposed from a position I would have been only too happy to resign. I found myself admitting to accusations that were false rather than make accusations that were true. (I was never anything more to Anita Sewell than a dear friend. At least I thought so, and I know in the end she did too.) Finally I was driven to absurd delaying tactics on points of procedure and constitutional issues – the kind of thing which has always bored me to tears as you know! – because I did not know what else to do.

In other words I had to make decisions. I really believe the majority of people are lucky enough to get through life without ever having to make a single greatly significant decision. I had to make such a one five years ago. I made it on personal grounds, unselfish I thought at the time, though I'm no longer sure, grounds of love, and respect, and hope, for an individual. The only grounds, I felt, on which such a decision should be taken.

So I concealed my knowledge of the death of Miss Girling and felt that I had done my lifetime's duty. No man should have to do that twice. Now five years later, because I did it once, I'm faced with the same decision again. Someone else is dead – Anita – someone much more valuable than Girling.

So, I'm confused. I acted once as I felt I had to act. I felt it was the *only* way to act. Out of that action came distrust, misunderstanding, contumely, slander, and finally another death. But the reasons for my original action still seem valid. So how do I act now?

Well, I'm confused. But not despairing. Living poses too many problems. Life – and death – are simpler and there is an easy way to get at their meaning, if any. That's the way I'm taking now.

As for this letter and any information, or hints of information,

it contains, do what you will with it. Burn it, or show it to that
ill-assorted pair of policemen. What you will.

Me, I've given up decisions. Except for this last one.

Your friend,

Sam Fallowfield.

'It's a terrible letter for anyone to write,' he said aloud.
The others looked at him, Landor sympathetically, Dalziel in irritation.

'It's a bloody useless letter,' he reiterated. 'It tells us
nowt. If Roote hadn't been so keen to get the first blow
in before the girl had a chance, we'd have been nowhere.
As it is, well I suppose it served some purpose.'

He leaned forward, groaned and rubbed himself
between the shoulders.

'If my lad hadn't come when he did, those two would
have had all the time in the world to get rid of it. Or they
might even have let us find it, for all the use it was. But
unread, that was different.'

'They were both so firmly convinced Fallowfield would
have told everything he knew and suspected, that they
credited us with this knowledge once Mr Saltecombe told
us to read the letter,' explained Pascoe. 'We just kept
quiet and looked confident.'

Dalziel nodded complacently.

'I told Mr Saltecombe to look accusing and say a couple
of nasty things to Roote when he appeared. That did the
trick. And once he thought that Fallowfield had put the
finger on him but not the girl, he went wild. I think he
even felt betrayed. Imagine!'

'It was odd,' said Pascoe. 'Roote was quite happy to
warn Cargo that we still had the letter, that's why he
came into the sick-bay and asked about Saltecombe. But
the minute he thought the letter *wasn't* dangerous to
her . . .'

'Yes,' said Dalziel. 'I saw her face then. And I remembered she was right on top of us when I told you I was

going up to the Common Room. Also I had a sense of *two* other people being over me when I got clobbered up there. So when I saw Halfdane's car making off, I wondered if she might not be in it also. So I put out a call. Poor lad. I feel sorry for him.'

You sound it, thought Pascoe, remembering Halfdane's face ravaged with shock and disbelief. You bloody sound it.

Landor shook his head in perplexity.

'It's hard to believe . . . it has hurt us all in more ways than we realize, I think. When will it all be over?' he asked.

'When someone decides we've got to the truth,' said Dalziel.

'But you just said you have their statements, their confessions?'

'Which are very contradictory. It looked as if Cargo was going to crack completely at first, but she pulled herself together in the end. She's too clever to go back to absolute denial – we've dug up all kinds of circumstantial evidence to tie them in together. We can prove they spent that Christmas together, for instance, so it would be foolish of her to deny it. But she's hurling all the mud back at Roote that he's slinging at her.'

'And who do you believe?'

Dalziel shrugged.

'Roote, I think. Mainly because he seems to have been motivated by something less or more than mere self-preservation all the way through. I don't know whether this makes him a more or a less horrifying character. This is the way I read the story, though God knows if we'll ever get the real truth.

'Roote and Fallowfield arrive together on that Friday in December. Fallowfield's a bit of a weirdo, king of the kids, one of your modern nothing-is-too-sacred-or-way-out-to-try philosophers who go down big with some youngsters. There was probably more than a touch of the queer there too. Anyway, they're spending part of the Christmas vac together and Fallowfield, who probably persuaded Roote to apply for admission here when he knew he himself was being interviewed, drives them both up. Roote has his interview. Is accepted. Even at eighteen he seems to have had a way with women, of all ages. He runs into Marion Cargo, practically the only student left in the place. She's hanging on because she's going ski-ing with Girling, remember. She's three years older than he is, though I doubt if she was anything like as experienced. Perhaps enough to make things easy for him, though he's obviously a very smooth operator anyway. By Monday, after a week-end of considerable delight, she is thoroughly infatuated. He asks her to spend Christmas with him – he was joining a party of friends, we've got all the details – and the prospect pleases. But Girling has to be told. Just how much she was being the mother-figure and just how much she fancied her chances with Cargo for a romp in the snow, we'll never know.'

Landor pursed his lips in distaste. Dalziel scratched his belly-button voluptuously and went on.

'Cargo gave me some story about Disney intervening: Disney denies it absolutely, though there's probably just a speck of truth in it, enough for Cargo to build on. Anyway she goes along and tells Girling the trip's off. Girling is furious, flies into a rage, cancels the bookings instantly, a kind of see-if-I-care gesture. Later that afternoon, after the governors' meeting and Fallowfield's appointment, Girling sends for Cargo again. Perhaps to plead with her, perhaps she has got wind of what's going on and wants to put the bubble in, perhaps Cargo herself let something slip. Anyway, Roote is summoned to the presence also. When he arrives there is a full-scale fight going on. I've no doubt he quite enjoyed it. Anyway, his version is that finally Girling slapped Marion's face in her

262

fury. The girl retaliated by pulling her hair. It was a wig and it came off. Roote says he fell about laughing. Quite beside herself with rage, Girling flew at Cargo's throat and she pushed her away so that she fell into the fireplace and cracked her head open on the sharp corner there.'

Dalziel pointed dramatically across the room. Landor stirred uneasily. He had obviously forgotten that these events took place in this very room.

'Accidental death,' he said. 'I suppose that's . . .'

'Well, it might be. But Cargo denies it and says Roote came up behind and struck the old woman on the head with the poker. I'm sure a compromise will be reached eventually.

'At this point, Fallowfield seems to have walked in. Whatever the truth of the matter he was given the accidental death story, I should think. And the way a man with his kind of mind would see it, he had a choice between ruining or protecting the careers and futures of two young people, one of whom he obviously thought was very special. It's remarkable how stupid you bloody intellectuals can be,' he snorted.

'Quite,' said Landor drily. Why don't you spit in his eye? wondered Pascoe.

'But how did Miss Girling apparently get to Austria?'

'A diversionary plan was put into operation, once Fallowfield agreed to help. First they lugged Girling out of that window and over the lawn to where Cargo knew there was a nice deep hole already dug. Remember there was thick fog. No one was going to be about to see them. A thin covering of earth. Cargo knew the concrete would be poured in the following day. There was an element of risk there, but it was worth it. After this, the diversion. Remember that eventually they believed Girling would be missed. The farther away she seemed to have got from the college, the better for them. Where better than the airport, a hundred miles away, to which everyone knew the principal was travelling that evening? Her cases were packed, they soon found her tickets, passport, everything. Remember they had access to her living quarters through that door and up the stairs. They had to move fast before anyone in college came to see Girling. I don't know who initiated everything, they both picture themselves as the passive member of the trio, merely carrying out instructions. But it was probably Roote who had the bright idea of going one step further when they reached the airport – he had driven her car there, by the way, in convoy with Fallowfield; it must have been a hell of a journey on a night like that.

'Still, they made it and, as I say, they pushed their luck a little further. Cargo, dressed in one of Girling's coats and wearing her spare wig, checked in the luggage. Things were chaotic with the fog and it seemed a clever move to establish the presence of a red-headed woman like Girling at the airport by more than just circumstantial evidence.

'After that, it was just a matter of waiting. If there was no report of the body having been found at the college, they could go off to spend Christmas with some ease of mind. But when the report broke in the paper of the avalanche, and Girling was one of those listed as having possibly been on the bus, this must have seemed like an act of God. They were in the clear. The statue was up, for ever it seemed. Everyone was satisfied about Girling's death. The brief nightmare was over.'

Not for Fallowfield, thought Pascoe looking down at the letter once more.

'How could they bear to come back here?' asked Landor.

'Why not? They could keep an eye on things. Every time they saw the statue, it stood as a surety for their own safety. There's something fascinating about such a secret. It's a truism that criminals always return to the scene of the crime. All it usually means is that people often commit crimes in places which are familiar to them. But the pull is there. Look at the way Cargo came back for a job here when she got the chance. Though something of her infatuation with Roote probably remained.'

'What happened next? All this business with that poor girl, Anita, I mean . . .'

'You happened for one. And Franny Roote grew older and wilder. Fallowfield had learned a little discretion, I think, especially among his colleagues. Perhaps Girling's death had made him seriously question his own philosophies. But here with Franny's help, a little cell of soul-mates, earnest seekers after the truth, was soon set up. It must have seemed the attainment of an ideal to Fallowfield for a while. But with Franny, the search for the truth was a lot less important than the kicks you got on the way. Fallowfield was delighted to discuss freely how drugs, or certain rituals, or sex, can bring about an enlargement of human awareness – have I got it right, Sergeant Pascoe?'

'Yes, sir,' said Pascoe, though he knew the question was rhetorical. 'He was interested in isolating those elements which all these sources of spiritual release and greater sensitivity to our environment had in common. Roote was more interested in the experience than the theory.'

'Niccly put,' said Dalziel appreciatively. 'So gradually they drifted apart. And in Roote's eyes became rivals. He had a great advantage – he was young, he was quite amoral, he was persuasive and he was sexually very attractive. The girls went for him; the young men were for him too, because he laid on lots of crumpet for them. Fallowfield hung on to one or two. Anita Sewell was one, but she leant more and more to Roote, despite all that Fallowfield could do. She had some kind of conscience-crisis at the start of the summer. That's why she got back late. But she'd made up her mind by then. She was with

265

Roote all the way. So when it seemed her division of loyalties had so ruined her academic work that she was going to be slung out, Fallowfield probably felt relieved. At least she would be out of Roote's way. Then came the appeal. She must have taken some persuading to lie, but Roote was a great persuader. Cockshut too, all the political bit. He'd got himself attached to the Roote bandwagon and pushed him for the Union Presidency, thinking he could use him. The poor bastard, he was the one who was being used all the time.'

'But why did Fallowfield appear to accept the story?'

'How to disprove it? He knew how the whole relationship between himself and Roote, and all the other young people involved, would sound. He was certain that reason could still prevail, especially with Anita. He was probably right there. So he tried to take the wind out of Roote's sails by admitting Anita was his mistress, or not denying it, but fighting the accusation of academic dishonesty as hard as he could.'

'I can't see why Roote *did* it in the first place,' said Landor.

'Partly enjoyment, plain and simple. Partly a real belief that Fallowfield was his enemy now. And doubtless other reasons we shall never know. But he overreached himself. Anita's relationship with him was based on love. They hadn't ever become lovers in the physical sense yet. He was saving her up for midsummer's eve; this was probably something else he used to get at Fallowfield with. But the girl didn't take any of his claims seriously, all this business with witch-craft and ouija boards and the rest. She went along with it for his sake, that was all. And when she and Roote together asked the ouija whose body it was that had been found under the statue, she knew very well whose finger was pushing the indicator round. When it turned out that it *was* Girling's body – and Elizabeth, the

266

girl who looked after our food for us, made sure the students got the news almost as quickly as we did – '

'It must have been that very night,' interrupted Pascoe; he reckoned he deserved at least one interruption a year. 'We know she'd already sent a note asking to see Fallowfield, so she must have been growing more and more worried about the other business. When she questioned Roote that night about Miss Girling, he was probably a bit high on something or other and he told her the lot – blaming Cargo of course. This, we think, was after they all got back from the dunes. No one else saw her unfortunately. She probably deliberately waited till they were all out of the way.'

Dalziel took up the reconstruction again.

'Off she went immediately to talk with Fallowfield. Unfortunately for her, Cargo had been there already. It was her the neighbour's kiddy saw going up the path. She'd wanted to discuss the discovery of the body with Fallowfield. God knows what they decided, but on the way back she met Anita. Once Cargo realized that she knew the truth, the girl was dead.'

'Oh my God,' said Landor, putting his head between his hands.

Embarrassed, Pascoe looked at his watch and stood up.

'Do you mind if . . . ?' he asked Dalziel.

'No. No. The principal and I will be here for a little while yet. Though it's thirsty work this talking.'

The whisky'll come out now I'm gone, thought Pascoe as he made his way up to Ellie's room. He felt he had to say goodbye. He wasn't really looking forward to it, but anything was better than sitting going over all the horrific details of the case again. He must be going soft.

As it happened, he wasn't even spared that. Ellie treated him as some kind of impersonal information bureau, shooting questions at him from all angles, insatiable for analysis of motive, reconstruction of event.

'I don't *know* any of this,' he protested. 'Nearly everything I say to you is theory. The two versions we've got conflict in so many particulars, all we can do is keep on digging till we see which the circumstantial evidence fits best.'

'All right,' said Ellie. 'I understand. I'm not stupid. But at least you can make an educated guess. Which of them wrecked the cottage? That's what you'd just found out on Saturday afternoon, hadn't you? When we met you on our way to the beach. Christ, to think of that girl – ! If she'd really taken me for a rival, God knows what she might have done!'

'You were very lucky,' said Pascoe ironically. 'It was Roote. He admits it. He was gilding the lily a bit. After Marion told him what she'd done to Anita, he went out again and shifted the body nearer to the place where they'd been dancing, and took off her clothes. He was just trying to confuse things, make it look as though it had happened immediately after the dance was disturbed. Later he got the idea of planting the clothes on Fallowfield and he wrecked the cottage, hoping Fallowfield would call us in and we'd be the ones to find the clothes. Which we did, of course, but poor Fallowfield by this time had given up the struggle. Inside, he must have been quite certain that Marion and/or Franny had something to do with Anita's death. But the poor bastard just wasn't equipped to deal with such knowledge, not after the first time. Anyway, we were left with the interesting question, why would anyone want to mess up his cottage?'

'So it turned your attention away from Fallowfield rather than brought it closer on him?'

'In a way,' said Pascoe. He wasn't going to mention Disney's part. There was nastiness enough around without helping it to breed.

'It's incredible,' she said after a pause.

'Read your newspapers,' he answered. 'The incredible's happening all the time. There's nothing that human beings haven't managed to do to one another, however vile. And no motive, however slight, which has not brought someone to murder.'

Another pause.

'What happens now?'

'Like I say, read your newspapers. We just collect facts, solve problems. Then the public prosecutor decides.'

'I mean about us. I take it you're on your way now.'

'Yes. Shortly.' He tried the light touch. 'It's only thirty miles; I'm not off to shoot big game.'

'No.'

She made a little motion with her hand.

'Do you want to go to bed with me before you go?'

The light touch was a bit heavy now.

'I'd better not. I don't like to rush. And it's a bit early for me, really.'

'It's a bit late. For both of us.'

Pascoe said the thing that he had promised himself not to say.

'Why? The field's clear for you now, isn't it?'

'Halfdane, you mean? That poor sod. Have you seen him? If the way he's cut up is anything to go by, I never had a chance there. I certainly haven't now. There are some rebounds you just don't try to catch.'

She laughed.

'Who cares? I'm not desperate for a husband. I've got all *this*.' She jerked her head in a gesture which included the whole college.

'Listen, Ellie,' said Pascoe urgently. 'If it's too late for me, it doesn't matter. All I'll do is grow up into a hard, beery, old cop. It doesn't matter. Besides the country needs hard, beery, old cops. But you'll end up like Disney. Or Scotby. An academic old maid, which is to womanhood what a Scottish professor is to golf. That's not for you. Not you. It's such a waste.'

'Christ Almighty! I'm only thirty-one! I'm not glued to the shelf yet.'

'No, of course not,' he said, slightly embarrassed by his own fervour. He wasn't really sure why he was getting so worked up. Other people's lives. Policemen couldn't afford to become involved in other people's lives.

'As long as you don't think ... . I mean . . .'

She laughed at him again. Quite convincingly.

'You know, sermons are for priests, not cops. You'll be sorry you said all this when I'm a famous novelist, pursued by all.'

'As long as you don't forget your friends.' He glanced at his watch. He could get out now, shake hands and go, leaving things between them much as he had found them. That would be the wise move. But sometimes the wise move just left you standing still.

'Time to go?' she asked, lighting a cigarette.

'No. Not yet. I was just thinking. That offer you made.' He imitated her small hand motion.

'Is it still open?'

She stubbed out her cigarette.

As they drove slowly along the drive, Dalziel heaved a great sigh of relief.

'That's that then.'

'Yes.'

'So that's what I missed when I didn't get a college education.'

Behind them in the driving mirror, Pascoe could see Landor standing before the Old House, watching them go. By his side, slightly behind him, was Miss Scotby who had turned up as they left. Would she make some move now or be content with her dreams on horseback? It was none of his business. And Disney, now her arch-enemies were defeated, what would she do in the future? Probably set about destroying Dunbar! Not a nice woman.

From the highest point of the drive it was possible to catch a glimpse of the sea to the east. Or to look down upon the complex of buildings which made up the college. Work had restarted on the foundations of the new biology lab and the green sward of the garden was now irremediably scarred. But no one seemed to be protesting any more.

In fact with the heat-wave still in full blast, no one seemed energetic enough to protest about anything. Pascoe felt a pang almost of sympathy for Cockshut as he changed gear and the car gathered speed down the hill to the main gates. The cool draught through the open windows was very welcome.

There were students scattered around the grass on either side of the drive. Some sleeping, some in close embrace, one or two even reading books. He could feel Dalziel's indignation beside him.

'Look at the sods!' he said finally. 'Just look at them. And this is supposed to be a place of bloody learning.'

Pascoe didn't answer and Dalziel as though sensing a criticism pressed the point.

'What do you think, Sergeant? What about you? Did you learn anything here? That's what these places are supposed to be for, isn't it? To teach the ignorant.'

A group of students walking down the drive hand in hand scattered laughing as the car came towards them. Pascoe felt an odd surge of tenderness for them, for everybody. And with it there came into his mind a line from Fallowfield's letter. *Pain is a risk we take in becoming fond of people, isn't it?*

The car passed through the gates.

'Oh, yes,' he said. 'I think I learned something.'